Frederick Lightfoot was born in West Cumbria and educated at Sussex University where he studied English and Drama. Spent many years in London before returning to West Cumbria where he now lives with his wife and two daughters. He has done many jobs, a lecturer in English, Drama and Creative Writing. He has also worked as a qualified general and psychiatric nurse, the training for which he completed after his degree.

He spent many years teaching drama and running drama workshops for people with Learning Disabilities and Mental Health problems. He currently works as an educationalist in End of Life Care, parts of which include working with actors to develop communication skills for staff and running workshops for people with advanced illness using narrative. He divides his time equally between writing and his teaching commitment.

MY NAME IS E

Frederick Lightfoot

SANDSTONEPRESS
HIGHLAND | SCOTLAND

First published in Great Britain by
Sandstone Press Ltd
PO Box 5725
One High Street
Dingwall
Ross-shire
IV15 9WJ
Scotland.

www.sandstonepress.com

ISBN: 978-1-905207-74-9

Cover design by Guilherme Condeixa
Typeset by Iolaire Typesetting, Newtonmore
Printed and bound in Great Britain by
Martins the Printers, Berwick upon Tweed.

Mixed Sources
Product group from well-managed
forests and other controlled sources
www.fsc.org   Cert no. SGS-COC-2959
© 1996 Forest Stewardship Council

FSC

Sea, base greys, moving, writhing, at eye level and unseen: writhing, rolling, in excitement or turmoil? She, signing, stood there and intimated it was all depth and weight. Dreams, she shared, of depth and weight. A mermaid, I saw her, adrift and free. The answer – a whim to wind, tide and the moon – all water is subject. In the caverns, she painted, dancing, her drifting mime up and down the shore, the beloved shore – the sands corrugated, black speckled, dusted with millions of coal grains, dotted over with lug-worm casts – in the caverns, she boasted, there would survive the sweet drone, the groan of a single vowel. Smiled, she, and said, whispered but announced, my name is E. A tiny figure, small, faceless, drawn of lines and circles, she made in the granular sand and sang aloud E, her signature, that of the artist, though she would not look for credit. Smiled, she, wicked and a-wing, witnessing the drowning moment, E lost beneath the drape of sea. Again, the claim, the sea says, E, my name, E, Eeeeee. Vibration, no lip movement, one chord, the most common of all vowels, Phoenician E, Greek E, Etruscan E, Roman E, Silent E, Magic E. My name is, coastal is, writhing, ecstatic, E.

Chapter One

The last time I stood here I was twenty-five and pregnant and determined to kill someone. I remember so clearly getting off the bus and strolling through the village, surprised as one always is by both alteration and continuation. There were more houses, new houses, where before there had been prefabs, and little cul-de-sacs built behind old terraces, the old houses that had known so many raised voices and beatings, so much primitive noise.

Walls don't contain sounds, though, whatever ghost hunters might say. They deflect sound and it goes off diminishing, losing voice, until it is no more and the violence that birthed it is rendered ridiculous and slightly obscene in the transformation. I think it was that which stuck in my throat, all those dead sounds, those dead aggravated calls.

By the time I'd followed the old, still familiar paths – the quarry rail-line across the bog land, navigated the old sandstone bridge with the coastal rail-line over it and the river beneath, then onto the dunes and finally the shore – the tightness in my guts was unbearable.

As I stepped awkwardly down the shingle towards the amphitheatre of rock-pools the possibility had become a certainty. Someone was going to die. Someone was going to pay. It was a vendetta, a need for restitution and justice, and she was the reason, the person the sea named, E, but who was it going to be? Martha, Harold, Agnes, Mr Drake? They were all guilty, in one way or another, all culpable. In fact, as that roar got the better of me I had the fleeting vision of them all dead. Was I capable of being such a nemesis? I believe I was. Centuries of abuse could be rectified and the morality of the conscript, those born without any voice to their name, constituted.

*

From the moment Abby was born she was claimed and had to go and live in someone else's home. Mother Sempie, the matriarch, Martha, claimed to have been too long alone, too long struggling against the senility and decay loneliness engenders – though still relatively young, Harold being born when she was still in her teens. She possessed Abby not with love but ownership. She watched over her in her crib, the bottom drawer of what had been Harold's chest of drawers, the matriarch not wanting her home unduly disfigured, and told her tales, family stories, stories of feuds, vendettas and acts of revenge. She even told her the one thing that no one knew, the identity of Harold's father. She laughed fiercely at the comedy of witness and told ever more daring things, the secret fantasies of her inner most thoughts.

*

You are a Sempie. She was told that until there could be no more doubt. It was a demand and an accusation. Of course, it wouldn't have been the case if Martha had told the truth. But a Sempie it was. Semp-ie! Abigail Sempie who later Grace named Abby.

*

Never go back.
   The old maxim tends to hold true. Of course it's something of a nonsense. How could such a thing exist anyway? Time erases the possibility. Looking at the sea today on this filthy, junk swept coast, could not be looking at the same filthy, junk swept coast thirty-five years ago, or twenty-five years before that, together making one lifetime at least. The

weather, the tide-line, the herring gulls, the oystercatchers, the plastic barrels, the dead, will not permit it.

The planet is round, though, the universe round, science proves impossibilities. Time must be round, probably a spiral. Points of likeness, of shimmer, of recognition, line up. The seer looks across them. Looking is greeted by a sigh. Is it repudiation, resignation, despair or wistful pleasure? Of course, it's impossible to say, unless you get closer, much, much closer, within better hearing distance, which really would be something.

So, I did the impossible. I disregarded the maxim, even though I steadfastly believed its truth, and returned, but I came as an invader. I came with a mission, a mission to correct time. Looking across these waves then – hard to believe it was thirty-five years ago now – I remember saying, I was born here – uttering the phrase aloud with slow, mannered syllables, making that declaration of origin, of beginning, into something of a challenge: a challenge for me, certainly, but more specifically, a challenge for all those I had never really left behind.

Of course, they would not have guessed I had any purpose at all, would not have imagined it even possible, though if they'd only had the skill to hear, the sea whispered the clue.

*

We usually ended up here. It was one of Abby's favourite places, not the only one, but special. Not that she ever felt particularly safe here, the beach is too exposed for that to be the case, but it's such an ugly shoreline very few people ever ventured here.

It is one long expanse that stretches in either direction like a long straight road. A narrow stretch of shingle attaches to a filthy strip of sand. Where we went – because that's where the interior quarry rail-line joined the coastal rail-line – there is a great bowl of rocks and rock-pools where we often watched giant crabs scuttle for shelter. It looks like the archaeological remains of an amphitheatre. The sand is corrugated and dark, flecked with coal dust. The shingle has lines of seaweed and flotsam.

The short tract of land on the seaward side of the coastal rail-track is composed of sand-dunes and tough scrub. It isn't difficult jumping down onto the shingle from it, but climbing back can be fraught. The bank is at least five feet high and has only been worn away into pathways in a couple of places, and they are forever collapsing or filling with rubbish.

The litter used to bother Abby. I don't know that it was because she was a tidy person; such notions didn't exist then, not around the dilapidated little farmsteads we understood as home. I think it was more the fact the litter was so outlandish. It suggested a life going on somewhere completely alien and hidden to us. The fact that that life was vulgar in some way we never questioned for a moment. Why an empty plastic barrel should announce such a thing I don't suppose I will ever understand; but understanding is so often like that, intuitive and prejudiced.

Of course we knew what attracted her, the roar that signalled her, and the persistence that guided her. It was the sea. That thing that was moving, writhing, sounding from some indefinable depth, spelling out her name, the only name she would have for herself.

Name, hers, E.

*

By the time Martha rescinded her claim Harold and Agnes were two children better off with another on the way and so were not best pleased to be landed with a deaf-mute, particularly one so reviled by the matriarch. Once the realisation hit home that her secrets had fallen on such infertile ground Martha was consumed by rage. When the nurse came round to confirm in her most diplomatic, concerned tones what was patently obvious to everyone, that Abby had never heard a single word of the family saga and was not ever remotely likely to repeat them, Martha flew into a fit of temper and flung her entertaining cups – the ones with saucers, produced for the nurse's benefit – right across the room, fortunately before any tea had been poured.

She went on to lash at everything within reach, condemning a tongue in brine she was pressing and a flank of bacon she was about to hang to the green flags of the kitchen floor. At first the nurse tried to reason with her, ridiculously pointing out the obvious that it must have been something of a shock. With that Martha rounded on the messenger and glared at her as if it were all her fault. The nurse found Martha's close attention more frightening than her previous eruption. She began to excuse herself, saying she had a number of visits to see to, she was also in the middle of immunisations, but promised that the doctor would call and someone from education, but she had only just begun to button her coat when the matriarch screamed at her to get out. The nurse defended her dignity for just a few seconds more, but as that merely resulted in a barrage of the previous injunction, she decided it was better to beat a hasty retreat without another word, leaving the child to the fury of the woman who had claimed her.

For a while Martha simply gazed at the back of the door through which the nurse had gone, and then slowly she rounded on Abby. Her eyes burnt with hatred. Her expression suggested betrayal. Abby had simply viewed the scene with amusement, tickled by the nurse's embarrassment, fleeting pluck and then hasty retreat. She had seen it all before. The matriarch was renowned for her temper. She had seen worse when Martha claimed Harrison the butcher was trying to undercut her, or Addison was overcharging for the use of his boar, but she had never experienced it. Martha had treated her like a favoured pet, something to stroke and feed with occasional tid-bits, though she was never unduly pampered. She had certainly never seen Martha eye her like that before, with malice and distaste.

Instinctively Abby backed away, aware that something had irrevocably changed in her master's manner. At that movement Martha smiled vindictively. She began to mouth things towards Abby, things she now knew the child couldn't hear, couldn't interpret. In all likelihood it was yet another family secret, possibly something very near to Martha herself, something very near indeed, but she was no longer gloating, pleased with herself for confessing to an infant, but tormenting herself with it. – Was that the insult, the complaint, that the child had made a fool of her and her confessional game? Or was it altogether blander than that? – As she began to mouth at her, mixing her last confession with threats and expletives, Abby scurried across the floor trying to find some place of safety in the kitchen.

She had found safe havens there before. Her memory was full of them. There was the space between the back of the small horsehair settee and the wall with the embossed flowers. There was only room enough for her to crawl in and no space to move, so she simply lay there, often with her eyes closed, touching the flowers, inhaling the dank rug that covered that half of the room, feeling the coarseness of the cloth of the settee against her. She didn't daydream there, didn't imagine vast open spaces, plateaux with sunshine, but was content in the confinement as it was.

It was the same in the lid of the enormous Singer sewing machine the matriarch produced from time to time. Occasionally Abby sat in it and paddled as if it were a boat, an ancient wooden galleon paddled by hand, but the seas were always stormy and she invariably looked for a port, any creek or cove large enough for her vessel. More often than not, though, she twisted and contorted herself until she was entirely contained in the lid, and she liked nothing better than to be able to pull over a covering, a pillow-case or tea-towel, so she was completely hidden. She liked the fact that the light still came through so she could see her own snakelike shape, and she loved the sense of her own breathing, even and moist in the confined space.

Indeed, the smaller the space the better. The matriarch often found her coiled around the bars of a stool or under a heap of sheets, her head under a pillow, her eyes peeping out now and again as if she were navigating some vehicle into ever narrower spaces. She imagined her bed was surrounded by four walls and she had to stay there forever, her food appearing mysteriously through a tiny hatch. She never thought for a second she might be bored, her imagination, which was as subterranean as her behaviour, would sustain her – which when the time came to need it, I hope it did, but by then the spaces she sought were far greater.

Of course, no matter her contortionist's acumen, her mole-like skill, she never uttered more than a syllable; purrs and grunts of delight or frustration depending on her level of achievement. So there is no reason that it should have come as such a shock to the matriarch when it was indicated and confirmed that Abby couldn't speak because she couldn't hear. After all she was five years old, in fact nearly six, when the nurse came to inform her of the outcome of the audiology tests they had conducted in the surgery. Martha had been against any investigation into Abby's lack of speech, and had somehow managed to keep all professionals at bay. She told the health visitor, who insisted on it, that it was simply a matter of time. Harold had been a late speaker. All her children were slow off the mark – by which she was presumably claiming Abby, as she had no other child than Harold. The health visitor was not to be gainsaid. It didn't matter that Martha lost her temper and accused her of being an interfering busybody, adding it was better before the war when people could get on with things themselves. The tests were carried out, the result scarcely in doubt. Abby was deaf and had not acquired speech. Perhaps the matriarch had simply refused to believe what was patently obvious, and thought as long as she could deny the evidence then everything would be all right. Her acquisition could remain her pet. The truth of it was presumably in the speech she made as she descended on Abby in that small kitchen, but Abby was never one to repeat that.

Abby had managed to entangle herself amongst the legs of the table, but Martha seized her and dragged her out, and whilst holding her firmly with her left hand began slapping her with the right, across the buttocks and thighs, all the while ranting at her as if she had wilfully deceived her. All round the small kitchen she beat her, barging her into the furniture and the grate, so that her body would be bruised for weeks, and the only sounds Abby made were mute screams of incomprehension.

Agnes was feeding chickens when Martha threw Abby across the yard, sending her skidding over the black cobbles towards the dung-heap, scattering the chickens as she did. Martha evidently thought it better to bring her to the rear of the house where there was less chance of the neighbours seeing – Harold having acquired all the land behind a small row of houses. Martha held herself upright and declared, as if she were personally accusing Agnes: "Your bitch is deaf." When Agnes made no reply Martha marched up to her and glared at close quarters, repeating: "Did you hear me? Your bitch is deaf, a deaf-mute." Agnes evidently didn't know how to respond and simply stood there squinting at Martha as if the sun were blinding her, though in reality it was a dull, cloudy day, the cobbles beneath her feet covered over with a grimy patina of mud. Martha threw up her hands with impatience, and made to leave, but before she turned away Harold appeared on the steps. She didn't hesitate but called to him with as much sarcasm as she could muster: "Your Shaughnessy woman has done you proud and spawned an imbecile, just like I told you, but you wouldn't listen to me. Well, I hope you have the stomach for it, because I don't." Harold gazed with the same vagueness as had his wife, his expression denoting nothing of what he was thinking, except

8

perhaps the fact that the matriarch didn't frighten him, even if she had once. Infuriated by his silence Martha screamed: "I warned you, I wouldn't care if I hadn't warned you." Harold gave a barely perceptible shrug, kicked his clogs against the frame of the door as if he needed to kick off mud, though he hadn't made it into the yard, and disappeared back indoors. Martha rounded on Agnes, defying her to comment, then when Agnes said nothing, screwed up her face and said: "I thought not." With that she took herself back out of the yard and was gone.

Agnes wandered over and peered down at Abby as she lay hunched up, her clothes smeared with mud, chicken shit and corn. She held her head to one side, weighing her up, as if the idea that she couldn't hear or speak was just too great for her to understand. Of course she was aware that her own father, Aidan, was partially deaf, but with him you wouldn't know. He could speak and was certainly no imbecile. This was new, incomprehensible, not something she would have expected in her own child. She skewed her face, shrugged, turned away and continued to scatter corn for the reassembled chickens, leaving Abby to find her own way inside, which she instinctively realised had to be the case.

After that Agnes took a shy, diffident approach to her, keeping her distance as if Abby was a possessed child, something to be wary of, her silence somehow devilish. It was the silence she found disturbing. She was certain something went on behind it, something deceitful, untrustworthy, something bad. Besides, as a woman who would have insisted she was as religious as the next person, though virtually never venturing into her church anymore, she assumed that if Abby's silence itself wasn't sinful, then it must at least be a punishment for something. She was far from clear in her own mind what the logic of that thought was, but wouldn't have argued against some philosophical notion of perpetual return. The child was guilty of some crime, some sin, some tremendous wrongdoing committed in indeterminate time. The question for Agnes remained as to what she was still capable of.

Harold took an altogether more forthright approach and decided to beat language into her, reasoning perhaps that if he made the assault loud enough she would surely hear. Agnes didn't argue with Harold, but nevertheless found the beatings upsetting. So, with unusual sensitivity to his wife's feelings, he took Abby outside into the yard, and on occasion into the pig-sheds, where he slapped her with both sides of his hands across her thighs and bare buttocks. There was no logic to the cause or frequency of these beatings, which resulted whenever Harold suspected some impertinence to her silence, to her refusal to hear.

It was after one of his beatings that I found her by the shore nursing her wounds, sobbing, probably in time to the waves, with scarcely any volume or any demonstration. Up until that point we had been kept apart, Abigail Sempie, Judith Salt and Grace Powers. Grace appeared like a vision. I would have to admit that I was unnerved when she materialised out of the blue, just standing, looking on, someway along the shoreline. She was the first to speak, to sign. She raised her hand. Hello. Hello, welcome, don't shun me. It was a benediction. We didn't know sign, only Grace knew then, but, looking along the shore towards her, Abby tapped herself on the right shoulder with the tips of her fingers pressed together into a claw, indicating herself, then she groaned a single sound, a vowel. E. My name is E.

*

One sentence to describe us then, one sentence to denote who we were, who we are, but which is the topic, which the central theme, the driving concern? Well, here goes. Deaf children, three, girls, all born in the same village, in the same year, in the last and final year of the war, 1945. A miracle, a coincidence, an omen, a tragedy, a triumph? All of those, to

10

different people, not all to all, but how is the conclusion of this cosmic configuration to be seen? Eclipse, luminosity, nimbus, corolla, glory? But then, who is to say? Who is to decide? Me? Martha Sempie? Harold Sempie? Agnes Sempie? Mr Drake? Deaf children, three, girls, born in the same village, in the last year of an appalling war. Miracle, coincidence, omen, tragedy, triumph? Let's see, so few can hear.

We called ourselves sisters. Grace was the first to say it. She approached Abby and handed her a small doll she had been indifferently carrying by its waist. At first Abby was hesitant, but then took it and held it as if it were a real baby. Grace screwed up her face at that. Abby's tenderness was too serious, too maudlin, by far. For a moment Grace considered snatching back her bruised and battered offering, but then smiled and said she was Abby's, indicating it, her open hands signalling the gift. Strangely enough, once the gift had been given Abby considered rejecting it. It clearly crossed her mind to throw the little doll across the sands, but just as her arm moved to eject it she stopped herself, and with an edge of defiance roughly pushed it closer into her chest. Grace mouthed her name. The doll was called Poppy. She let Abby know with great inflexions of her lips. Poppy, her name, the doll, the little pot thing with smudge marks and knotted hair. Abby understood but treated the information, the name, as if it were of no concern of hers, nevertheless she hugged the thing ever closer, but with deliberate petulance, and then it must have crossed her mind that she really should have responded in some way, so she looked up at Grace, who was still standing over her weighing up her handling of Poppy, and groaned her own name again, E, E like Pop-py.

Grace screwed up her face again in a show of indignation and irritation and told Abby that she was Abigail, a Sempie, she knew about her. She turned to me and told me we would call her Abby. To underline the point, she looked down at

11

Abby again and shouted it aloud, Abby, name, her. Abby replied that her name was E. Grace was satisfied, content it was the confirmation of what she had just said. With that confirmation she said we were like sisters.

Sisters, three, deaf, Judith Salt, Grace Powers and Abigail Sempie, Abby. After that day on the beach when we found her, found each other, discovered her sobbing against the force of the waves, the day Grace named her for us, we always called her Abby, Abby with a pleading, questioning affection on the second syllable, and it seemed to please her, more often than not eliciting a groan of approval, the confirmation of, my name is E. It wouldn't have crossed Grace's mind or mine that we were claiming her, claiming her in the same way Martha had claimed her, naming her for something, naming her in the same way Poppy had been named, for pleasure and ownership. Poor little Poppy. She had been treated roughly, scolded every day of her life, until she was given to Abby and Abby cradled her, hugging her scruffy little figure to her with defiant affection. Grace couldn't have predicted how much Abby would love stupid, little feckless Poppy, but she did, loved her without hesitation. What could Grace have been expected to predict, though, she was just a child, headstrong, determined and impatient, but still a child, as were her newly discovered sisters, children.

Grace was perceptive though; we were sisters, sisters of a kind in so many ways, three similarly made but distinct patterns, three shades of deafness. Grace and Abby even looked alike, Grace being a tidy, well-groomed version of what Abby might be. The lines that made up Grace seemed more complete, more definite somehow, as if strength of personality was repeated in physical outlines. Even her colour was more striking. Of course, her clothes were so much brighter than Abby's, brighter than mine, and her skin took on the sheen of her red checked pinafore, her face suffused with the tone. Abby was simply drab, her features

12

washed of colour, her hair untidily swept across her head, her dress too large, hanging crookedly from her shoulders. Martha had kept her but never preened her. It is unlikely Martha would have known how. There was a quality about Martha that was neither masculine nor feminine but an aggregate of both, making something new, not asexual but hermaphroditic, epicene. She had never given any thought to the bringing up of a young girl, the only issue being possession. Abby might as well have been a species of chicken or pig. It was all the same to Martha. Harold and Agnes had not seen fit to improve on that.

Funnily enough, although I had as much in common with Abby and Grace as they did with each other, I looked nothing like them. I was already noticeably taller, and even then stiffer, with my plumb-line back, and my propensity to purse my lips and screw up my eyes, and whereas they were fair with smooth skin, albeit one pink and one drained, I was dark, my skin mottled, its surface rough and blemished. I felt older than my sisters, even then, felt a responsibility for Grace's playfulness and impatience, and Abby's desire for confined spaces. I was the big one, awkward and exposed, but with enough physical strength to stand up for myself, for them, to some extent anyway. Isn't that how sisters are though, no matter how close, particularly when there are three, two alike, one different, one the elder.

It wasn't surprising that we were related, everyone in the village seemed to be related in one way or another, there wasn't enough population for it to be otherwise, and it was rare that anyone travelled, not then, except in desperate circumstances, which meant unemployment or homosexuality, never simply boredom. The village was a mile from the coast, one of a number of small hamlets, made up of farmsteads and terraced houses, ex-mining houses when the coast was pitted with coal and iron-ore mines and quarries, and on the fringes estates of post-war prefabricated houses which, despite their oddity, we took for granted. The prefabs meant nothing to us, nor did the disused railway escarpments, the spoil banks, the flooded workings, the tumbledown red brick walls that criss-crossed the country-side. They had always been there. It didn't mean anything. Nor did the fact that we had been kept apart; but we found each other out and discovered we were sisters of a kind.

My mother, Flora, was a Sempie. Her grandfather Jim Sempie and Martha's father, Wilfred, were brothers. We didn't know what that made us except sisters. Grace Powers' grandmother, Nora, was a Shaughnessy. Nora's brother, Aidan, was Abby's grandfather, Agnes' father. Again they didn't know what that made them, but assumed it could only be sisters. Besides, Aidan was deaf, as was his Auntie Honor, as were Grace's uncles Peter and Paul. – It was Aidan who taught Peter and Paul how to sign, then all three taught Grace, which was the only way it was taught then, through families, through clubs, then Grace taught us. – There was a lot of deafness in Grace's family, but Grace hadn't been born deaf. She had acquired it at some point in the few years leading to our discovery on the beach, as I had. It might have been scarlet fever, influenza, measles, no one said, not then. Perhaps we were ill at the same time, feverish together, dreaming vivid dreams – I remember a whole tribe on camels chasing me through a desert and my mother trying to hush me, not the camels, nor the men, but me, her frantic child, not realising that shouting out was for my own sake because that's how it would have to be from then on, shouting to be heard. At least we could talk a bit, Grace and I, awkwardly and amateurish, and hear something, in fact, quite a bit, all told. We were Grade II deaf, but whether that was Grade IIa or Grade IIb was still to be discovered. Abby was Grade III deaf and had been from birth, but whether Grade III a, b or c, who could know? Of course, there was no deafness in the Sempie family, certainly none the matriarch would lay claim to, but then Abby's grand-father was a Shaughnessy, a deaf Shaughnessy, deaf Aidan.

14

Whether Aidan, Honor, Peter or Paul were born deaf or acquired it no one will ever be sure about. Certainly Martha detested the Shaughnessys, but that wasn't because they were syphilitics or defectives – the way the deaf were usually seen – not that she ever claimed anyway.

Chapter Two

There was a tradition in the Shaughnessy family that Owen's sister Moyna, Owen being Grace's great-great-grandfather, had been the first victim of the Great Famine to be recorded as died of starvation. It was said how she bought a love-token, a charm of some kind, from a tinker man she called Panax. She confided in Owen that Panax had promised her that Michael Hoy couldn't fail but love her. They were teenagers at the time. Owen himself went out onto the bog, but whether to chase the tinker man away or purchase his own token, his own charm, is no longer recounted. He remembered that the curlew and snipe were silent, and that he had never known silence like that before. He thought he saw the tinker man, someway in the distance, like a hunched monkey he said, described him, lolling off in the distance out of their lives.

The next morning there was frost in July, a frost that wasn't cold or crystal but powdery, forming a sheen on the potato leaves. Memory jumps then to the stink of rotten tubers. After that all the dreams of Panax were over. It didn't matter anymore that Michael Hoy, handsome youth that he was, was the illegitimate child of Catherine Hoy, and that she had brought him up in the teeth of the most fierce opposition, shunned and excluded by unforgiving neighbours. Except, at the end, Owen remembers how a crowd went to feed them, but found they were already dead, and that someone else fell down beside them, relieved to have the permission to do so.

Most people tried to sit it out, just waiting for the inevitable evictions when rents couldn't be paid, but Owen decided that emigration was the only hope they had. He remembered Moyna's reluctance and the terrible scene she made being taken away from Michael Hoy, the possibility of Michael Hoy, in a place that wouldn't have allowed it anyway, and he could never remember it without, in his own mind, seeing her famished face with her thin lips, toothless mouth and purple gums, though he insisted to any audience that she was beautiful right to the last.

She told Owen that Michael Hoy wasn't dead, he was famished, and that wasn't dying, it was a mistake. In the end she went with him, though. What choice did she have? There was no one else. On the road they passed bodies in the wayside, crystal ornamented bodies, frozen in brief time. From that time on Owen always maintained that wandering into the snow, into the cold, scarcely believing they would find the coast, was dying. Don't look at me and believe I am not dead, he lectured two more generations, because I am, and I died in a place where there was food to feed them that had to be exported. He never said when Moyna died. The Shaughnessy myth was that she died en route and Owen carried her across his shoulders all the way to Wexford where a coroner registered that she had died of starvation, not disease but hunger.

There was a scene in the snow that Owen kept to himself for most of his life, only telling his daughter Honor, whom he claimed was the image of Moyna, when he was dying himself. At the point when Moyna was certain she could go no farther she started cursing, swearing and blaspheming, then moaned and cried without ceasing that Michael Hoy had never made love to her, that no man had ever made love to her. She then ripped at her clothes, which were little more than rags anyway, and revealed her shrunken, wizened breasts and her childlike hairless sex, after which, she refused to cover herself, her rage never allayed.

Whether it points to a cruel streak in Owen to have

17

divulged the secret to Honor is not part of the Shaughnessy myth, because history would have it that Honor was a virgin, a deaf virgin, at the time, though Martha did scoff at the notion of any Shaughnessy being pure, even their imbeciles.

Owen Shaughnessy in England didn't exactly prosper but survived, though as everything is relative, survival to Owen seemed profound. He stayed in Liverpool for a while and considered America, but couldn't face the prospect of another voyage with a boat full of corpses. In the end he drifted north with a group of farm labourers, who dwindled en route until he found himself alone at the extremity, the North West Cumberland coast. They were still digging iron-ore in bell-pits at the time, then taking it up into the nearby fells for smelting. He met Eistir and decided to stay. Eistir's family worked in the nearby coal mines in Whitehaven.

Nothing much was said about Eistir's family, other than they found themselves in England in the hold of a coal-boat. Owen said she was a more sophisticated person than he was and even knew Dublin very well, though he never explained how. She died whilst Honor, their third child, was still young, there being something of a gap between Honor and her brothers, Dermot and Edward, called Ed.

Apparently, before Eistir's death Owen was quite a grim, humourless man but afterwards became quite the opposite. Of course he was drinking by then. At the time she died he had already finished with the mines and had been renting a small plot for a few years, having previously been forced to move his family on three separate occasions when the mines laid people off. As his drinking worsened and his health deteriorated Dermot, Edward and Honor kept it going. By the time he was ready to admit to Honor, his deaf child, how Moyna had died half-naked, completely starved, he was considered a bit gaga. After all, what was the sense in confessing to Honor? Except, of course, Honor was a marvellous lip-reader and wonderful signer, which she had learnt before oral education was made compulsory in 1893, by which time she was already twenty-three.

When Dermot married, another coal-boat migrant like his mother called Maura, Ed and Honor stayed on. Obviously Honor was deaf and didn't have an opportunity to leave and Ed was either simple or lazy. Given the scale of the house it was evidently a crush when Nora, Christian and Aidan were born, once again the third child being deaf. Presumably Honor taught Aidan to sign because he could certainly do it, though there is no account of Aidan sharing any of his newfangled oral education with her, in fact it is very unclear whether Aidan had any schooling at all.

Martha was surprisingly diffident in complaining about Aidan, her future daughter-in-law's father, though for some reason no one could fathom was quick to brand his eventual wife, Hazel, little better than a whore, pronouncing it so that it rhymed with sewer. Nora, though, Aidan's sister she hated absolutely.

I learnt all of this later, not when we were kids, sisters, working out who we were, what our sisterly ties amounted to. I was a woman before I realised I had to confront that hatred, though even when we were just kids it was obvious she did hate them, despite her insistence that she had nothing against them, certainly not for being Catholic – an irrelevance above all other irrelevancies, she said – claiming she simply didn't want them as her neighbours.

As far as she was concerned the Shaughnessys were from somewhere else. It didn't matter where. The difference was what mattered. The problem was they were making here there, stamping themselves on everything. Honor with her quiet devotional ways symbolised the complaint. She was so childlike in her submission to the practice of her faith she was altogether in her own world, devoid entirely of nostalgia or regret for any other. There could be no real telling where she came from because her reality was always the here and now. In truth it wasn't God who was with her, who

19

was altogether too great an idea for her to comprehend, but candles, saints, the altar – trappings.

Of course, Martha refused to concede that Honor wasn't actually from anywhere, but lived in the village in which she was born. Nor would she concede that Honor could be anything but a simpleton, an imbecile, despite having never made any attempt to really know her. Honor's only saving grace was that she hadn't married, because as Martha proclaimed it, her sort should never be allowed to marry, never bear children, then as if to excuse Aidan blame of that indiscretion added, certainly not with each other, anyway.

*

With Poppy held firmly, if roughly, in her arms Abby watched the tide close in, green, turquoise, with filthy cream streamers, the wind blustering across the coal pocked sands. She felt exquisitely alone, triumphant, released, though none of those words would have come naturally to her. The only natural word would have been no word at all – a groan, a groan of recognition, a groan of non-recognition. She had an undisclosed knack, call it a talent, for ambiguity. It was the essence of her charm.

After that we always knew there was a place to find her. She had discovered her element. She was drawn by depth and weight and farther still by the defining and containing horizon. It all rose in her mind from below and formed itself into a note, a voice and ultimately a vision. She lived between pig-shed and shingle, between punishment and pleasure, and the mid-ground was a sequence of discovered confinements. We were all to learn more as time progressed.

We never realised at first, even though we were sisters, that she could hear the sea, at least its floor, the lowest notes it could sound. We had no inkling that it called her name.

The frustration was that it sounded from such a depth, the tragedy that it called to her more and more, time after time.

It is certainly the persistence of time that brings me back

here, having served my time, my long hours in so many hallways, work-rooms, behind locked doors, each space as absurd as the one before. In time everything returns, though never the same, never freely, always with intent, as I have returned, as I returned, with the certainty that someone was to die, something I felt, sensed, as only someone with a special sense could, because reading time is a special sense, very special indeed.

*

My name is Judith Salt. I am sixty years old. My hair is dyed supposedly pale russet-brown, but tends to have a copper, metallic, unnatural sheen. I have been advised by my hairdresser, who is an incredibly talkative young woman who seems to find the greatest pleasure in the minor skirmishes of life, to soak it with avocado and vegetable oil, which she reliably informs me will bring back the natural tint, texture and shine. She assures me that thirty minutes soaking is enough, followed by thorough washing of course; but my natural tint is grey, my natural texture like wire, and I have no recollection of shine, so I politely decline her well-meant suggestion.

Standing on this shore it is something of a relief to bring her to mind, visualise her posturing around me, talking to my reflection in the mirror, though well aware of her own alluring presence in the glass, generously listing the options for new styles, new images, a new me. I know what she's getting at, what she means without actually saying it. Why don't I hide my hearing aid? Why do I simply sweep back the hair from my face into a neat little bun? As she says, there are so many possibilities.

I listen appreciatively and even smile from time to time, warmly, without pique or embarrassment, as if to say, no it's just not me, and all the time I watch as she sweeps back each strand from my face and think, it doesn't matter, I have worn much worse, a small behind the ear device is really nothing at all and, after all, wouldn't I be something of a let-down if I started hiding it now? My God, what would Donald's face look like, knowing I had listened so quietly to such beauty tips? Even after all these years – can it be so many? – I can hear the storm of rage.

It is almost comical letting it wend and knot itself with the waves. The waves are so simply suggestive of time, and yet also of time's opposite. That is such a pleasing thought.

I am sixty years old. I have been deaf since I was four or there about – scarlet fever, influenza, measles, I don't know which, no one said. I have hidden it, hated it, denied it, hugged it, loved it. I have never been without an opinion. I still have an opinion.

I smile at my hairdresser, who really is so vivacious and lovely in a clumsy, informal way, with her blond and black hair cut so waywardly around her head that it always brings to mind a cactus, which isn't fair on her at all. I think I get my hair trimmed so regularly simply to enjoy her company, her brazen certainty and her ridiculous incredulity. Why should I abuse her? Besides she is so gentle as she eases the comb behind my ear, around my aid, as if she were afraid of hurting me, which is misguided, but kind. Really I would like her to be rougher. I like my face pulled slightly tauter than it is.

To be honest, I don't think my face has ever looked better. I am obviously thin enough for its natural shape to emerge without looking ill and skeletal. The cheekbones are smooth and look almost polished beneath the somewhat reptilian eyes. I suppose I look as if I have had a face job, but I haven't. I am lucky though. I smoked far too much as a young woman. I guess that accounts for the yellow, ma-hogany tint the skin has, but at least it hasn't wrinkled up like most. Maybe I gave up in time. Funny but I never missed it. Absurd that I should ever have started, but people did then, started things they couldn't easily stop, though we didn't call ourselves addicts, or even consider there might be a problem. Funny how easily everyone forgave themselves.

I was still smoking the last time I was here. In fact, I was frankly chain-smoking. In my memory I see myself calmly taking a cigarette from the pack – I smoked Rothmans in those days – and putting it to my lips so slowly and thoughtfully that the whole process is charged with deliberation. I strike a match – always matches never a lighter – and guard it from the wind, then inhale so deeply that it feels like drawing a life breath. The mind reels with it. I am capable of anything. I can kill what it is necessary to kill. I can stand up for my moral right. To hell with it! If there was a God he left us to it when we took to residing in caves. Besides, the existence of evil doesn't assume the necessity of its opposite. So, I had few qualms. I had to be right, though. I had to work it out.

Donald was always trying to get me to quit. I knew I should have. I was pregnant for God's sake, but then no one stopped smoking because they were pregnant, not then. I don't know if it was the baby that prompted him. I can't remember that. I just remember his attempt to smile as if I were being a stubborn teenager, though behind that easy gesture I knew there was real anger. Donald was always smiling and angry. It was a disastrous combination really. I don't mean angry over smoking, but angry over everything, everything and anything that didn't fit with how he wanted things to seem, and I believe it was the seeming that mattered, the surface of things, the bright shiny outside of existence.

I had already been living in London for almost five years when we met. I was seeing someone called Michael at the time, a well-meaning, churchgoing boy who collected for Christian Aid and took me to church dances in a large basement hall in Somers Town where I was noticeably made to feel welcome. The small world of Christian charity throws wide its arms to all who are heavily burdened. Of course the very welcome points to your difference, points to the fact that you are being owned.

It gives me goose-bumps now to think I finished with Michael because of Donald. It stands for something, even if it is only prestige. That Michael was hurt doesn't subtract from that. – Was he hurt because he couldn't even keep hold of a poor little deaf girl, or because his charity was found wanting? Or am I being deliberately uncharitable and he was hurt as a human being can be, as human beings learn to be, let down, disillusioned, betrayed. What would we ever feel without our knowledge of suffering?

I felt physically sick at those dances. He thought I was shy and nervous. On the contrary, I was overconfident. One of the many things I believe is that there is an absolute lack of separation between mind and body. I suffered from nausea because of the overfullness of mental capacity. I still suffer from bouts of nausea, nausea being far worse than actually vomiting, but perhaps not with the frequency I once did.

I was living in a rented room in a house in Camden Town, sharing with a midwife and a nun. They were good women. On the night I moved in I wrote on a piece of paper: Tonight as I lie down to sleep I have never been happier. I had eaten fish and chips and drunk a couple of glasses of London Gin. I slipped the piece of paper inside the lining of my suitcase. I still have it to this day. Tonight as I lie down to sleep I have never been happier. Such an amazing sentiment really. It points to the ability to sleep – with or without the assistance of London Gin – and to the ability to feel at peace, not removed from life, but as a participant, a willing traveller.

Of course, it also points to a past where such a feeling of excursion was impossible, points to the stunning panic of childhood, the abysmal hours of its unwinding filled with the filthy images of Victorian and Edwardian sentimentality. Nothing quite provokes nausea as much as those horrible colour plates in children's nursery rhyme books. There is nothing I hate more – unless, it is childhood itself, anybody's, everybody's.

I would like to kill it, but then resurrect it, see it live in exactly the same sentimental plate. After all, I was pregnant, stuffed with the happiness of Donald's child, possessed of the genes of Donald's dark brooding, and my own fiery, quiet temper.

Did Donald ever realise how much I detested nursery rhymes?

He came from a solid Scottish Presbyterian background, which maybe didn't take nursery rhymes quite so seriously. He spoke about his parents, his life in Argyll, with fondness and regret, his regret one of disappointment and anger rather than nostalgia. He was always at war with himself, contradicting himself. His father was at once sincere and sham, too easily instilled in the Calvinist dogma that there was no salvation outside the church, yet principled, holding an idea that went with the name, McCloud: his mother, a nurturing compromise of pleasure and virtue, a person constituted by time and place, yet befitting it. History had made them, and they knew it, trusted it and bequeathed it, but the younger son needed to disclaim it, Donald's elder brother staying put whereas he had to go.

Donald didn't know what to make of my assertion that my family believed in nothing, nothing except perhaps a permanent present, time fixed forever and ever, recounting the same stories day after day. He would insult me with his mother's reading – how many books a week was it? – and his father's speeches and maxims, such as the whole world's inability to hold the stick by the thick end. What did I have to put up against that?

My name is Judith Salt. My father is Robert Salt, an iron-ore miner who worked permanent nights in a paper-mill when the mines closed in the early seventies. My mother's boast was that her man never drew the dole. There is contempt for existence itself in that assertion. There is no salvation outside survival. There is no past or future, just an endless struggle with time present. My mother would have been ashamed of anything else, the same way she would have been ashamed of love, the same way she would have been ashamed of any sentiment other than contempt for those who drew any sort of dole.

Not that she was ashamed of me. I was like the mine, the paper-mill, or the thermometer factory where she worked, another factor of the permanent present, simply her disabled offspring on whose part she was never angry, down-trodden or in love – nothing to resist, nothing to condemn, nothing for which to hope, nothing to stand up for. I was another of the life events that you just had to get on with, though I suspect there was an inkling of pride in her ability to say such a thing, another version of never drawing the dole; after all she was a Sempie, Flora Sempie, she couldn't help but be proud.

Donald didn't believe it. I was overdoing it, the primitive world from which I had fled to eventually lay down to sleep happier than I had ever been; but then, he didn't trust anything. He certainly didn't trust my happiness, and never trusted his own. I have to take much of the blame for that. At first I refused to believe. I berated myself, devalued myself – though I never meant a word. I openly declared my doubt and distrust of his wanting to date a deaf girl. It wasn't about the ears at all, though. In fact the ears were attractive in their own way, not too large, nicely hugging the side of the head. It was the face, the plumb-line stance, the whole essence of Judith Salt, clerical assistant in a social services office, ful-filling the 3% rule of disabled staff, the whole essence that I had learnt to love and hate, pity and revile, respect and reject.

You don't love me, I accused him, immediately regretting the use of the word, the presumption of it, the scale of it, wishing I had said something else. Of course if I had said, you don't care for me, he would have flashed me his impatient, energetic look and told me plainly that I wasn't a candidate for care. I was relentless though, picking up his unguarded looks, the expression of wistfulness, pleasure, pride. You don't love me, I'd say, you love some ridiculous image you have of yourself. I cast him in the role of twisted, holy pervert, his martyrdom my deafness.

He could see through me though, but then, he was a radiologist. He worked in the basement of small hospital on Hampstead Road. He complained of never seeing the day-light, of not knowing one season to the next. Sometimes he would rant about it, but I never believed it. He wanted to be in a small space complaining about the urge to a wider world. He was domestic and conservative, but couldn't bear that in himself, couldn't bear to be seen in that light. When I said the only reason he wanted me was for the conspicuous fact of my hearing, he looked me over with his eyes as only a radiologist could, boring right through the skin, right through soft tissue and flab, to the naked core, the grey bone, and uttered: But you love me pitying you, though I don't, not for a second.

The trouble was, his great flaw, his human reversal of fortune, was that he did pity, pitied greatly. In fact he was worn-out by pity. I remember on one occasion sitting in a café with him when he couldn't eat, and finally had to give up and leave, because on the next table there was a man with an almighty tic and twisted face who kept letting morsels of food drop from his slack lips. There was no way Donald left because he was in any way offended or disgusted. His pity drove him away. The radiologist wanted the world to be a beautiful place for all of its teeming life, but as that struck him as impossible he instead chose to hate it.

Pity like that stinks of bigotry.

He took my head between his large, yet sensitive hands, making sure his great fleshy fingers hugged my hearing aid and said: You have to let me in, trust me, believe me.

And then there was the baby. It took away all the other

27

questions and concerns, such as: why he didn't turn up for days and when he did was so morose and timid? Why he had so many nightmares, shouting aloud in the night and waking panicked, insisting the next day that he couldn't recall a thing? Why he drunk quite so much, helping himself to copious amounts of my London Gin? Why he was so flirtatious with the midwife and the nun? They all vanished away, sucked up into the one great question: Will this child be deaf?

But you weren't born deaf, he said, reminding himself, reassuring himself, convincing himself. Nor was one of my sisters, I replied, teasing him with it, taunting him, but the other was. There was a great deal of deafness in my family.

I believe I wanted him to say, get rid of it, get rid of his own child taking form within me, the radiologist who couldn't examine it in its amniotic pool and shout at it to see if it would turn its head or not. I wanted him not to want it, to reject that portion of himself, to give up and deny his enormous pity. I know I wanted it.

Why else would I have crawled over him, naked, the child yet hidden, tiny in the womb, and licked his easily masculine body, his solid, down enriched body, from belly to chest to neck to earlobe then whispered, as if it were an intimacy, a secret sexual desire: Of course, it might not be able to hear; then immediately deserted him, my lips wrapping around his penis, surprising him, shocking him, providing him with dubious pleasure?

Chapter Three

Of course, there was a great deal of deafness in my family, the family my sisters and I knew we were, no matter how violently the matriarch would object, which I imagine would leave her decidedly unsure whether she should shout the denial at the top of her voice, which was her natural predilection, or simply mouth it in an attitude of quiet menace, though the gangster was never her natural style – which isn't to say she wasn't capable of horrific crime, because she was. Though I was the one to serve so much time, so much silent, solitary confinement, I was never as criminal as Martha.

She was the first person I went to see when I returned here, twenty-five years old and pregnant; unless Abby's outline can be counted, crouched then standing, curved lines in air recounting her, replaying all of those people she had been whilst listening to her name. I even spoke to her, determined she had to be the first person to hear my voice on returning, determined someone should die.

Why do we return here, you and I, I said, bruising ourselves with this unpretty, clumsy, unmerry, murderous dance, scarcely able to tolerate our hand in each other's, our self in each other's pockets, in each other's debt?

Was that true? Was I so much in her debt, or was the nastier truth that in owing her I owed myself?

We remember because the dead cannot tell, and I was willing to dance to that, there on the shoreline, as wave upon wave reached towards me, white crests all, coming back to that shore, as the tide must have been doing for thousands of years, speaking someone's name, from somewhere in the depths.

All the while I was there I saw her eyes peering at me, the surfaces glossy and moist, two tiny mirrors reflecting the dull coloured world wrapped around her, the shore winds blowing, rifling through her, but without sound, her bruised and abused figure taking it in in silence, with a patience and expectation that only silence can engender. Then I left her on the shore where she was safest, where in memory she had always been safest, in as much as that can be relied on, left that impression of her, which is not mine to ever be parted from, and went to call on the matriarch.

If she was surprised to see me she showed no sign of it, though from her general lack of greeting, little more than an inclining of her head, she was suspicious of my coming.

"You seem to be wondering about me," I said.

She considered for a moment, then shrugged, threw more seed to her scrawny bantams and pullets, then eyed me calmly, a smile apparent around her lips: "Wondering what?" she asked. "What would I have to wonder about?"

"I didn't expect that you'd still have chickens."

"No one grows tired of poultry, no one throws up at the repeated taste of fowl."

"There's a supermarket three miles away."

The ghost of a smile vanished away, replaced by something far more bitter. She dispensed two more handfuls onto the muddy ground and made to go indoors, but turned on the threshold and asked me if I was through. I shrugged, as much as to say I didn't understand. It wasn't an interrogation, not openly declared anyway. She said she had nothing against my coming inside. It struck me as a singularly guarded welcome. She had nothing against it, but presumably nothing for it. I followed her in without another word.

The house had never been modernised in Martha's lifetime, the floor still lain with green flagstones, half-covered with an old threadbare rug, the walls whitewashed over rough plaster. We had gone down the lobby to the back room she called the kitchen, the front room, the parlour, closed. I had never been in there but could guess it, the cabinet with a few ornaments and the sideboard with her best crockery and cutlery which she had probably used twice in her lifetime, when Harold was married and when she claimed Abby. Certainly in one of the drawers, probably a top drawer, the one most accessible, would be her shroud, stowed there for decades, along with the policy book to pay for the funeral and perhaps a spot of tea, though who would be there to celebrate or mourn who could guess. Someone like Martha commanded respect or fear, or some intermingling of the two, but whether that would mean a well attended funeral only time would tell. There was something brutally lonely about the prospect.

I commented on the fact that everything was just the same, nothing changed, noting a marked defiance in it. She scowled at the comment as if I were being needlessly romantic, my language embarrassing. She was right, I suppose, my language had become embarrassing, for her, for me, the old accent overlaid with niceties, with new words, new tones, new subtleties, though the old hesitancies, knowing my place, knowing my point of permission, remained. Donald revelled in picking out those inconsistencies, the new voice and the old voice. Martha simply sneered at the existence of either.

She began to make tea, spooning out loose leaves from an old, grubby caddy, adorned with cartoon sketches of Indians and Chinese. She commanded me to sit. There were two chairs tucked up close to a leather based hearth, one a rocking chair, the other a rough horsehair armchair, a settee of similar style was pushed against the wall at the back of the room. An extendable table was shoved against another wall covered over with an oil-cloth. In the centre of the table, pushed against the wall, was an old box radio. I sat in the armchair, keeping to the edge, determined to show my discomfort, the extent to which my skin was crawling and tightening.

To think that Abby had lain, silently, like a resting faun, pressed between settee and wall, as if in a sanctuary, a haven, a place in which to grow into her natural self, hearing no evil, was almost unbearable. I felt a rising tide of revulsion for this graceless woman arrogantly making me tea, but I had to contain it, swallow down the taste of bile and cabbage the room emitted, she emitted, the stink of camphor, the digest of a different era, different timescale, different life expectancy.

As she put down a tray with teapot, cups with saucers, milk jug and a plate with slices of ginger bread and apple cake, she informed me I was mistaken, entirely wrong. Everything had changed, everything worsened, everything was now incorrect. She said incorrect with the glimmer of a hard smile briefly altering the tough, weathered fissures of her face, but the satisfaction of that complaint quickly receded and the former sullenness and anger at something unspecified but constant reasserted itself. There was no doubt about it, Martha, the matriarch, was a frightening woman, effortlessly disclosing an absence of pity. Should she choose to find a person unworthy, there would be no forgiveness, no respite, only gloating punishment. I had only one option, to brazen her out, defy her with likeness.

I thanked her for the tea, the excellent cake, which was in fact disgusting, half-cooked apples squeezed together in glutinous layers, the ginger bread, which I simply picked up and quickly replaced, stale and solid. She eyed me sceptically, certain of the joke, the preposterous insulting hospitality, yet bothered to treat me to a speech about home baking, the dying art of ingredients which my precious supermarket was doing away with. I told her I had never made any claims for the shop, simply pointed to its existence, an existence she obviously wanted to do without. She swallowed, frowned, and assured me she could manage

32

quite well without all manner of things. She picked up a piece of the stale ginger bread, sat in the rocking chair and began to munch, rocking gently as she sucked and gnawed at it. I eyed her all the while, growing dispirited and deflated by her easy arrogance, her apparent sway over me. I had to resist. After all, I had made the move. I had entered her kitchen, willingly accepted her tea, even suffered her cake. She wasn't going to dismiss me with such simple symbols of life inconsequential.

"Why do they name you the matriarch?" I asked, making sure I betrayed no excitement or true meaning in the question.

"Do they?" she replied, as if she really doubted such a thing.

"They always did."

"That's an altogether different thing."

"Why?"

"Because a family was a wholly different thing, a family was a family."

"Still," I persisted, pressing her.

"I was a Sempie," she flashed, as if the name alone justified any query. I don't know that she understood what I was asking, simply knew there was something she needed to defend.

Maybe the simple truth was that neither they nor she knew what the word meant, other than it was something about family, about something which legitimises a family, legitimises the past to which that family claims to belong, thereby stating a claim on the present and the future. Martha was the matriarch because she was a Sempie. It was a statement of ownership and defiance. It named physical violence, threats, intimidation. Martha was a Sempie mother. Except, she wasn't. Harold wasn't a Sempie, not entirely, unless Martha had fashioned it so that only her blood ran through his body, sluggishly to be sure.

"And now," I said, as if my new tone, my polished diction

33

could question what she was claiming for herself, "don't they call you that? Has the name been consigned?"

"I wouldn't know," she replied flatly. "I don't listen anymore, I don't bother. I find most conversation tedious, dull, most people gutless. I talk about the weather and seed and that's enough to keep me correct."

I was lost for words. How dare she say she didn't bother to listen? I wanted to strike her down where she sat, where once Abby must have sat, perhaps in her lap used as a breed of pet, a dog of kinds, though without canine ability to detect sound and sincerity, but I controlled myself. It was imperative. There were things I needed to know. I couldn't let her refusal to hear, or my failure to speak, win out. I had to confront her with meaning, with deafness, with sign.

Matriarch, with son, you, who, a name.

I signed at her, signed and watched her shock, her disapproval, her disability.

"Sempie, Shaughnessy," I uttered, still signing, outlining Abby's known lineage. "The Shaughnessys, family, like . . ." Then I brought it to a close and began again. "You must know of Owen Shaughnessy's epic journey as well as anyone," I said.

She altered her position, not suggesting unease or anger, just a change of position, weight redistribution. Of course, the suggestion was absurd. Even if she knew of it in finest detail it meant nothing to her: not epic, triumphant or tragic, but squalid; not human endurance or faith, but depravity, dirt, the Shaughnessys trash. I didn't let it go though. I wasn't here to play games. I was here to tear open and expose, lay bare the hatred and revenge it. "You never had a great deal of time for the Shaughnessys."

"Tramps, criminals, no, I never had a great deal of time, I never had any dealings."

"But Harold married one."

"Yes Harold married one."

"And there was Nora."

34

She conceded there was Nora.

After that, she was through. She adopted silence. I was raging. I had determined to choose when to stop, but I let it go. It was all right. I would take all the time it took.

I stood up to leave. She made no effort to see me out but remained seated staring obdurately into the empty grate.

From the door I spoke to her, demanding the right to one more question. "Tell me this, what did you say to Abby the day you dragged her out?"

"I want you to leave now."

*

Sometimes Abby saw herself, felt herself, was sure she had to be, a beetle: certainly some species of crawling creature, something with a preference for dark, confined habitat. Even on the shoreline she sought concealment. Even when we signed for her different shapes, new shapes, fantastic shapes, shapes personal and peculiar to three newly discovered sisters, she stuck by a certain exclusion, refusing to accept she didn't possess some insect life.

She sidled away with baleful, disbelieving eyes, pulling herself across the sands as if her body were a dead weight, her legs, which were perfect in every way, devoid of function. We couldn't work out the line of her thinking, but we fully recognised that only a creature with reason would have crawled towards concealment the way she did, just as only a creature with reason could have learnt to love the way she learnt to love, trusting it and believing it despite so much evidence to the contrary. She signed it. I you love Judith Salt, you love Grace Powers. I deaf you love.

Harold tried to beat that love out of her though, in the same way he tried to beat all reason out of her. She couldn't work out what he was scared of, none of us three loved sisters could, but she knew it. She signed fear whenever he was named. The same way the chambers of the sea made her say her name, so Harold made her quiver with his fear. I

35

don't suppose even Harold could have said just what it was that terrified him, but there was no doubting it. Why else would he have lashed out at a quiet girl who had learnt the sign for love?

*

At first I didn't love enough and then too much.

Donald never understood that. It would never have crossed his mind that I was sick of feeling nauseous, sick of honest charity and wanted to stop acting the cripple. He took all of my protestations for the truth and never for a second recognised I was another of the world's great liars. I always knew that love, real love had to be painful, as painful as a dagger.

When Abby crossed her two hands in front of her chest, signing love, the pain of it cut right through me. Her love was like violence, my body scarcely equal to its explosion. Many were the times I thought love would tear me into pieces.

Donald didn't threaten to destroy me like that. He didn't come close. Not to begin with anyway. I convinced myself it wasn't love I felt for him but a desire for exposure, the desire to be tall, plumb-straight Judith Salt. So, I revealed small frames of nakedness. This is my breast, Donald, which you are free to suck, this is my anger which you can observe without comment, and this is my shame which I am trusting to you, a gallery of staged intimacies given without constraint. Donald wouldn't have guessed such a thing, though. Not that he was either certain or complacent about love, but he was certainly less interrogative than I was.

Mind you, when I stand on this shore now, not old at sixty, certainly not as old as I felt when I was twenty-five determined that someone was going to die, though burdened by a certain sentimentality, I wonder how I can ever have had the confidence to assume to know his thinking. Isn't that the whole reason we tame existence, because at heart we are terrified of the gross freedom of someone else's thought? Ultimately all understanding is based on guesswork and trust. One's loneliness is never ultimately breached. We invent an inexact language to try and achieve some compromise, but my blue is never yours, your hurt singular, your frown all your very own.

I can still see the look of perplexity as he tried to reason with my self-doubts, my absurd accusations of unworthiness, never interpreting for a second that it was all in reverse, that I was bloated with self-confidence. I just wanted to hear his praise and protestations of love, though I never did touch him with anything other than lust and pleasure, never with that longing indicative of pain, never with those two hands of Abby's crossed at her chest.

In the end, though, when he was squirming and the cleverly crafted man began to slip, leaving him intolerant and quick to anger, I loved him, loved him too much, loved him so that it was a drain on all of his inner resources, but what went into that love, what terrible words, I don't know. It wasn't necessarily a turn around, just a change of emphasis, the same signs with slight inflections.

Of course existence is not composed of a single love, the brimming essence of the one God, despite so much wishful thinking that it were. There is a whole directory of love. We dipped in at different pages. I deaf love you, like a whore, like a witch, like a demon, like a woman. In response to my crossed hands he threw up his, signing the certainty of the thing being untranslatable. We don't mean anything forever though, only at the point of saying, within context, always within context, and besides who ever chooses to hear?

*

No, one is not old at sixty, though solitary confinement, punishment and separation do exact a heavy cost, the bonded body and mind pitted and pockmarked by the experience. Nevertheless, Judith Salt at sixty feels like a much younger woman than she once did.

When I stood here at twenty-five, pregnant, determined that someone should die, I was crippled with age, with no space left for another thought, time against me. I wanted to beat back the waves that threatened to overwhelm me, but scarcely had the energy to lift my arms, the energy to sign my being there at all. Any strength I had was claimed by the child. Already it was demanding primacy. I was determined to stand firm, though. Abby was indelible. Her sign was everywhere, her name all around me, her waste abundant – and the fact that someone would pay, Martha, Harold, Agnes, Mr Drake.

They never saw that time was a donation, a fund, a stipend. They treated it with contempt, but nevertheless stole it, stole it from her, from me, and it turned out we had so very little at our disposal. They were guilty of the most horrendous crimes against time.

Wave after wave confirmed it.

Me, old, a prisoner: Abby not even able to say her name; figures of eroded beauty.

Chapter Four

After Martha I went to call on Harold, called Sempie because Martha never would say any other. Whether in her heart of hearts she believed Sempie was his rightful name or not, I don't know. My guess is that she did, except in those moments of brutal honesty when she admitted to herself how disappointing he was – though he was never the slow-witted, numb-skull she made him out to be. Deep down, I don't suppose she ever really believed it herself. She never ceased insulting him, but only went so far. Of course he had committed a terrible wrong in her eyes. He had married a Shaughnessy.

She treated Agnes like a wilful, disobedient child needing a firm hand. There was no doubting which she assumed the dominant family. Agnes had married into the Sempies. It was not the match Martha wanted, probably none could have been, but once made Agnes had to take her place as one of the matriarch's subjects, in her case, the lowest of the low. That status to a certain extent immunised her from the worst of Martha's bile. The significant feeling the Shaughnessys provoked was tempered by the insignificance of Agnes herself. Agnes was cast in the role of idiot, who could at least be bullied into some semblance of worthiness.

Agnes, for her part, never retaliated, and on the whole played up to the role made for her. She allowed Martha to name her children – Abigail, Joseph, Ruth and Dennis, motifs the matriarch felt set the right tone, though she never explained what that tone was, but needless to say was something about propriety. Agnes even deferred over the question of religion. Her children could never be Shaughnessys as long as they were Church of England. Not that any of them were ever expected to go to church, though they did attend Sunday schools, alternating between the Church of England and Methodist, depending on which had a trip in the near future, as it got them out of the house on a Sunday afternoon.

Even before Agnes married Harold she understood that it would be at the cost of her own faith. Martha never considered for a moment what a bold act of defiance that must have been for Agnes, what a fight she must have put up against Aidan and Hazel, demanding her right to be with Harold. Martha couldn't countenance that the Shaughnessys might hold an opinion, a set of values: least of all in this case, given that she insisted Hazel was a whore and Aidan, who didn't earn any comment, was deaf.

In fact, it had been a struggle and a strain for Agnes, and much to her surprise, the most adamant opposition came from her father, not because of any religious sequel to her marriage but simply because it was to Harold Sempie, someone of whom he had never previously expressed an opinion. Her father was usually a tolerant, easily humoured man who openly allowed his daughter to manipulate him in order to get her own way, much to the annoyance of her mother who took an altogether more astringent view of her daughter's upbringing, but he was totally inflexible over Harold Sempie. He wouldn't hear of any relationship.

At first he simply denied it, forcefully putting it from his thoughts, insisting to Hazel that if nothing was said the situation would pass. He resorted to deafness. As Hazel tried to reason with him, at least to the point of admitting that Agnes was actually infatuated with the Sempie, he simply refused to hear. When he finally had to admit that deafness wasn't sufficient to hide the truth he became incensed. He begged and threatened Agnes, even offered to pay for her to go away to work in order to give herself time, though time was something she had never thought about once before in her life. He insisted that the age difference was too great, Harold being twenty-nine, Agnes merely nineteen.

Hazel found herself in the strange, not to say invidious position, of having to champion a Sempie. She pointed out that there was a war on and maybe Agnes was lucky to have any man at all. Aidan countered that Harold Sempie was no soldier, just a stay-at-home thug. Hazel made the case that Harold himself didn't attempt to boss the area, he was simply Martha's shadow and couldn't help being a Sempie. Aidan was quick to point out that Harold wasn't a Sempie, the reality of which struck Hazel as something of a relief, but for Aidan was virtually infernal.

Neither Hazel nor Agnes could understand why he should be so obdurate. The situation threatened to become a major rupture between father and daughter, maybe one that would prove irreparable, the danger of which Hazel was not slow in pointing out to Aidan, when suddenly he surrendered and gave his consent if not his blessing, making no attempt to mask the fatalism in his voice. If there was any lasting consequence to the crisis it was in the fact that Hazel told Agnes that her father was rather deafer than he had been, and even when she shouted as loudly as she cared he sometimes couldn't hear her at all.

Not that Martha would have believed the struggle Agnes had endured, considering her hopelessly unequal to such a thing. The very fact she offered no protest when Harold forbade her attending mass – a move certainly inspired by his mother, Harold himself having no religious affiliation – seemed to prove the point. If she could so easily give up a fundamental, then she was fit only for Martha's firm direction. That the nineteen year old had already rehearsed such a possibility with her own parents and gained their sympathy – evincing the uncharacteristic comment from Hazel that Agnes would always be a Catholic in her heart, as would her children when they came, and the mysterious addendum that it was God's burden to be acquainted with evil every bit as much as good – would never have entered Martha's thinking. Agnes was an inconvenience, an embarrassment, an act of stupidity on the part of her plodding son, but easily controlled, easily held in check, in fact so accommodating that if Martha had ever chosen to forget that she was a Shaughnessy, which she certainly did not, she might easily have affected the trick. Her real anger, her most bitter rage, was levelled at Harold, her contrary, offending child, the real culprit in inflicting such a ridiculous marriage on her.

He took all of her abuse, her fits of temper when she became breathless with shouting and her mouth filled with spit, like a large, patient hound, seemingly unperturbed by the attacks, but with a steady, watchful gaze ready to retaliate if the capricious master crossed the line. Not that he ever did retaliate, or even defend himself. He never crossed her and never had, except in the one but amazing choice of wife – which is not to suggest that the courtship was in any way romantic, Harold being a man of too few words for that to be the case. In fact, it is difficult to envisage just how he made any approach towards Agnes at all, but then, the situation should not be overstated. Harold was a man who used language with obvious infrequency, but who certainly was not devoid of confidence. Indeed, on occasion, given the right company and the right amount of drink, Harold could positively gush with words, depicting someone's misfortune without malice but real comedy. Those occasions were rare though, rarer still as he grew older. No doubt there was an element of convenience in his wanting Agnes. He evidently reached an age when he felt he should have a woman, certainly one additional to his mother, despite what she might think, and Agnes was on hand.

As to what Agnes gained from the match, enough to abandon a religion she loved and was devoted to, and relegate a family she loved – she never claimed for herself anything less than a happy childhood – is difficult to say. Perhaps the simplest explanation, no matter how unlikely, is that she fell in love. Her nature, which was essentially simple, allowed for it, love and obedience, the latter absolute once the match was made. In later years, particularly when Abby was returned to them, the two things, love and obedience, probably coalesced into something entirely new, something that meant Harold had to be right and that all he did was for the best. She grew into that compact with him. It was predicted long before by her absence from mass.

There was the added advantage in accepting Harold that he had his own place. It's likely he didn't tender her the possibility of himself, but of property. He probably invited her to walk with him, presented her with the front of his small terraced house and asked her whether she would like it. He may even have hinted at the certainty of gaining his mother's farmstead one day, but as Martha was still a relatively young, robust woman, perhaps he avoided that. On accepting the property, and therefore accepting she was ready to be woman of her own home, the marriage contract was sealed. No objections from Martha or Aidan would have meant anything after that.

Why Harold had his own place is difficult to fathom. He had left the farmstead some years previously, though he still took his washing there and frequently his meals. From the way they approached each other, Martha and Harold, warily, skilfully, like two predatory beasts, it seemed they recognised that it was dangerous for them to be penned up together. The thing that bound them, and it was certainly strong, – one would have killed on behalf of the other – also burdened them. It was a weight they could only shoulder for so much of each day. For Harold the sheer scale of his mother wore him down. Then, on his twenty-fourth birthday, as she sang to him, he knew he had to get out before one of them killed the other. For Martha there was a certain satisfaction in his leaving, which was evident in the pride with which she explained it to people – though no one would have asked outright – saying forcefully: He is such a Sempie, through and through, thank God.

It turned out to be a fortuitous move given that within weeks the war broke out, by which time Harold was an iron-ore miner, a reserve profession, no longer a pig and hen man – though he had erected pig-sheds and hen-huts in his yard, and taken a piece of the field behind to have somewhere for his sows to run. On paper he was a miner, his animals a pastime. In fact he spent very little time in the mine, which suited him fine as he detested the stain the ore left on his skin, which was becoming increasingly permanent lending his naturally dark features a distinct orange tincture, but was occupied in seeing to the transit of black market meat. Martha was behind it. She became quite the criminal as far as pigs and poultry were concerned. Not only did she have her own to sell, she established a whole network of farmers and smallholders keen to cash in on soaring prices. She didn't have enough say-so to authorise Harold's absence from the mine herself, but knew someone who did, someone making far more money than she ever would. If she expected Harold to show her any gratitude she was sadly mistaken.

Still, despite the surliness with which he saw to his task, those years of marketeering were some of the happiest of his life. The thrill of watching for the police as he made his round of the fell farms in the hours of dusk was one never to be repeated, and perhaps contributed to the moroseness of his later years. He was also pleasantly impressed by a driver who regularly came up from London, a powerfully built West Indian with a craggy, pockmarked face who went by the name of Nurse. Nurse told him all manner of amazing stories, usually involving near misses with the authorities in his numerous wanderings around the globe, accompanied by peals of screeching laughter. In comparison to this man's life Harold's seemed like a prison sentence.

In fact towards the end of the war Harold wasn't unconvinced that he should have joined up and seen a bit of the world himself. He was particularly taken by news accounts of the gradual taking of Italy, but left it too late. It became a regular refrain when he was bored or irritated that he should have been a soldier and had missed his opportunity. It was never clear whom he was blaming, Martha, Agnes or himself. Agnes was invariably sympathetic, whilst Martha simply scoffed and suggested he was better off with pigs. He always spoke about Nurse with affection and regret.

After the war he took to doing odd jobs, usually farm work, and still had his own sows and porkers, anything in preference to the iron-ore mine, though his skin retained a mild glowing tincture. There was still a great deal of illegal trading, post-war shortages ensured that, but Nurse had disappeared and there was less money about than there had been. Once the fighting was over there was an admission of bankruptcy. Within no time it was as if Harold had never known any other life. He and Agnes settled down to a routine of stasis and boredom. Whether either of them dreamed of anything different is impossible to say. It was an existence outlined by habit; habits formed through lack of money.

Then there was the child, Abigail, my sister, named by Martha, claimed by Martha. She never cried so everyone said she was a good child. We never cried, except Grace, occasionally, so they thought we were all good, and if not good, at least appropriate, children of the age, sharing its bleak realisations, its lack of funds and goods, silent in the teeth of the uncertain future. The miracle is that there were children at all, let alone three, three sisters, born in the same year, with grades of deafness, grades of non-hearing, but nevertheless the same scale of vision, visions that were biblical, apocalyptic, ruined.

Abby always had that sense of seeing, of peering at something sketched across the horizon revealed only to her, which she accepted without enthusiasm or fear, but nor with negligence. There is always that which defies and denies us, that which bars access to the world of inner visions, so that everything is always partial, even her touch, the sign for love, Poppy cradled, the hurt like a light on her face, displaying her but never unmasking her, decoding what the horizon had just given.

*

I left the shore, the horizon having given me Abby, at least a trace of her, her looking, seeing something without enthusiasm or fear, signing a muted declaration of love. I needed that after my encounter with Martha, needed to hear her name, the urging that drew me on, her vowel.

It was growing dark when I climbed from the shingle onto the dunes then re-crossed the river and followed the quarry line back to the village. From the railway bank I could still see the mud-flats spread along the coast, despite the mustering greyness. There were probably waders calling, perhaps the occasional drum of wings, but I left it to silence. I was glutted on Abby's name. As I'd stepped up the shingle bank, the gathering darkness muffling the sea, bending sound, I'd turned off my aid, leaving only the planet's bass notes to rumble through me.

A barn owl hunted silently across the plain, etching the twilight with a movement of drifts, stabs and falls, each swoop to the bog floor unsuccessful. I waited, hesitating maybe, watching the bog, the owl, the imagined life below it, merging my thoughts into the shadows, the vanishing contours, wanting to lose definition myself, wanting to assume spectral beauty, my veins frosted, crystal rich, an element amongst those receding but life rich elements, and called to it with an animal intimacy, like a she wolf, baying an understanding beyond reason, because reason had let me down.

The trick could not be effected for long though, because as is always the case we insist on reducing everything to meaning. Besides, I had an appointment to keep, one I had made with myself. So I went on, departing from another of Abby's spaces, the bound world of the marsh flats, where she looked and signalled no name, no animosity and then love.

And, of course, I had to re-admit sound.

Harold was alone. Agnes had gone to her parents because Hazel wasn't very well, nothing too serious, he didn't think, but Agnes was doing their dinner, presumably because Aidan didn't cook, which he immediately corrected to couldn't cook. He smiled at the thought, but didn't say any more. The smile, though, loosened something in him, some stream of thought that amused him, pleased him. He smiled more broadly and invited me in. I was astonished. He was little short of flirting with me, his invitation, the look on his face, signalling his hints.

He remained in the doorway as I stepped inside, forcing me to brush against him and encounter his weight and substance. He slammed the door behind me like a prison door at night, his hand going with it, demonstrating its closure, the absence of an escape route. Despite everything I felt my heart rate wind up. I too felt excitement and distinct pleasure, but of a wholly different nature and order.

He smiled at his achievement, the closed door, the display of himself, then removed his hand from the door and eyed me more coldly, with a revelation of dislike, or perhaps more accurately, disregard.

Speaking with slow, mannered syllables he told me I was looking well, that he would have been hard-pressed to recognise me, except of course he knew it was me. Well, it was obvious, the telltale sign was on display, as always, my hair pulled back into its usual neat bun, the hearing aid exposed.

He stepped up to within inches of me, the aroma of moist earth and stale sweat emanating from him, and uttered that the life must suit me. I met his insistent gaze and shrugged my agreement. Yes, *the* life did suit me, *the* life if not life itself, life happening in so many places and times at once, memory and desire overlaid on event, making one, one Judith Salt, twenty-five years of events, currently enjoying *the* life.

"I fancied London myself at one time, but I don't think I'd want it now," he said, accusing me of something in saying it. He shrugged, smiled, and then, as if dismissing any further thought of it, quietly demanded: "Can you hear me?" Again it sounded like an accusation, a threat, but I quickly realised that I had yet to speak. I had appeared on his doorstep, accepted his invitation to come inside, but hadn't said a word. It was a question. He wanted to know if I could hear, but there was no concern, sympathy or embarrassment associated with it, just blandness and bluntness. He was used to it, of course, the query, the doubt, the suspicion: can she hear, can you, can you hear?

"Yes," I said, "yes, I can hear, sorry."

The apology seemed natural, though I hated myself for so easily giving it, but he didn't pursue it, didn't want explanations. He had already moved on. "Well sit down, go on, sit down."

It was only then that I took in the room, freed from his attention, his grip. I was surprised. What had been two rooms had been knocked into one, and where there had been flagstones with rugs there was now a wall to wall fitted carpet. The walls were an expanse of red roses. The old grates had been taken out, replaced by coal effect electric heaters lit by light bulbs. – There was no gas in the village.

"It's very different," I said, without excitement, not wanting to reveal surprise over anything.

He pursed his lips. "It's not new."

"Your mother's is exactly the same, exactly as I remember it."

"You've been there?"

"Just to say hello, be polite, and I noticed that the house is just the same."

"At her age people don't change."

"But she isn't old. What is she now?"

He eyed me coldly, suspicious of insult, before responding: "No, she isn't old, but she likes it the way it is, that's how she is, likes things as they were."

"I guess so. I wasn't sure she even used the supermarket."

"Of course, she uses the supermarket. What do you take her for?"

"There used to be a meat van."

"There still is. He sells meat. That isn't everything."

"There used to be a van for everything."

"Well, now there isn't."

"But a meat van."

"A meat van."

"The world used to come to us, but now it doesn't, except for a meat van, that must be quite a change."

He didn't reply but watched me steadily, alert to what I was saying, searching each word, uncertain of his ability to decipher hidden meanings, annoyances, cleverness. It wasn't his strength, which was in all ways physical. He was flabbier than he had been, though, his outer coating softer because of it, but that was a new layer, the bulk and heaviness remained, the size, the imposing expression, the constant vigilance, the disappointment.

"I mean," I continued, "once upon a time there was no need to ever leave this village, this tiny village with its handful of families. You could die here without having seen anything else."

"You can die anywhere without seeing anything else."

"Don't you think it's surprising though? There must have been people who never went anywhere, simply waited for the meat van."

"They were all right."

"I'm not saying they weren't, I'm saying, it's surprising."

"We can't all bugger off to London."

"You said you fancied it."

"But I didn't do it."

49

"Why not?"

"I had kids."

"Before?"

"I didn't know anything about it, not till the black told me."

"The black?"

"I wouldn't say out against them. I liked him. We got on well."

"I remember, remember hearing, you talking."

"Funny, I don't remember telling you."

"Well, it wasn't Abby." He flashed me an angry look. I laughed and went on: "I mean, it couldn't have been Abby, could it?"

"No, I don't recall telling her," he replied slowly, but with triumph, pleased with himself.

"I don't suppose you do."

"Which means what exactly?"

"Nothing. It means nothing."

"Is there a point to your being here?"

"Just visiting family."

"But we just carry on. We don't know you're gone. Only you know that. Only you know you're not here. We don't know it. So don't expect a big welcome, the red carpet, because we didn't know you weren't here all the time."

"Was it like that with Abby?"

"Abby was different."

Yes, she was different.

*

She was here and away, never entirely present but not absent either. We were never sure about the other places, what she saw whilst listening to her name, listening to the voice that urged her, made her part of saying. When I recall her now in one of her spaces, relentlessly and tirelessly staring, she doesn't seem to be looking but interrogating, not content but not disappointed either. It's as if she were certain there were things behind things, that she could peel away the sky, the sea, the mud-flats, the rail lines, the walls, to reveal . . . to reveal what? We could never fathom it.

At times Grace became angry with her and demanded an explanation, access, I suppose. Sometimes she answered with her name, pronouncing it over and over, in ecstasy with the vowel, her face twisted with the pleasure of it, and other times she turned her shoulder, tucking Poppy closer to her with the same rough compassion she always showed her and refused to divulge anything of her secret. Grace was determined though. She was sure the things Abby saw must be like the things in her picture books. Grace had lots of picture books.

Her father, Seamus, Nora's eldest, set great store by reading. He was an avid reader himself and had completed numerous evening classes at a Technical College, managing to become pit deputy in his thirties and eventually, in his late forties, a primary school teacher. He read the first and second readings and the psalm in church every Sunday. He was an awkward, troubled man, devout and disciplinarian. Despite the uncomplicated faith of his two brothers, Peter and Paul, he believed the deaf were incapable of proper education and therefore of true religious experience. He considered Grace's deafness a punishment, his rather than hers, though he never declared the nature of his sin. He handed her the picture books with an air of hopelessness and regret, but Grace accepted them gratefully, in her own feisty, offhand way.

He refused to learn sign, refused to acknowledge there was a great deal of deafness in his family. We never realised he was ashamed of it, in fact, considered nothing strange about his attitude at all.

Grace put her idea to the test and brought a book and shoved it into Abby's arms, displacing poor put upon Poppy. She pointed to the cover picture and demanded to know if that was the kind of thing Abby saw. It was a book of angels. Grace opened it onto a white robed angel leading a red robed child over a two plank bridge, the child carrying a small willow basket and clutching the angel's robe. There was a prayer written underneath, but as none of us could read that remained a mystery. Grace asked Abby in her savage, frustrated voice, whether that was it? Did she see angels in the sky? Abby cringed, turned away and tried to thrust the book from her, but Grace wouldn't allow it. She was convinced Abby was possessed of visions, but then she was only a child and possessed of visions herself, visions that even she couldn't find the sign for.

Grace's own favourite book was the Boy's Book of Marvels with its fantastic and grotesque pictures, which included an etch of five different breeds of snake strangling the body of a cow, a picture of Pizarro's terrified crew contemplating the New World, the flat earth on the backs of elephants, and Dr Faustus signing his soul to the devil. She brought this one to Abby and showed her each picture in turn, then back to the first and through them all again, and then she cross-examined her, demanding to know whether they were the things she saw, the flat world, the undiscovered world, the violent world, a world of devils? Abby studied those images with much more interest than she had the book of angels, peering at them as if they too were surfaces, a sheen covering another truth. She giggled and then she moaned, but she was attentive, enthralled by the images, and then she marked it off with her name.

Poor Grace persisted with her books but was never satisfied. She nagged Abby time and again, her voice inflexible and absurdly grown-up. Sometimes she threatened to take Poppy away unless Abby co-operated. At those moments Abby held Poppy more loosely, whether to feign indifference or because she accepted Grace's authority to claim ownership, I don't know. I do know that Grace never would have taken her. No one could have loved Poppy with the same unsentimental devotion Abby showed her, and no one could have shared such visions as those two did, cuddling together. Still, it was always amusing to hear Grace admonish Abby, as if Grace were a tiny, strict adult – which she would have learnt from Seamus – confounded and infuriated by Abby's behaviour.

Indeed, Abby's stubbornness rankled more than Grace.

*

I smiled at Harold, the smile enriched by Abby's image between us, which I wanted him to know, willing him to see it, share it and wonder about it. He recognised it all right, recognised the strength in the smile, the outline of the figure in its making, but decided to outface it.

"Did you love her?" I asked, the question arising spontaneously, because of that deliberately vacant gaze of his, but I regretted it immediately. It gave him power, released him from me. The word was so stupid. He didn't know anything about love, only impulse and instinct. My using it, uttering it in that quietly melodramatic way, removed me, allowed him to think of me as an intruder, albeit one that used to belong. "She could be very stubborn," I said, trying to retrieve something.

"Yes, she could."

"Is that why you hit her?"

"I thought she was playing games, having me on. I didn't like that."

"And what do you think now?"

"She liked games."

"I suppose she did."

*

I don't know that it is possible to call such intensity of feeling a game, but I suppose it was. We never thought we were playing games. We were sisters engaged in battle, in conflict with a recalcitrant nature. We knew it could yield secrets, but it was stubborn and niggard, determined not to give up its pearls, but we were dogged too. We crossed the fields like

53

Pizarro's conquistadors, clambering amongst escarpments of exposed iron-ore we called cliffs, dropping into craters we called valleys, mapping out the extent of our world, the boundaries of our existence, and they were vast, we found them so, and named them, Red Steps, Hawk Cliff, Ghost Valley, Lost Plateau, Frozen Fields, Waste Land, No Man's Land, Lost Girl, signing them like pathfinders, scouts, enthralled and frightened by our finds.

Beneath Hawk Cliff there was the rusted gut of an abandoned car, little more than the metal frame and busted seats. We had no idea how it had appeared so far from any road or track. It stunk of mould, saturated horsehair, dank leather and rust. Nevertheless, we sailed for miles in her, feasting on stolen turnips, Grace signalling rapids, giant squid, hurricanes, jumping from running board to roof to bonnet, whilst I held the wheel, and Abby crouched on the ripped up bench in the rear, shielding Poppy, sometimes eyeing the dangers with a look of grim resistance, sometimes violently rocking and moaning aloud, signalling fear, enthusiasm, ecstasy, we weren't exactly clear which. We called our vessel The Inca because Grace's father told her that's what the caption read in the Book of Marvels beneath a picture of a tall, lean, hollow cheeked Pizarro standing over his newly baptised enemy, the Inca king, though he fell short of admitting it was just prior to his garrotting him, and how we would have felt about that, I can't say.

At the time Pizarro was a hero. The Book of Marvels said he had been abandoned as a baby on the steps of a church and suckled by a pig. That made him like us, intimate with pigs, though Grace did sign that it was pretty disgusting, all the same, even if he was only a baby and didn't know any better. Grace's father went on to explain to her that lots of people had been brought up by animals, he knew a few himself, it wasn't so rare: Tarzan by apes, Mowgli by wolves and the founders of Rome, Romulus and Remus also suckled by wolves. Learning such things about wolves was strange.

It forced us to rethink our geography and rethink our dangers. The Wasteland had always been overrun by them and we had considered that terrible. We had to rethink everything that frightened us or pleased us. I don't remember who was the first to wonder about Pizarro and Atahualpa, the Inca king, but eventually we all did – but, maybe I'm making up the past now as much as we made up the present then, and always made up the future, though whether we ever recognised we were in the future, I really don't know. We certainly never knew when it had begun.

In my memory it is Abby who first wondered about Atahualpa, Abby and Poppy, indefatigable investigators of the Book of Marvels, Abby's index-finger tracing the outline of the soon to be garrotted king, after which, the sketch being complete, she moaned aloud like a mourner expressing the magnitude of her loss. I seem to recall that our games were spiritual that day. We sensed that the wastes of bog land, escarpments, shallow ponds, the dun coloured earth conjoined to the low lying, leaden sky, was overviewed by a sad and disappointed watcher, though whether from the highest cliff or higher still we couldn't say. Perhaps it was the spirit of Atahualpa himself, his or like his, perhaps made up of many.

Maybe I am being fanciful, though. How could we have thought that? We never knew the word, the sign, for Atahualpa, which is knowledge of a much later life altogether, though we certainly could have touched the top of our heads with the fingertips of a curled hand and lifted it indicating king, though if someone were to insist we didn't, I wouldn't argue.

I would insist on the day though, and many others like it. So many lead heavy, flint-grey days, days when the silence was almost complete, when colour was bleached from everything, leaving only a tincture of pale blue, days that made us aborigines. It was invariably Abby who set the tone, initiated those strange, sombre games, ourselves haunting ourselves and relishing the terror. Grace sometimes objected, but never for long, rarely marching off in a huff at Abby's intransigence, her spook filled gloom.

Grace did regularly stamp her feet and berate Abby when she refused skipping or hopscotch. Grace liked those, the faster the better, but at the start of the game Abby was always reluctant and hugged Poppy tightly to her as if her sense of responsibility wouldn't allow her to put Poppy down for a moment. That made Grace livid who would start her war dance and sign all manner of insults at Abby. If Abby looked crestfallen Grace would relent and try to coax her, pointing out that Poppy could watch. No sooner would Abby begin, rotating the rope in her right hand, than excitement invariably got the better of her and she would make the crudest noises of enthusiasm. Sometimes she went too far and the rope was too fast even for someone as proficient as Grace, then the recriminations and insults would start again. The peace was usually restored by reverting to hopscotch, which again Abby always refused then overdid, which more often than not ended up with her stamping her foot on a numbered square as if it were an insect she wanted to trample under foot. Grace would calm her by signalling that Poppy was watching, implying that she wasn't setting a good example. That tended to cow her. She recognised from very early on that there was something in Grace's expression demanding, be a good girl, and that it was imbued with the question: Have I been a good girl? I am sure Abby always hated that question.

*

"She was a good girl though," I said, "stubborn, but good."

He didn't respond, but eyed me steadily, letting me know he was refusing me, wasn't going to play games.

"Did you not think she was good, a good girl. That's what she wanted to be, a good girl. She always said that."

"I don't remembering hearing it," he replied coldly.

"But she said it all the time. Have I been a good girl? It was pathetic, really. Have I been a good girl, over and over, the same awful question."

"I said, I don't remember hearing it."

"Now that you mention it, I don't think it was her. Silly me. She wanted to be a good girl, but then she didn't. You're right, it wasn't her who said it at all. Your memory's better than mine. I wonder what else you remember, better than me I mean."

He raised his eyebrows, pursed his lips and looked thoroughly bored. He finally sat down, slumping heavily into an armchair that was pulled up close to the electric fire at a slight angle to a television on the other side of the grate.

"What do you want?" he asked, complaining, telling me of his boredom and impatience, his indifference to everything.

"I don't want anything. I'm in the area. I thought I should see you."

"I told you, we didn't know you weren't here, had no idea, you might have been round the corner, not in London at all." He sat forward, his right palm cupped around his right knee, his left elbow across his left thigh, and tried to smile, the effect being one of a muscle spasm around his jaw which merely contorted his face, making him disjointed. He shuffled further forward until he was on the edge of his seat, both elbows on his knees now, his fingertips touching, forming an inverted v across his lips. His eyes were moist and sharp, weighing me up, quartering me. The fingertips slipped and became a fence of eight digits across his chin, the thumbs hidden behind. He smiled again, more successfully, all the pleasure within. "Everyone wants something, don't kid yourself." The smile broadened out vividly. "And don't kid me."

I repeated that I didn't want anything.

He reached across the space of the grate, his backside scarcely in touch with the chair anymore, and placed his right hand on my knee. "You know, you really are looking well, really well."

"Despite everything."

"Now why do you say that?"

I half-cocked my face, inquiring, but almost smiling, the gesture of it, no more. He warmed to it though and pressed his fingers into my flesh.

"Will Agnes not be back any minute?"

He grinned triumphantly, but sat upright, his torso full and straight. "She just might at that," he said. "But we're not finished?"

"No?" I queried, my attention coquettish, submissive and amused, all for him to see, to interpret.

"We all want something," he pronounced, satisfied, wanting to show it, "no one's any different to anyone else, as far as that goes."

"Except Abby."

He scoffed and looked offended, distrustful of my going over old ground, angry at me.

"You said, that's all, said Abby was different."

He pursed his lips severely, acknowledging, distastefully, that it was certainly the case.

*

Sometimes with her contortions, her body like a rag-doll, with less definition than Poppy, less solidity, her muscle tone absent, a soft yielding bag of a being, I felt she was enacting the Book of Marvels, mutating into a species of snake, strangled cow, flat world, demon, scuttling across the dunes or shingle banks, terrified to be found in such a metamorphic state. I failed to grasp the honesty and confession involved.

Our changes, Grace's and mine, melted one into another, the past sloughing off, shed like dead skin cells, but with Abby it was a struggle, a fight between forms, her, the owner, uncomfortable with any, and her nature was offended, embarrassed by such incompleteness. I guess it was her knowledge of the world of transformations that drew her so doggedly to the marvels, to those moments of transition, things that she saw through and was amazed by, though never shocked by.

Nothing shocked Abby, not since she had witnessed Harold and Agnes butcher a pig in November, neither of them revealing any compunction as Agnes pinned it down and Harold passed a knife across its throat. Abby obviously had no awareness of the fart of air, the animal's squeal and the dying whistle, but couldn't escape the redness of its blood, the pale tincture of its nude pink skin, its kicking body. All her protests and anguish simply resulted in a backhand from Harold and a glare of disgust from Agnes. She ran from it and discovered the shoreline where she rolled around on the sands like the animal in its death throes, her soul wedded to the creature.

There was no talking to her then, no knowing what she wanted, what her attempts to fit into ever smaller spaces amounted to, though Grace tried and tried again to reason with her, until Grace lost her temper and left her to her immediate fate, which made no difference at all.

I never said Abby wasn't stubborn.

*

"We both know what we want, don't we?" Harold announced, keeping his torso braced, upright.

I shrugged mildly. It amused him. He saw that the gesture wasn't denunciation, rejection or threat of exposure, simply non-committal. Of course, at first, I had been taken aback, shocked that he should be propositioning me, Judith Salt, deaf, grade II, but I very quickly recognised that, as always, he was acting on impulse and instinct. Nothing else motivated him. The realisation was liberating. I knew exactly what he wanted, and it wasn't sex with Judith Salt but control of Judith Salt, authority over a deaf, grade II woman. Well, I could cope with that. I held up my hands, palms

facing my body, and then moved them forward and out-
wards, as if I was indeed offering him something. He
grinned at the possibility, the sign.

*

For some time Abby gave up her second favourite book, The
Adventures of King Arthur and the Knights of the Round
Table. Grace only ever let her look at it, never keep it for any
length of time to secrete away in one of her many dens. It
was too beautiful to part with, picture after picture of Dark
Age knights, painted predominantly in various shades of
vivid blue, in combat with serpents and witches, overviewed
by beautiful, wretched women. Abby was particularly fond
of a plate of Sir Galahad witnessing the Grail. She gazed at it
with naïve joy, her face turning slowly as if to see it from
every possible angle, but then one day, completely out of the
blue, she gave it up, thrust it aside as if looking at it had
become fraught with danger. It was as if she had realised,
without having any skill to put it into words, that purity, the
worldview of Sir Galahad, was incompatible with life. It was
a sense that went right through her and really put a stop to
any tendency towards sentimentality, though it didn't stop
her attempts at escape, doomed searches for the door
through time that would allow access to such a chivalric
world, a world of myth and magic. Little did we expect that
she would find a door, a door into the dark.

*

"Just tell me this one thing," I asked. "Why did she scare you
so much?"

I knew before I had even asked, responding to my own
impulse and instinct, that he would find the question unanswerable, but I failed entirely to predict his response. He
took it seriously, patiently, trying to work out an answer that
would make sense. He must have calculated that this was to
be the cost of my compliance; the pay-off for allowing him to

manhandle me, an answer to an unanswerable question. It was comical watching him squirm with its possibilities. In the end he gave the only answer possible. He wasn't scared of anything. He smiled and corrected himself. He was nervous of heights, uncomfortable in high places, didn't even like nailing down tin sheets on the pig-sheds. He didn't like heights at all, but I shouldn't go away with the wrong impression, he wouldn't let it get in the way.

I had no idea what he meant by that. The accompanying smile was dreadful, not asking but telling me he had passed the test, successfully answered my question. I felt sickened. His filthy smile was turning my stomach. I wasn't prepared for it. He had always been so lazy with expression, to my mind only really capable of hostility or suspicion, and yet here he was trying it on with me, a deaf sister, a sister he would once upon a time have bullied and dismissed. So, what was going on? Was he feeling his age? Was it desperation in him, awareness that all he was equal to was a deaf sister, a sister who brazenly declared her deficit, who ripped back her hair to exhibit it to the world, who outfaced bigots with *strength of purpose*, as Donald called it? Is that how he saw me, a measure of his failing?

I stood up, straight, rigid, and stepped towards him, until I was only inches from him, until he might have touched me with just an accidental movement. He eased himself back in his chair, his eyes slowly scanning my figure, up and down, though avoiding my face, sticking to the space between neck and thigh, making filthy calculations. I said: "Maybe I'm a high place, maybe you should be careful."

He emitted a low groan, a purring sound. Was he excited or disgusted? Was he sinking or soaring? And how dare he make a transaction out of me. My instinct and urge was to smack him in the face, to smack him in the face and never stop until it was a disfigured sop, a parody of a face. I wanted to wipe his entire history from him, eradicate it feature by feature. However, I wasn't so blinded by my mission not to recognise that I didn't have a hope against him, so I smiled, gave him a signal of humour. Yes, I was having him on. Nothing to fear from a deaf sister. I was just being playful.

He made a move to get out of the chair, a move towards me. I stopped him, laying my palm firmly on his shoulder, whispering, reminding him that Agnes might be back at any moment.

He eyed me with his usual primitive vigilance. I laughed quietly and promised him that we would have our day. I even told him that he shouldn't worry, we would definitely have our day. I can't disguise the fact that there was a hint of relief in his expression. He had won what he wanted, secured enough. The prize itself wasn't worth more than the winning. Well, we would see about that.

I smiled again, coaxing and reassuring him, then lifted my palm to his face, and made an indentation along his cheek with my index-finger, like a blunt knife carving him. "She wasn't a high place, was she, so why be scared of her, scared of someone in love with the shore, someone who'd learnt the sign for love."

"I don't know what you mean."

"I'm just wondering, thinking about then, that's all. I don't mean anything, don't mean anything at all."

"She was an oddball, got people's backs up, played games. You said so."

"Yes, I said so. So you hit her?"

"It was my job."

"Job?"

"She was mine, wasn't she? I had to take her in hand."

"But not yours to begin with. To begin with she was your mother's."

"She didn't want to be saddled with a dummy, did she? Who would?"

"Is that what you thought?"

"That's what I knew, what everyone knew."

"But she . . ."

"I've had enough of this."

He stood up, forcing me back a step. My hand fell away. We were at eye level, Harold just a few inches taller, but enormous in comparison, his interest slow but menacing.

"I'm sick of your questions," he said.

"I'm sorry."

"So what are you playing at? Why are you going on and on?"

"The past, I don't want to lose it, that's all."

"To hell with it!"

"But I don't want to say that."

"We don't have a past. We're still here. We didn't know you weren't."

"And there's still a meat van."

"Of course, there's a meat van, a high-class butcher, but that isn't everything."

"I don't suppose he's getting any younger."

"Who is?"

I thought: I am, Harold, getting younger every minute, minute by minute, time sloughing off me, my tissues packed with collagen, all those years of smoking too much banished, an imago. Can you not see Harold, the female perfection of Judith Salt, standing in front of you, negotiating the charade that is human business? No, Harold Sempie, or whoever you are, I shall not let go of the past, I shall not be left high and dry, a tragic clown. I don't ever expect to lose the past, though I accept I shall change my relationship to it.

I said: "I don't suppose there's anyone to take his place."

He glared at me, his anger at breaking point, without understanding why.

"Still," I said soothing him, telling him it was still playful, "all the more reason to take your chances, seize the day."

He pouted his lips as if he were about to swing for me.

I smiled and repeated that we would have our day.

He made a move towards me. I shook my head.

Not now.

I suggested I should be getting on and slowly stepped away. He shrugged, letting me know again that he didn't know I wasn't here. I said we would meet again. I would make sure of it. A promise. He shrugged again, but the meaning wasn't remotely the same.

When I reached the door I asked: "How is Agnes, by the way?"

"Just the same."

"What did you say to her when you hit her?"

"Stop playing games," he said, then immediately turned towards the fire and slumped back down.

Chapter Five

Abby saw a spotted woodpecker dance up an electricity pole and held a chicken claw in her hand, which she looked at, and from that time onwards the two things became inseparable, creating the same feeling of sickness in the base of her stomach.

The chicken claw was the only gift Harold ever gave her. He threw it at her and when she ducked he was moved to take her into the pig-shed and beat her. It wasn't easy for him to provide a present and he expected her gratitude. He grabbed her by the arm and dragged her across the muddy yard, barking at her to pick it up, but she didn't understand. In the end he threw her down, picked up the waxen looking thing himself, held it at her face and commenced to pull the severed tendons, giving the impression that the thing still had life. After that he threw it at her again, this time meaning it to hit her, and marched off cursing.

When he had gone she crawled across the mud and picked up the claw from where his wayward aim had let it fall. She dabbed it clean with her dress and then sat there, not bothering to get herself out of the corn streaked slurry, just pulling at the tendons, watching the thing contract and relax. Then she saw the woodpecker. She looked again at the claw, imagining it contracting against a solid surface, and was just about to pull it again when she was knocked flying, landing face down in filth. Her stomach contracted and she felt a deep agonising sickness, but this time she decided to fight back. She suddenly leapt to her feet and began reaching up, tearing at Harold's throat.

She never forgot the shades of expression, the shades of meaning that crossed Harold's face as she scrambled to tear out his wind-pipe. At first he looked shocked, non-plussed by her ferocity, and then, with his arms held out defending himself, a half-smile formed itself on his features. He realised he could enjoy this, and that his enjoyment would be saving face. He started shouting at her, swearing and goading, which even if she had been able to hear she wouldn't have registered, she was too possessed by her need to fight. She was driven by fear, retaliation and something else, some-thing so abstract that she wouldn't have been able to name it, and for which I only have a few supposed words: dissent, shame, ecstasy, avowal – which was her name, but maybe that is too clever by half.

Eventually, Harold subdued her – after all she was just a small thing, scarcely turned seven – grasped her firmly by the bodice of her pinafore with his right hand and lashed at her with his left. After that he began to throw her around the yard, until she fell face down inches from a manure heap, small rivulets of the slurry running against her. He glared at her for a moment, his massive torso heaving with the weight of his breathing, and then turned to march away. His temper hadn't quite abated though, hadn't been satisfied. He couldn't stop himself from coming back to her. He lifted her up in one hand by the loose cloth of her pinafore, screamed right into her ear – presumably words to the effect that if she ever tried anything like that again, then the next time he would kill her – then flung her, as if she had little more body than Poppy, across the yard so that she ended up in a disjointed heap by the door of the pig-shed.

Harold would never forget that fight, and even though he laughed about it, dismissing it – uttering threats of what would happen should she ever try anything like that again – he was aware that it had taken a great deal of brute force to subdue her, which embarrassed and troubled him, and determined him never to be caught off-guard again..

He remembered hitting her across the buttocks and feeling that it was like striking a pillow, the flesh absorbing his blows, rendering them useless, and becoming so frustrated it crossed his mind to break her arms. Something stopped him, though, a residual commandment submerged somewhere in his subconscious, something he was absolutely certain wouldn't interfere again. He would never be so lenient in the future. Nevertheless, the damage was considerable.

We found her in the church grounds curled up at the base of a lichen crowned angel, a yellow capped angel smiling enigmatically, overviewing the dead, guarding, with its slow growths. This was another of her places, her favoured places, spaces into which she made herself fit. She was stained with mud and chicken shit. It was raining heavily, coming down in straight, visible sheets, with not the slightest breeze to divert it. It made the mud and shit run down her face, patterning her with filthy lines. Grace kept her distance, standing stiffly, occasionally commanding Abby to get up, shouting it and then signing it, growing increasingly scared at Abby's lack of response, whether inability or refusal she couldn't work out. I think she believed Abby might be dying. There always was that never admitted belief between us that she might be dying. We lived with it all of the time. It never crossed our minds that she was simply the living embodiment of what we all were, tiny tricks of life trying to work out an arrangement between body and reason. I was altogether braver. I went up close and peered at her, studying her as if she were some kind of specimen, after all she herself was convinced she possessed some essence of insect life, but it wasn't the case. She wasn't crushable, though she could be disfigured.

Her eyes were vividly red. She had been crying but had stopped, stopped with a determination to deny she ever had. It made her face taut, vigilant and yet quick to cringe, her expression, her shiny red eyes, rushing between a near ground and a far ground, dealing with two worlds at once.

There were small veins, tiny capillaries, apparent beneath the mud and shit. Within the next three days she would obviously be a patchwork of blue-purple bruises. Of course she still had green bruises, brown bruises, scarcely discernible bruises, bruises of all ages. We were quite skilled in knowing the age of a contusion, knowing just where the blow had fallen, the mark it had hit or missed.

I made small oblique signs that we should go, but she wouldn't entertain the idea. She curled into herself even more tightly and gazed straight ahead, in the direction of the angel but not at her, not at anything, nothing apparent anyway, which was how she was in her favourite places, in them and elsewhere at one and the same time.

The geography of her world was definite and we learnt her territory very quickly, and more to the point learnt its ambition, her need for small spaces within big spaces, small worlds within big worlds.

The village was small but scattered. At its heart there were rows of terraced houses, for the most part small houses built to accommodate mine workers and farm labourers, but a number were on a grander scale, presumably built to house higher ranks such as deputies and foremen. There were also a number of quite large dwellings, Georgian in build, occupied by land managers, factory managers, pit managers, the doctor and the vicar. These people all owned a car, which was still a novelty. On the fringes of the village were the prefabs, small kit houses constructed of rusted metal sheets, without gardens or yards.

Around this congregation there were numerous scattered cottages, in rows of three or four, tied cottages that had once been attached to farms secreted amongst spurs of the nearby fells and at the head of bluffs that led up from the coast. Everything was built on low hills, in troughs or on escarpments, the land buckling before the great heights of the interior.

The village had a single room school and two churches,

one in the centre, St John's, skirted by a beck which flooded in the winter and formed a small moat around the hill on which the church stood. The other, St Bridget's, was on the track towards the coast, close to nothing, half-ruinous but not abandoned. In fact, though there were only half a dozen services a year, most people were still buried there. There were no graves in St John's, not even a church yard, though there was a demarcated field about half a mile in the other direction with a neat brick wall and beautifully carved wooden gate. Despite the fact that most burials took place in St Bridget's, its grounds were over-run, its ancient graves toppled over and smothered in grasses, its surrounding wall, high and crenelled covered in mosses and lichens. The church itself was simple and unadorned, its frontispiece surmounted by a very small, triangular bell tower. Inside it was bare and austere, simple wooden pews like boxes, with plain whitewashed walls, one wall only inscribed with a poem for sailors and beside it a list of parish vicars.

The track went on from St Bridget's, becoming smaller and smaller, until it was only a narrow path passing between a number of ponds and bogs, some natural but most man-made created from flooding of the deeply subsided mines that had worked there. Once there had been mines all around the area, but already by the end of the First World War there was little new ore to be extracted and the major mining activity was *robbery* from areas which had already been worked. By the nineteen twenties most of the mines were abandoned, leaving only a handful still in operation, by far the major activity being large scale quarrying farther inland.

The path joined a rail track that ran along an escarpment connecting the quarries to the coast. Below the escarpment was an enormous plain of bog land that spread all the way to the coast, to the other side undulating farmland, and then, near to the coast, an enormous factory complex producing bricks and cement, with great constructions of chutes, towers, kilns and chimneys.

From the rail track there was a short footpath to a sand-stone Victorian bridge that crossed a large slow moving river, the footpath mounting one side of the bridge, crossing its top length and then back down onto the other side where it ducked under the bridge parallel to the river, after which it petered away amongst sandy dunes. The bridge was part of the coastal rail track; the iron-ore hops shunted from the inland track as far as the brick factory, then reversed and shunted north following the coast, one train a day, mid-morning. The river, which ran parallel to the coastal railway, exchanged the interior rail bank for the seaward bank beneath the bridge.

After the sand-dunes there was a corroded bank, with a steep jump down to the shingle. The coast was long and bare, with rocky outcrops skirted by blackened sands, lead-ing to a long esplanade where sand and sea met.

Abby's spaces were St Bridget's, amongst the long grasses on the grave before the lichen crowned angel, and on the coast, her shore, listening to her vowel, her name, hugging something close to her, sometimes Poppy, sometimes herself, looking from a small space to a big space. There were other spaces amongst the crevasse, troughs and fissures of the fractured landscape, the places we named Red Steps, Hawk Cliff, Ghost Valley, Lost Plateau, Frozen Fields, Waste Land, No Man's Land, Lost Girl, maybe quite often in the disused car beneath Hawk Cliff, often inside a disused shell of hut along the quarry train escarpment, but never as frequently as those other two, never so regularly alone. In the named landscape we were pathfinders, explorers: in her confined spaces, small world within big world, she was a fugitive.

I tried to touch her. She flinched and withdrew from me as if I was one of those who wished her harm. She eyed me with close attention, alert to my slightest movement. I don't know why but I began to speak, so quietly I couldn't hear myself, it

70

was so below my frequency, and nor could Grace, so what hope was there for Abby? I don't suppose the fact that her vigilance informed her that my lips were moving held any meaning for her. She was in no state of mind to try to understand or even wonder about it. She just wanted to know that she was safe, but in that moment we were all the same to her, all liable to hurt her, all tarnished with the same human contagion. Grace and I had lost all identity. We were hallucinations, figures of an inner world, unreal.

In so many ways, that has never changed. I am her hallucination, a voice inside her head, because all other voices failed her. I am a spook, a story-teller, her conscience, her madness. I would never let her go. I go on and on, speaking between her ears, prising apart the understanding she had of the crimes people perpetrate against each other, demanding proof of her reason, exulting in her unreason, celebrating her wilful pleasure. I was with her, a stowaway in her dreams, a parasite, a lover, and I never renounced her, or proscribed her. At times I was her, and was never wise enough to know when I wasn't. We were sisters, conjoined, two of three equal angles, an equilateral being, making sense of all we failed to hear, dependent on the voices in our heads, the voice in her head.

Eventually I stalked her like a predatory animal, inching towards her, whispering to her deafness, certain in my own twisted mind that it was soothing her, consoling her, keeping her tame. However, at the crucial point, I didn't pounce, but carefully fingered her, shaping her, restoring life to discreet portions of her flesh, as if she were a delicate work of art, a priceless acquisition, which she was. She looked at my hand, the fingers gently stroking her, as if it were independent in itself, an animal of some kind, a thing with its own mind. It was the hand, the probing fingers, she was unsure of, not the mind that lay somewhere else completely. She was reduced to her immediate world, capable temporarily of only re-sponding to the stimulus of touch.

71

I signalled to Grace to help. I don't know why, but I had to move Abby, remove her from the averted gaze of the lichen crowned angel. It wasn't that I considered one shelter superior to any other, I just knew it wasn't good watching the rain wash chicken shit into her lashes, and her too removed to care, too hurt to consider there could be an alternative. Grace was reluctant. She was afraid, afraid of what her senses told her: that her sister had been hurt, maybe permanently disabled. It suggested things she wasn't ready to know. She shouted at Abby again, shouted with the most childish voice she could muster, demanding that Abby get up and that she take charge of Poppy, though Poppy wasn't with her – whether her loss was to be permanent or not we couldn't guess – but Abby didn't respond to her childish appeal. How could she? It wasn't in her earshot. For her it didn't exist, as so much else at that moment in time did not exist.

I rebuked Grace and told her we didn't have time for games. I know that hurt her. I was loading maturity onto her which she wasn't ready to carry, and really, why should she have? Certainly her father had a deep seated belief that Grace was the physical embodiment of God's punishment, but he didn't try to drive any demons from her. He never resorted to violence against his pitiable child. It was his sin, not hers. He treated her with cold indulgence, providing her with anything he thought might occupy her mind, not because he believed it would educate her, but would at least keep her at peace. Her mother though, Eileen, was a Boland – who had certainly been around as long as the Shaughnessys – and simply loved her daughter. For Eileen, family took precedence over all else. The fact that one of its members was different was simply how things were. There was no mystery in misfortune. It ratified luck. Grace had no desire to part with her state of ignorance, her own state of grace, certainly not for the shit across Abby's face, not without some resistance anyway. Eventually though, she came to Abby's side, still rebuking her for being stubborn and a fool, neither of which made any mark on her, and together we got her to her feet.

She allowed herself to be led. Even now I don't know whether she knew where she was being taken, nor whether she guessed my intentions. My feeling is she suspected something drastic and had given up all resistance. She walked like an automaton along the track, then the path, along the railway, over the bridge and to the shore, her favoured place, where Grace had named us sisters, named her Abby, and we took her right into the water – at first Grace hadn't understood but quickly caught on – and we held her underneath the waves, held her under with our four stubborn hands, her own waving about her, lashing against the weight of the depth, then we dragged her, right up, lifting her from the pull of the water, the break explosive like a tearing of muscle, and again, until she started calling her name in loud repeated ecstatic chants.

Then we stood together, up to our waists, the water bitterly cold around us and we carefully scooped water onto her face and removed the final traces of the yard floor from its surface. She stood there, awkwardly hunched, shivering, but clean, purified, quietly repeating her name through chattering teeth.

Later we ran back to the village through ever heavier rain. The wind had picked up and blew fiercely across the bog land and lashed across the escarpment, making it difficult to even keep our feet. We went to Grace's house, expecting the least of harsh receptions there. Grace's father was out at work, so there was only Eileen to contend with. Eileen was remarkably generous though.

She herded us into the loft and made us strip to the skin, and she stared for a while, until really it felt uncomfortable, and then with sudden energy she brought blankets and handed one to me, one to Grace, but Abby's she wrapped around her, draping it as if she could avoid it touching her,

73

yet at the same time cover her. Even then, I don't think I realised she had been studying the marks on Abby's skin, the telltale blemishes and blotches, the red sores, the heated flesh, and just at the base of her spine a great tear, exposing the pink flesh beneath that seemed to be oozing from her. I thought she was weighing us up, considering us wicked and wayward, being so wet, so obviously in the wrong. I wasn't unconvinced that she was preparing to pronounce punishment, but none was forthcoming. In fact, she said nothing, nothing at all. She disappeared for a while then brought us a tray of tea, with a plate of ginger biscuits, still silent, obviously of the opinion that there was little to be gained in admonishing those who wouldn't hear anyway.

Abby was ill after that. I heard she was hallucinating, had even been found one night frantically running around the hen yard, desperately looking for the door out, which for some reason eluded her. She was always seeking a door into the dark but certainly we never expected her to discover it, a door, a door into the dark.

*

Donald made much of the fact that I spoke about Judith Salt – meaning a tall, inelegant girl on a northern coastline watching the distant thread of horizon with a wonder at the total inadequacy of the words at her disposal – as another person entirely. Today is not the last day of the past or the first day of the future, he insisted. Each exists within the other. You cannot escape Judith Salt.

I found that a strange conundrum.

Was he telling me I couldn't get away from him, from where we were, or was he informing me that some figure called Judith Salt would hunt me down, no matter where I ran?

Perhaps he meant both, but more probably the latter. He seemed to take great pleasure in using the abstract past against me, accusing me of niggardliness, compliance, defeat. He would never believe me when I said it didn't matter. He thought I was promulgating some form of forgiveness or resignation, by it; something without true catharsis to his way of thinking. Of course, I didn't mean that at all. I never saw the sense of letting the past destroy the present, though I had no such aversion to the present destroying the past, or at the very least correcting it.

Surely we owe it to those confined forever to speak out for them, to revenge in their name, to rectify the wrongs, otherwise the future will be impure, predicated on untruths and compromise. I don't compromise, and yet Donald accused me of it all of the time, but how could that be, unless I had to compromise to him?

We spent the first few months we knew each other indoors. He would come to the house in Camden Town and spend much of the evening talking with the midwife and the nun. He made them laugh with simple stories of the absurd things people say to someone who is about to expose their bodies beneath the skin, reveal diseased bone and tissue, the malevolence of the body in not holding out. All the elderly women who thought he could see them naked, and would readily admit that it was more than their husbands ever had, laughing about it as if it were of no consequence, yet no doubt smarting at the absurdity. The little old man who had heard that if x-rays got inside you it made you impudent, meaning impotent, and flatly refused to have it done. Donald sat him down and gave him a good talking to and made him see sense. Unfortunately the x-ray was to reveal a right lobe loaded with cancer. Funny, absurd and poignant, Donald's stories, all at the same time. At first the absurdity made him laugh, telling the midwife and the nun, an old man stuffed with cancer worrying about impotence, but eventually it would transmute into anger, and I would have to succour that.

Except, I never could. How could I when he never wanted it to happen? He didn't want that anger allayed. It nourished him, or at least he thought it did. I believe he had a real distrust of contentment because it wasn't really happiness, but then happiness would always be flawed because it wasn't ecstasy and could never be universal, and if it was how could it be particular, and so on and so on. So he chose discontent.

I think I always knew he enjoyed it, the way I knew he really wanted to shock the nun. Why else would he always joke about sex? Sister Lavinia never was shocked, though. She was a teacher in an inner city school, for God's sake, and there certainly wasn't anything the midwife hadn't seen.

Naturally, I didn't matter. At best I was simply over-hearing what was said, but then I was deaf, so how could that even be possible? I was to be protected from the modern world. I think that's why it took him so long to sleep with me. He just couldn't bring himself to try it on. I told him, coaxing him, humouring him, or so I thought, I'm not a little deaf girl, in fact, I'm a tall deaf girl. At first he didn't get the reference, the quasi-joke, so I told him, all his lame characters were little, little old men, little old women, all little. He sulked for the rest of the evening. I'm pretty sure it was because I called his characters lame.

Was that piece of word play deliberate?

Naturally.

Even Michael, with all his religious zeal, had had no qualms about sex, even if he did ask whether I would prefer to keep my hearing aid in or not. He was so sincere I couldn't be angry. It was as if he were offering absolution. If I wanted I didn't have to hear, so perhaps I hadn't really taken part. Silent sex was no sex at all: not hearing the same as not knowing, the world of encounter entirely optional.

Donald was like a clumsy kid, not knowing what to touch, where to put his hands. It was as if my whole head was out of bounds, taboo, and yet not to be ignored. I told him I liked to have my ears licked, liked to feel the tip of the tongue flicking inside. That sent him wild. He fucked as if he were thrashing me, licking at my face like some overpowering dog. I could tell by the look on his face that he wasn't turned on, not in the way he wanted it to seem, the way he claimed later. He was enraged. He was trying to fuck the past away, fuck away the trace of any previous life. The very thought of someone else's tongue anywhere near my offending ear was simply unacceptable.

So, I told him about Judith Salt. I told him about the many things that Judith Salt had never thought might happen, like being there with him, in a North London house, in bed, with a nun just two rooms away. I told him Judith Salt was grateful. I told him Judith Salt was grateful because that's what he wanted to hear, that Judith Salt was his mission, his strength of personality. In that way I told him he resurrected me.

Judith Salt should not dismiss who she is. Judith Salt is worth everyone else.

As always he demanded something, and then when he achieved it complained about it.

He said I should be more independent, and then accused me of letting him down when I was.

It was certainly me who pointed to the fact that we never went out, never went anywhere, but remained holed up in Camden Town like fugitives. He claimed it was him, that he was the one to complain about our segregation but that I was reluctant, as if I were ashamed of myself. He made much play of the fact that I shouldn't be ashamed. I'm sure when we finally emerged, dinner together in a small, unfussy Italian restaurant – café by day, restaurant after six – I was a trophy, symbol of Donald's grace. I hated him and loved him, at the same time, in the same look, in the same bemused, untruthful manner, admitting neither, saying only what was needed, or rather what was wanted.

So we started going out, Donald insisting on it. I think for a time that we were really quite happy. It seems strange recalling it, as if it couldn't have been, as if the simplicity of it was in some way a deception. I believe, though, for a time, we did indulge in simplicity and stopped questioning what did and didn't motivate and drive the other, stopped questioning how we found ourselves in the position we were. Richmond, Kew, Greenwich, then farther afield, Leeds Castle, Rochester, Canterbury and then the south coast, Brighton Pavilion and the beach.

I said it was so strange that Judith Salt should find herself on a different shoreline, the continent just a stone's throw away. I said Judith Salt had never been aware of the continent and that the sea could lead to a real otherworld, a tangible world. Judith Salt had only ever been aware that it had depth, that it called to her sister with a terrible but dignified insistence, championing a name, a source, a place where mermaids were adrift and free. Judith Salt could hardly believe in Judith Salt, but there she was, and was somewhere she must have been, and despite everything still was. Judith Salt poised at the edge of the known world, without ever realising she was at the brink.

As I spoke, staring out at the horizon, Donald began a war dance. He marched around me, shaking his fists, signing incredible frustration, incredible perplexity. Then he started to berate and question me. How could I do it, stand there like some lunatic dredging up dead lives? Why did I have to dramatise it all in such a childish fashion? What about him?

I told him the sea at Brighton was like a domestic animal, whereas Judith Salt was used to a wild creature.

He shouted at me to stop it.

Judith Salt was alone and depressed, brought low by the factors of a seaside resort.

I told him I had to go, return to London. He went wild. I suppose it was understandable, after all, he had paid for a room, at the very least could have expected some sexual satisfaction in return, even if he was deep down concerned he was indulging a fetish. – At least he never asked me whether I wanted to remove my hearing aid or not, which I would have to admit I often did.

Of course I stayed. We ate in a steak house because Donald felt in Scottish mood, which I didn't really understand but assumed alluded to the tartan décor of the place, though now I'm not so sure. I was to learn that whenever he evoked Scotland it meant something to do with purity.

In the event the steaks weren't very good and Donald insisted on complaining, making more of it than he needed. Sure the waiter wasn't very apologetic, but Donald acted as if he'd been insulted. He went on and on about knowing good meat and knowing good service, and wasn't that what was wrong with the whole damned country, waiters like him trying it on. It was as if a whole mask had temporarily slipped and some rabid reactionary was reasserted. It ended up with Donald marching out with me following, apologising in his wake. On the doorstep he rounded on me, angered that I should have felt the need to apologise.

Without any great demonstration of the fact I switched off my hearing aid and then removed it from my ear. Later, when we knew about the baby, he claimed that I'd removed it because I was sick of parading my deafness, that in Brighton I was deceitful.

I hate to think the baby was conceived in a small, rough and ready hotel on the south coast, the window open, the sound of the sea presumably drifting in, though, as with all other sounds, banished, but it was probably the case. A baby conceived through mannered, impersonal sex, ovum and sperm conjoining in a silent world, a world in which speech was optional and largely regrettable.

I guess it was inevitable.

*

From shore to shore, the earth is not round, but spiral, image lain over image – though never so completely that any should become a blur, a corruption. So, here I stand, Judith Salt at sixty, at twenty-five, wondering just what it is that has happened to me that I find myself here? What it is that has

79

happened to me that I am under sentence to formulate an answer, delegated to fashion an action?

I have no way of knowing how I feel about that.

In fact, the most singular, strongest feeling I have is one of claustrophobia, but that is a somewhat ambiguous feeling, as it certainly has nothing to do with space. There is abundant space here. The amount of ground available per person is generous, some of the most generous in the country. It is something of a boast. Here there is enough space not to realise you weren't here all along. There can't be many places in which that could be the case.

Nevertheless, I sense myself quietly choking, quietly succumbing to the dreadful weight of some unseen, unheard burden. It isn't a new feeling. I could have predicted it long before I stood here, no matter which year I might allude to. I knew it would happen just as certainly as I knew the sea would be here, writhing up and down the shoreline. It is an old adversary, an old friend, as all such familiar things tend to become.

I have worked out, even after such meagre visits, that the sense, if that's what it is, is of time: a claustrophobia of time, time or rather time's end, time closing in, closing in with a laughing, mocking, ridiculing, insistent weight. It is the same time that lingers in the dark sitting-rooms of former mine houses where two ageing people have decided they can tolerate one another, but certainly no more; the same weight that hangs over empty village streets behind the walls of which there is a yearning for entertainment but an absence of spirit to make it happen; the same claustrophobia that makes the hour before dusk last forever.

I can't accept we felt it dragging us under when we were so young, so long ago, recently.

I long for the night, fish and chips and London Gin.

*

We never realised our childish games had so much latent reality, but isn't that the case with all such games, that they end up being a prediction, a prophecy, a warning. So, when we served pretend cups of tea, with very fine biscuits, though we didn't know what they were called, or what went into their making, signing a conversation we didn't remotely understand, certain only that that was how grown-ups went on, we had no inkling it should be the living image of so many later tea-parties. How were we to know that hide-and-seek was actually running for our lives? How could we have guessed that poor, put upon Poppy, who suffered terrible travail – Abby pulling her about, wayward doll that she was, never sitting just so, and Grace Powers admonishing her for being the scruffiest, careless doll ever – was a maquette.

Grace threatened to cut Poppy's hair one day, right down to the scalp, it was so knotted and filthy, forming her fingers into scissors to signify her complaint and mercilessly flashing them in front of Poppy's unblinking eyes. Abby looked horrified, but as always when Grace asserted her rightful ownership of the doll her hold loosened and poor Poppy looked likely to fall to the sand. That only made Grace lose her temper and stamp about, kicking out and lashing at the coal pitted sand, whilst she ranted at Abby to keep hold of her, keep hold of her as she had been. Abby didn't understood Grace's fit of temper, she rarely did, though as she watched her, flinching from moment to moment, she surreptitiously pulled Poppy back into her clutch, so that by the time Grace calmed down, normality was intact.

We bought, sold, stole, cheated, captured slaves and freed captives, never knowing they were grown-up themes, never realising we were imitators, mimic sisters, making the only play we knew. We never completed Nora's role, though.

Chapter Six

A woman, wet and laded, dressed in a thick, threadbare overcoat, bound with string around the waist, appeared at the fringes of the village. It was a filthy day in November, not cold, indeed very mild for the time of the year, but with frequent heavy showers, falling from a dull, uniformly grey sky. There were pools of mist trailing amongst undulating fields and spoil banks and the air was heavy with the scent of rotting vegetation. She looked as if she had been walking for a long time, her boots and coat caked with wet and dry mud. She was bent with the weight of her bags, which she had strapped together with rope that trailed across her shoulders. She gave the impression that if she stopped to rest she wouldn't be able to start again, so plodded on slowly, relentlessly.

To begin with she was entirely alone, head bowed, careless of ruts and puddles, her boots splashing up to the ankles in iron-ore stained water and clay, but soon she was stalked by a group of children, though whether they thought they were cowboy scouts or Hun spy catchers – it was, after all, 1916 – no one can know. Christian Shaughnessy, Grace's great uncle, claimed they trailed her long before she reached the village, growing in number as she came on, until there was a crowd of them, at least a dozen, but in most versions of events she is said to have arrived at the edge of the village unaccompanied. Not that she was molested by them in anyway. They were too scared by half. That was the point of the story. They followed her, not because she was a tramp, wet, scruffy and easy bait, but because she appeared so formidable, carrying her load like a dogged mule. My father, Robert Salt, who was never prone to florid speech or exaggeration, who was matter of fact in acknowledging he had married into the easier Sempie line, claimed that his father maintained Nora Shaughnessy was the only woman able to stand up to Martha Sempie and that day was always cited as the proof of it.

Of course, as with so much regarding the Shaughnessys it is never easy knowing whether something is part of the family myth or whether it is true. The picture of her entering the village, weighed down but steadfast, her face clenched with determination, is a vivid one, but who was there to draw it? The fact that a dozen children appeared with her at the Shaughnessy household is never queried, but they are never named. Nevertheless, the events of that homecoming have become part of the collective memory of the village, certainly etched deep into the minds of the Shaughnessys and Sempies. I remember it as if I was there, and Grace Powers always spoke about her grandmother with undiminishing respect and fear. Even Abby used to laugh, hacking out the first letter of the alphabet as if she wanted to shape words with it, and clap her hands as if she were viewing a comic show, at the mention of Nora Shaughnessy.

I can see her now making her determined, fearless approach to the village, towards people who must certainly have realised she hadn't been there and had obviously ruminated why that should be, and I am guilty, despite coming from the easy Sempie line – Grandfather Dan being Martha's full cousin, but according to my father as ordinary a man as one could meet, which he meant as a high compliment indeed – of making much of her, much of her endurance. She has become symbolic of a woman's ability to experience suffering and foster regeneration through it. It was never doubted that she had suffered, not simply because she had returned a tramp, but because she was so aged. She must only have been in her mid-twenties at the time, gone from the age of sixteen, maybe seventeen, but already was weather-beaten, drawn. She must once have been a good-looking woman, maybe even a pretty one, but her surface was roughened up, damaged. It was later claimed, and never refuted, indeed, accepted as part of the Nora Shaughnessy myth, that she had earned a living as a prostitute, the weathering coming from street corners not open fields. Certainly Martha insisted on it as incontrovertible fact.

Nora had only just made it to the Shaughnessy household – which at the time consisted of Ed, generally considered simple, Honor and Aidan, both deaf, and Christian, who had a terrible reputation for drinking, home on leave (Dermot and Maura having died during separate influenza outbreaks before the war) – when Martha arrived. Martha shouted out her name, Nora Shaughnessy, as if wanting to identify her for the dozen attendant kids, her tone incredulous, accusatory. Nora immediately rounded on her, her cumbersome baggage forcing her to turn a full 180 degrees.

Nora didn't have the physical presence of Martha, particularly bent under her burden as she was, but she certainly wasn't perturbed by her. In fact, as her eyes lit on Martha – who in reality was little more than a girl, Harold just a year old – the pressure on her back seemed to ease and she physically rose with the relief. She glared for a moment, her expression consumed with hatred – hatred and maybe resentment that such a young person could exact such feeling – and then quietly, surprisingly, she smiled, and her smile seemed to erase all of what had just gone before. Indeed, her smile threatened to erupt into laughter, though what quality that laughter would have had was impossible to predict, but just at the point of manifestation it drained away, drained away as if it were formed of liquid. After that her expression was devoid of easily read meanings, though taken together her various shifts of attention seemed to denote one overriding feeling: satisfaction, its coldness, its freedom. It blossomed around her eyes and mouth, igniting the ghost of a once good-looking woman, a ghost untested and unknowing.

Eventually, encumbered as she was, she pulled at her overlapping coat until her hand slipped inside and she produced a small slip of an envelope that she immediately offered to Martha. Martha didn't hesitate but stepped up and snatched it, though as she did a part of her self-composure broke. She quickly looked around as if she felt exposed, but finding only a dozen bemused kids looking on she immediately shouted at them, shooing them away. She turned back to Nora, her defiance intact again, but seeing Aidan and Christian, who had appeared on the step, her composure failed her once more and she froze. Nora spoke up, her voice quiet yet charged.

"We're through now," she said, and then hesitated, evidently considering whether to say more. Eventually she shook her head and said, "You're just a kid," her voice lowering and failing, as if that fact cancelled out all other considerations. She realised she was through so turned away and went indoors, ushering Aidan and Christian before her with a single nod of her head, leaving Martha to bluster in wordless rage, which far from appearing frightening looked decidedly absurd.

For Nora her liberation from Martha drained her, so that on entering the house that she hadn't seen for so many years she seemed gripped by a terrible grief. Perhaps it was an awareness of the absence of Dermot and Maura, or a recognition of herself, of what she had become that so affected her? Whatever the cause, she couldn't abide herself for a while and flatly refused any attention from her brothers, despite their coaxing and their evident disappointment.

*

There was never any doubt that Nora was paying off something and the most logical assumption was she was purchasing the deeds to the Shaughnessy plot that had come to Martha after the deaths of her brothers Tom and Will in the Battle of Loos – her mother having died of a haemorrhage

85

after giving birth to Will and her father dying in the same influenza outbreak that killed Dermot. Even as a teenager she was already the matriarch, a fact that hadn't escaped Nora. It was assumed she threatened the Shaughnessys with eviction at that time for no other reason than that she could. After all, it was well understood she despised them, though later, a chance comment from Mr Drake suggested something quite different.

There is no doubt that this place is capable of fermenting hatred, severe, intransigent hatred such as that Martha seemed to possess, though what provokes it is difficult to perceive. Maybe it's the isolation, people compelled to live with the same others, year after year, building up resentments and dislikes that finally erupt in outright detestation: and maybe some is spontaneous, the same hatred that has driven human beings from the very beginnings of socialisation. Maybe Martha's hatred was as unaccountable as that, but when she stood blustering outside the Shaughnessys crowded hovel, her feelings palpable and physical, there could be no doubting its reality, its fixation.

As to why Nora should have taken on the family poverty so fully can best be explained by a story she regularly told, in which she recalled her father, Dermot, describing one of three evictions he experienced when his own father, Owen, was laid off from the iron-ore mines, and in particular a detail that stood out above all others.

He remembered the speed with which the family possessions were loaded onto the back of a cart and being surprised, even frightened by it. It was as if they expected to be attacked at any moment and had to get the job done without delay. He couldn't really understand it, they were simply moving into a barn just a mile or so away, but nevertheless found himself caught up in the panic. In and out of the tiny cottage he went, bringing out any small bits and pieces he could manage. At one point he had to wait, his arms wrapped around a dolly tub he was only scarcely managing to hold, as Owen and Eistir struggled with a large wardrobe. As they slid it along the back of the cart a door swung open and a full length mirror pinned to the inside fractured into seven distinct cracks all emanating from a single fracture at the top. When Honor – whose first and only eviction this was – saw the mirror she began screaming, but Owen and Eistir were too busy to help her. She was left standing alone, crying and moaning, complaining incoherently. Dermot never did find out what it was about the mirror, other than the tragedy of its breaking that had so affected her, but it never left him. To the end of his life he regretted the fact he hadn't even attempted to console her.

He remembered as they settled down to sleep in the hayloft Honor still crying, saying to Owen she wanted to go home, and Owen answering that he was sorry but he had no home now. Of course Honor never heard his reply, but Dermot did and it was the worst sentence he had ever heard in his life, and even though it was only a story to her, it was also the worst sentence Nora had ever heard, enough to send her off and do whatever it took to ensure that her simple Uncle Ed, deaf Aunt Honor and kid brothers Christian and Aidan never had to hear it.

Of course all that might be Shaughnessy myth.

*

My palate is sophisticated these days. I was brought up on brisket, pork, bacon, black-pudding and root vegetables, carrots, turnips and potatoes. We didn't have lavish help-ings, after all things were still rationed, but I grew tall, if awkward, on what I was given. But now, I favour Medi-terranean flavours, anything with olive oil. I love bone-dry Sauvignon wine. I am old enough not be surprised or embarrassed by new things, and when I want I can dismiss so much as fad. Which corner of the world will provide the next culinary delight, I mockingly muse? Personally, I am always rather surprised that East European dumplings have been so shamelessly neglected, or Norwegian boiled cod with liver sauce. I have come a long way.

I can't escape the fact, though, that my life stretches back over a hundred years, to a time when diets were probably very basic indeed. A whole period before I was born lays claim to my attention, to my time, to me. So, as much as the afterlife will only make sense by what happened in this life, so this life must only make sense by the life preceding it, and yet it eludes me. There are voices there demanding restitution, ease, forgiveness, but even at maximum amplification I just can't hear them. So many hidden lives, then, so much unfinished business, so many intrigues, so many bewildered people, surprised by more than anchovies and clams, abandoned, lost in time.

As is Judith Salt, lost at Red Steps, Hawk Cliff, Ghost Valley, Lost Plateau, Frozen Fields, Waste Land, No Man's Land, Lost Girl. Each time I hear something, a note, a murmur, a whisper, I reach out, certain that this time I'll be able to hold it, keep it still, fathom it, but each time I just miss it, and the moment is gone, replaced by another, another whimper, another giggle, so the present never exists because it will never be still, never be contained, never held, and like everyone, I look, and look again, and can't quite account for the fact that the present has vanished away.

We sleep-walk to extinction, playing catch up.

I have felt relatively free in London, able to make up names and games, make up me, with my delicacies and friendly hairdresser, with my insistence the past was another country. London doesn't care about its tribes, it survives them all, is bigger than any of them. In London everything is significant and insignificant at one and the same time. I can't help but stay.

I still have the occasional London Gin, sometimes far too much, but not like the early days, then I didn't know anything else. And as for fish and chips, I really wish I enjoyed them as once I am certain I did.

Chapter Seven

There was always a great deal of killing in Harold's yard, some of it seasonal, the slaughter of pigs and poultry, but most of it sporadic, the elimination of things intruding onto his tenure, moles, mice, rats and crows, the carcasses hung out on wire fences as deterrents and trophies. Abby had seen him stamp on frogs and toads, crushing them underfoot, with neither a smile nor a grimace of satisfaction on his face, just an understanding, that's what was done. There was so much killing Abby was accustomed to it. I don't know why she found it any different the day they brought in dogs to kill a rat, but something clearly bothered her.

Earlier that day Harold had shown her a cleft pig head. He held it on his palm, showing her the face. He smiled at her, and obliquely drew her attention to the animal's features, the human look of curiosity and naïve trust. Maybe he smiled because he saw a similar look on her face, her features responding to his invitation. She moved quite close. She thought it looked like a fat woman with a wart and whiskers. She signed pleasure, amused by the pig's unblinking eye. He slowly moved it towards her, his hand hidden, as if the face were floating. He gestured that she touch it, feel what dead skin was like, cold yet pliant. She didn't understand but knew it wasn't worth refusing, wasn't worth making him mad, after all, it was only a funny fat woman with a wart and whiskers, long single whiskers. So she reached out to touch it, opting to stroke the cheek because she didn't want to feel the eye, but just as she was about to make contact he quickly changed hands, passing the cloven head from palm to palm, replacing skin with brain. He made a noise to scare her, but she never heard. She didn't know what to do, because still it wasn't worth making him sore at her, and besides, she had already seen too much to be squeamish. She held her hand poised, uncertain where to place it. However, before she had made any decision Harold began to trace structures with his index-finger, outlining brain, cortex and stem, jawbone, teeth, tongue and spine, talking his way through an anatomy lesson. Of course, she missed all of it. Still, it hadn't been his intention to educate her, but having failed to scare her, it was a means of saving face.

When he was through with his description, which had given him a strange feeling of pride he couldn't account for, he tossed the split head into a tub full of similar slop – heads, tails and trotters – which he boiled until the meat came away from bone which Agnes then stripped into bowls for brawn.

When the time came though, Abby didn't watch her mother strip the heads, her interest was taken by Harold's sows which ran free in the field behind the sheds. Soon after he had moved into his house Harold had laid claim to all the land behind the terrace, leaving only a small yard for each neighbour, though he also allowed them to string washing lines to his pig-sheds. He worked on the principle that no one actually owned any of the ground so he simply built on it, and as he expected he didn't receive any argument. It was, in fact, owned by the coal-board, but as no one had ever been to view it, or fix a rent on it, he assumed it was his for as long as he chose. He had made it into quite a smallholding, more than Martha's, with a substantial yard. He had also fashioned a fairly rugged track round one end of the terrace by gradually filling hardcore into the ruts he had made with his van.

It was from the track that Abby watched the sows, viewing them over a corrugated tin sheet fence. She never leaned on Harold's fences, not because they weren't robust, despite their thrown together appearance – everything in Harold's yard was made from cast-off goods – but because she was never so relaxed. She always stood to attention in her father's domain.

From the same sacks out of which Harold had produced the pig's head he had taken flanks of fat and rind. When he spread them out on the butcher's bench he kept in one of the sheds she expected he was cutting them up to render into pork dripping. She couldn't quite believe it when he threw it, raw, to the sows, and she was even more surprised by the speed with which they gobbled it down. She couldn't understand how it was that they couldn't smell pig, it was, after all, a potent smell. It wasn't the first time she had witnessed cannibalism – she had seen birds eat other birds, a magpie even taking another magpie's young – but it was certainly the most intriguing.

She was still watching the sows when they came for the rat. She was only aware of them when a terrier made a lazy snap at her ankle. Surprisingly she didn't jump, but simply turned to investigate. There were three men and six dogs, small, wire-haired terriers. She followed automatically.

When she trailed them into the yard she saw Martha standing at the other side, in front of the lean-to that served as the kitchen. Martha's face contracted with animosity, her bitterness at her pent-up confessions being so pointlessly scattered never allayed. She was torn between a desire to outface Abby, and a need not to see her. In the end looking won the day. For one reason or another she just couldn't finally reject her, and that failure, as she saw it, infuriated her. Seeing Martha's attention Abby immediately announced her own name. Martha turned aside in disgust, cleared her throat and spat onto the cobbles. She always resented the fact that Abby was the beautiful singer she was.

As she was spitting Harold produced the rat. He had a number of large, semi-circular wire mesh cages placed in his sheds. The rat would enter through a narrow funnel, which led to a weighted platform, from where it would drop into the cage, the platform springing back into place. He held up one of these cages, right above his head. The rat moved around inside. He banged the side with his free hand, causing the mesh to shiver and the rat to dance from side to side. Abby quaked. She found rats repulsive, frightening creatures.

Harold put the cage down onto the ground and told the men to slip the dogs, which immediately gathered around it and began pawing and snapping at it, sending it rolling across the yard floor, the rat inside turning over and over, the mesh dripping with slurry. Harold and the men laughed at the antics. Of course, Abby couldn't hear any laughter so how was she to know it was funny, the frustrated growling dogs and the somersaulting vermin with its piercing whistles? She wasn't given any such permission. She began to rock forwards and backwards and call aloud, unclear in her own mind whether she was scared, pleased or enraged.

The dogs became increasingly incensed and began ripping at the mesh, so much so that blood from their jaws appeared on the wire. The cage flew around the yard, and with it the laughter grew stronger. It was at this point that Harold strode into the small pack and held them back from their quarry, sweeping them away with his boots so as not to damage them. He bent down and released the pin holding the gate in the back of the cage. The rat bolted, but the dogs instantly descended on it and within seconds had torn it into bloody shreds.

Whether Abby wanted to retrieve it, sew it back into one ugly whole, or wanted to share in its dismemberment, she never could recall, but as the dogs gathered together, licking at the ground, their heads bobbing together, licking at the stain that had been rat, she plunged amongst them and fell to the floor, her whole body twitching as if she were in the midst of a fit – epilepsy was a Shaughnessy trait, both Honor and Aidan having once had regular convulsions, which in both cases more or less ceased in adulthood, not a Sempie thing at all.

The dogs jumped and danced around her. A couple of them yelped, those pitiful squeals small dogs make indicating surprise at any level of hurt, their hindquarters scraping the ground, scraping their firm genitalia. Then they all began to growl and snarl. She was rolling on the memory of dead rat, rolling on its trace as if she wanted to be scent marked. Her contracted limbs, her muscles in spasm, struck against the six dogs numerous minor, repetitive blows. They jumped and collided, snapping and nipping each other, as they tried to avoid the thumps of her writhing body, and then they began snapping at her, at first tentative bites, the jaws not clenching, not breaking skin, just grasping, but she didn't stop and her convulsions sent them mad. Eventually they began nipping at her clothes and exposed skin, small tearing bites. Whilst this was happening the three men were shouting, telling her to get out of it, telling her to stop acting the fucking fool, but doing nothing. Perhaps they were certain the dogs were out of their control, after all, they had just eaten hot blood, hot entrails. It was common practice to feed young dogs fresh hot liver to make them mad for the kill. They probably presumed Abby's liver doomed.

Harold and Martha said nothing, Harold too angry to speak, Martha too embarrassed and disgusted. Already in her mind she could hear comments about the sick Sempie kid, the graphic descriptions of Abby rolling herself in the mud and chicken shit, her mouth salivating with the pleasure of it, moaning as if she were being fucked not nipped to death, and certainly Martha's initial wish was that the dogs would finish her off, though common sense told her such small dogs probably weren't likely to do more than hurt her. It may have been that thought that prompted her to intervene, or maybe the fact that there were witnesses to what she did or didn't do, or maybe it wasn't thought out at all simply automatic, but whatever the reason, she finally strolled from the end of the yard nearest the house from where she had been watching events, kicked her way through the dogs and picked Abby up bodily from the ground – one terrier dangling for a while by the tip of its teeth to her buttocks – and carried her away, dropping her at the entrance to a pig-shed. Usually Abby would have run for cover, bolting inside, but not this time. She sat upright on her knees, her backside resting on her ankles, and wrapped her arms right around herself, her palms resting flat against her back.

The men took their dogs and left. There was no word said to Harold. He remained rooted, simply gazing ahead, staring at the spot where the rat had been ripped up, angered and sickened by the irregularity of it all. Martha stood a few feet from Abby, completely still, stiff and formal, guarding her captive, her eyes flickering between Abby and Harold. The three of them remained like that, rigid, fixed objects, for some time. Harold was the first to move. He turned from his contemplation of the scene of sport and rested his eyes on Abby, looking at her steadily for a few moments, and then he pursed his lips, marched towards her, his pace slow and even, and slapped her forcefully across the face sending her sprawling.

It's likely that might have been the end of it as Harold was obviously intent on marching straight indoors, had Martha not spoken up, asking how they were ever going to live it down. She hadn't directed herself to Harold, simply spoken aloud, letting him hear the uppermost thought in her head. He stopped and turned back, which Martha took as a cue to commence her interrogation. She bombarded Abby with questions – what the hell was she playing at, what was she up to, why did she enjoy bringing them all down, what possessed her, why did she put on them all of the time? The logic for Martha, which she made plain to Abby, was that Abby wanted to give the Sempies a bad name, was hell-bent on it. There was something wicked, evil, maybe even devil possessed, certainly unnatural in her personality. Not only was Abby stupid and an idiot, she was a liar, a cheat and, for some reason, a thief, and also a disease. As Martha listed her

94

insults Harold picked Abby from the floor and slapped her across the backside and legs, punishing her for each charge made against her, until Martha declared she wasn't worth it, she was just a piece of filthy corruption, and he dropped her back to the ground. Nevertheless he stood over her for a while like a dissatisfied fighter, until Martha announced it was enough, and they left her.

When he reached the door of the lean-to he ordered Agnes inside. How long she had been there only she could say.

*

The feeling of dreams, that everything is a dream, is a terrible one, but one that is hard to escape. I always assumed it was something to do with being deaf, the world and all its habits thrown onto a screen, only to be seen and not heard, at a distance and out of reach, but that supposes touch deficient too, and I can make no claim that deficient ears lead to deficient fingers. My fingers were never frail or failing, in fact quite often they assumed a life of their own, crawling like spiders, sometimes tiny elephants – my hands like two playful mates, their trunks touching so tenderly at times it was obvious they had witnessed upheaval, the loss of herd, displacement – towards another's unsuspecting skin, but wasn't that another attempt to solve the dream puzzle?

Of course, everything becomes a dream because everything is a memory, the present lost and irredeemable. So, Abby lay in the mud, she prostrated herself before a lichen crowned angel, and she surveyed the horizon, decoding it, loving it, but as soon as I picture one of those images and work something out it's gone, she's gone, and inevitably so am I.

It calls for something special to crack a dream, but maybe it isn't worth it. Sometimes when my delightfully vivacious hairdresser lifts my hair from my head in her two hands in the cusp between thumb and index-finger revealing the elongated, birdlike face, the mottled, tarnished skin, the offending ears, I have to admit that the face in the mirror is Judith Salt, first person, second person, third person Judith Salt, but if I consider all that Judith Salt has witnessed, it is simply a miniature on a screen. I used to think that the persistent sense I had of being in a dream meant I was devoid of sympathy, simple decency, tenderness, but I am not immune. It's just that when you have died once but survived, you are never quite fully alive ever again.

I don't mind. I think it would take too much stamina and courage to be entirely alive: the dream of it, the suspicion that this can't be happening to me, seems more than sufficient.

With dreams I can be patient and tolerant; after all there is the likelihood of its sudden conclusion, its disappearance, a loss that can't authentically be mourned. No one in their right mind would mourn something never real to begin with, however delightful, or fulfilling the moment. So, I sometimes smile at my hairdresser and gently close my eyes, or I look straight ahead and seek something on the other side of the mirror. There is usually something comic or novel to discover, such as whole forests carved like privet into the shapes of birds, a parade of Morris men on stilts dancing to a pig band. There is no end to invention, perhaps only to the point of it.

Donald often asked me what I was thinking as if he was accusing me of something in the question, some secret, some betrayal. In many ways, of course, he was right. At one time it must have been the thought that I didn't love enough, and then later that I loved too much. So, how do I remember Donald, remember that shift from loving too little to too much, recall my playful, elephantine, arachnid fingers inching towards him, the mise-en-scène in my mind, something that may or may not have happened?

I was always weighing him up, taking in his features and figure, and wondering how they would weather and wear. How would his thick sandy hair be in a few years? Would the dull orange freckles that lay dormant in the layers of his skin, like so many dead blooms, smoulder back into life, so the old man would be stippled by stale flowers? Would the flesh that made him big and meaty go flabby on the bone so that the torso, stubbled by coarse, colourless hair, would bulge and soften like a dough ball? He was so non-descriptive in his white coat, his suit, his corduroy trousers and jumper, but unclothed, naked, very fine, a surprise, a gift, as so many people prove to be, stripped of the things that define them.

I was certain I had no right, no reason, to do such a thing, to weigh up and categorise him, to wonder about his smile and his anger, his roar and his pity. I was lucky to have him, surely anyone would have told me that, but why should anyone trust in luck, yet alone believe in it? I suppose the truth was we fought out an emotional version of equality, not political economy or class but its physical equivalent, without ever admitting we were doing it. When he prompted me, saying I needed *strength of purpose*, and then later applauded the fact I had *strength of purpose*, wasn't he saying he was more perfected than me, not necessarily better – though the conclusion is difficult to avoid – simply more complete. I had everything to learn, and he could be my teacher, my emotional coach, the person who would brandish my deafness on my behalf: the man who would teach me to love myself. He could make me and unmake me.

We are always making and unmaking each other. We are all mimics, dabblers in make-believe, wishful thinkers, play-ing our parts with all the experience we can bring to it, all the ingenuity at our disposal, attempting to outthink the instinct that could debase us, expose us, show us up for the ancestral failures we are. Certainly my sisters and I spent much of our time perfecting games, making games so seamless only a true player would suspect the guile.

Players, then, Judith Salt, Grace Powers and best of all,

Abigail Sempie. Abigail Sempie, I miss her so much, her life in my life, my life hers. I am dumbfounded that such sisters could be so casual as to miss the obvious danger. I dream her like words.

I don't know how many times a person can fall in love, or how many grades of love exist, but eventually I loved Donald, not with pain and longing, but with comfort. It was suddenly like lying in a warm bath, with an overarching question of why not. Why shouldn't things be as they were? Why should it have to be laced with a sequence of doubts, apprehensions, suspicion? Why should it necessarily be hard just to be remotely true?

I gave up on me.

I gave.

He obviously felt the weight of what occurred, but I think the equality shook him to the core of his wonderful nudity. That wasn't in his game, that he shouldn't have to be my cheerleader, my angry guardian, shouldn't challenge dragons on my behalf.

There was a night when we went out to eat, opting for a small place in Kentish Town that appeared a little better than the usual day and night places we frequented. The lighting was subdued, and there were high backed chairs, almost as if it were a proper restaurant, which it, like all the others, wasn't. The waiter smiled gravely, formally and even offered a discernible bow, and then asked what the lady would like. He asked Donald what the lady would like. Donald was incensed. I could see it in his face, could predict what was coming. He was about to give the waiter a dressing-down, threaten a complaint to the manager, followed by a very public exit, but before anything occurred I reached out, placed my palm over Donald's forearm and declared: "I don't mind, I really don't mind. I'd like you to order for me, knowing my likes and dislikes as you do."

Donald was still determined to protest.

I smiled and added: "It's very nice here, thank you."

Donald ordered Chicken Kiev for us both and when he cut into it and the garlic butter burst out all over his plate I expressed my surprise at his choice, given that he must see some disgustingly infected, suppurating wounds, or did he only ever bother with the bones beneath the skin?

He neither laughed nor scowled, and I can say, I didn't mind at all.

*

The two hands can still perform the trick of elephants, wild elephants not circus creatures, beasts of mountain and plain. They clamber with slow determination over the arms of chairs, and then descend warily to the cushion below. They stand on the thigh upright, looking across vast distances as if the whole globe were revealed to them, a planet yet in its infancy but already old, already witness to mass extinction, privation and struggle. At some point they will have to find water, shelter, grazing, but more immediately they need to find each other. Sometimes the reunion is affected easily, sometimes it is tortuous, and indeed sometimes the right hand really is devoid of all knowledge of what the left is doing. Sometimes it feels as if they have been denied each other's company for years, but no matter the length of separation, the reunion is always the same, a mannered, tender dance, the index-finger of one pawing at the other, which is immediately mirrored by the other, and then the trunk of the long middle finger carefully takes in the aroma of its partner whilst the index-finger still paws at the joints, until there is an embrace of fingers. The two then take to the hill paths and mountains, and sometimes they even come to a shore, but that is extremely rare, extremely rare indeed, it is so infrequent that their world comes to any end, even when the wilderness has occupied them for thirty-five years or so. Being truly wild creatures they have no name of any kind and are not going to look for one now, still that could never stop my recognition of them. Strange that they of all things

99

should never have changed in all the years, but I should never forget, an elephant's memory is legend.

*

We found Abby in the graveyard curled in front of the lichen crowned angel. She wasn't looking at the angel, wasn't looking at anything in particular, despite the fact her eyes were wide open. She was simply gazing at her knees and whatever fragment or patch of colour lay beyond. We didn't realise she'd taken herself there for sanctuary; it was just one of the places where we knew we might find her, playmates wanting to play. I should have recognised immediately that something was wrong; she was after all, a creature of habit. Usually she lay coiled towards the angel, her knees and arms tucked up before the plinth, the angel's gaze passing over her, beyond her – its gaze always enigmatic, perhaps not even a smile at all, but a frown, a scowl of disappointment, of disapproval. This time she had her back to the angel, rested right up against the plinth, and if she had cared to see anything, which by the stasis of her eyes she didn't, it would have been the walls; but it was only when we stood over her, when we saw the tears in her skin, the small gaping wounds, the smears of blood, that we understood her change of routine was deliberate. Not that we could have guessed how deep that alteration went, that declaration of apostasy.

From a distance she seemed her old self, full of her usual defiance, snuggled in one of her spaces, despite the rain and the wind. We were sure she liked it best when it was awful weather, when the space was framed, the borders of her comfort clearly marked by discomfort. Grace was impatient as always, and even shouted Abby's name, insisting on formality – Abigail Sempie, what on earth are you playing at? Why can't you be a good girl? – She knew fine well Abby couldn't hear. She would never have assumed her full name if she thought she could hear. Still, as Grace came closer, she signed her disapproval, a version of the question, why can't you be a good girl, wagging her finger and setting her face in little masks of objection. I don't suppose she expected Abby to see. The grimaces weren't really meant for Abby; Grace was just practising what she had learnt, playing games.

Grace was horrified when she came up close and saw the raw wounds on Abby for which she could not account. She recognised that they were something different to the scrapes and bruises we'd become accustomed to, but she'd never seen a dog bite, or any other bite before. She started to shout, as if she could chase the effrontery away, and run about, at first away from Abby and then towards her, until it seemed she was caught by elastic, forced both to see her and recoil from her. She knew Abby wasn't dying – a mistake she had made before, seeing her curled before the angel – her eyes were too wide, too bright and filled with depth for that to be the case, but she recognised that there was something seriously wrong and she just didn't know what to do about it, and I couldn't help either. Neither of us knew how to deal with such a wounded sister. We were too young. We didn't know how to be angry, how to retaliate, how to dismiss the idea that this was normal, we only knew how to be scared and how to whimper.

So, I never stopped Grace running about or her ferocious roars, which Abby couldn't hear at all. I didn't know how to, how to calm her, reassure her, replace something the dogs had banished. I had to leave her be. I went and leaned over Abby. She was curled into an uneven ball like an animal in a den, her eyes wide, fixed. I assumed she wanted to be in enclosed space as always, but I couldn't work out why she had opted not to face the angel, opted to view the nearer wall. I touched her and she flinched as if my hand was burning heat. I stroked her. She looked at me, her expression fearful, disbelieving. She had no trust in human touch, couldn't work out its meanings. She inched away, scraping across the floor like a cringing dog, her back rubbing along the angel's plinth, and then she leapt up and began to run. It

101

was crazy. For some reason, despite being in known territory, she was disoriented and ran in all directions, flapping her arms as if they were awkward, flightless limbs.

Seeing her dash about, dodging between fallen headstones, stamping over broken masonry, brought Grace to a standstill. She came and stood beside me and eyed Abby as if she were some kind of carnival lunatic, her expression quizzical but relieved, thankful to be able to contemplate Abby in the old light, that of perplexing, wilful sister. She began to nod her head in rhythm to Abby's running, and then wheeled her hands, her loosely held fists turning one over the other.

Abby didn't need any encouragement. She ran and ran, and eventually she discovered a portal of escape. The strange thing was she didn't choose a familiar route, didn't inevitably find the track to the coast, to the waiting tide calling her name, calling her, but opted for a different direction completely. She found herself, after some fantastic convolutions, in the most overgrown, ruinous portion of the grounds, beneath the western tower. The most ancient graves were found there, the headstones all skewed and too weathered to provide any legible information. Nothing had been cut back there for years. She kept running, though, or tried to run, despite the fact she had to drag her feet and pull as if the undergrowth were trying to haul her down. Eventually she found a dilapidated door in the high wall, which when pushed fell to the side, hanging from a single hinge.

The moment she went through the door we followed, yet by the time we left the graveyard she was already some way ahead of us, her arms still thumping against her sides like stubby wings. From this side of the church the landscape rolled towards the interior high-ground, its features distinguished by bellying fields, inclines with streams and slender but fast flowing rivers, spoil banks and wetland. Chasing her was strange. Everything changed from soreness to pleasure. Her running was wild and random, so much what we would have expected of her, and her stamina bewildering, but we managed to keep up with her – until she went to earth, that is. It never crossed our minds that she might have felt like a hunted creature and that it was the dread of a hunted animal that kept her going. We were sisters. Surely they couldn't have removed that. We were sure she was laughing by then. It is something I have never been able to verify. It seems naïve now, but that doesn't mean it wasn't the case; after all, we were all three naïve, three naïve sisters.

When she vanished I thought it was magic. One second she was there and then she was gone, miraculously removed. For a moment I even thought she might burst across the skyline like an avenging angel, a sudden brilliant luminosity, an incendiary. Grace was rather more down-to-earth and signed the probability that she had tripped arse over tit, and knowing her luck had ended up in some filthy crevasse. Finding no trace of her was on neither of our minds.

We stopped running and began searching, Grace expecting a casualty, whilst I expected something more wonderful altogether. What prompted that hope is difficult to say, except I had always recognised that Abby was looking for a door through time, a door to a different age. It began from the very first time Grace had let Abby look at her book The Adventures of King Arthur and the Knights of the Round Table and Abby had gazed with such rapt pleasure at a plate of Sir Galahad witnessing the Grail. I really hoped it might be true, never stopping to consider whether it meant we would never be reunited this side of time.

Grace executed a wonderful job of signing her impatience and pleasure at Abby, at her vanishing trick, but couldn't wave away the fact that really she was scared. Deep down I think she wanted to go and fetch her parents, Eileen and Seamus, but somehow had already learnt, without understanding why, that Abby was our responsibility. Some of her facial expressions clearly insinuated the scale of the problem, and of course she was right. How could Abby have disappeared? What did it mean? It was all too big for us to deal with alone. Nevertheless, we plodded around looking for signs of her, aware that one sense was severely lacking, that if she was crying for help, it was something we really might miss.

The ground streamed red. In places bare rock protruded through the vegetation. Everything was saturated. Our legs were splashed with mud and ore. The rain kept coming, not heavily, but with persistence, drenching us, making us cold right through the skin. I picked up a branch and began thrashing it through the undergrowth. I don't know what I expected, but at least I was doing something. We were both aware of the fact, without having to share it, that there was no point in calling out. Abby was always beyond calling. The reality of that singular fact had never been as real as at that moment.

We found ourselves on a high, gently inclined bank, one side of a shallow valley, looking down towards a v shaped pool, into which ran a large rust encrusted tube, like some vast segmented earthworm, its head sunk in the water, its tail ashore. The bank was jagged, split boulders and sheer faces of bare red rock exposed through short tough grasses. There were numerous paths down to the pond, where the rock had been worn down to gravel. We carried on along the brink, following the separating lines of the valley, the banks to either side deepening, the pool widening, the segmented creature sinking deeper and deeper until finally it was completely submersed. The water terminated in an arcing shore of low ruined walls, tall reeds and subsequent marsh. The bank reached its zenith at the same point and then fell away to all sides, forming a hill of scrub, boulders and scree. The landscape beyond was an irregular fissured and broken outline of green and red slag, green fields and marsh. In the far distance were the broken outline of mountains, their shapes lost in cloud, colours distilled to pale turquoise and mauve. In all directions the sky had come to earth. Mist pooled in gullies and ran trails across the disorganised ground.

Without a sign we began to make our way down the bank. The rain continued to fall in a light persistent sheet. The rocky outcrops were treacherous. We didn't know whether to laugh or cry. Was this a real crisis or a game? I desired Grace Powers' comic impatience, without knowing how to demand it. I suppose it was all part of the growing awareness that Abby missing was frighteningly real. Silence was also space and space was immense. She was in the world, somewhere, but what was the world in. In the lap of God would have been an easy, and maybe beautiful answer, but we believed that as much as we believed in the flat world on the backs of elephants from the Book of Marvels, even if Grace would have been obliged to confirm it was indeed the case if Seamus ever put her sense of God to the test, which, of course, he wouldn't do, wouldn't risk.

We are in the world, but what is the world in? Is that what Abby pondered whenever she gazed tenaciously at the sheer horizon, taking in its implied line, its simulation of time, of centuries? I can only guess her answer – her signs were vague on that score – but despite the presence of sisters, however naïve, it seemed to imply solitariness, though whether awful or desired, I couldn't say.

Eventually, after a difficult descent we reached the foot of the slope. Looking back the valley was like a funnel, its vanishing point, following the edges of the banks against the sky, lost amongst a dense concentration of shrubs and trees. The tube also disappeared into foliage. We walked ahead. The ground remained uneven, still a mixture of exposed rock and scrub, with numerous spoil banks where the ground had been quarried. Everywhere was a new nature, man-made but disowned. Before long we came to a group of dilapidated buildings, a number of low sheds and a tower. The sheds were sealed, the windows and doors bricked up, but the tower had been broken open, a metal door forced, the hinges fractured. We went inside.

There was a narrow stairway. There was a stink of rotten vegetation and clay. I was sure we would find her; after all, it was just her sort of place, a place of concealment, protection maybe. In her imagination it would have been timeless: a castle, a sanctuary, a place of wonder. It was inconceivable she wouldn't have found it. I signalled to Grace. This had to be where she had gone. The fact that she had vanished in front of our very eyes was of no account. Somehow she would have found this. Grace nodded her agreement. We both knew her, her urge and desire. We ran up the steps.

Of course she wasn't there. No magic had transported her.

We found we couldn't make it to the roof; the stairs came up against a brick wall. The brickwork was a different colour to the rest, obviously erected to seal the tower's open top. We made a quick inspection of the chamber we were in. It was regular and bare, and despite its height from the ground the floor was covered in dry clay. It had obviously been occupied as there were scorch marks on the floor and wall where a fire had been, and there were empty beer and spirit bottles, though probably too dirty to be recently left. There were two small square openings where presumably there had once been windows. On one of the ledges there was a dead baby bird, its feathers and flesh almost entirely rotted, though the shape of its head was still distinct, particularly its large bulging eyes and stabbing beak. Grace brushed it away with a grimace of disgust and it made a solitary heavy flight to the ground below.

She turned and flashed me a look of defiance, as if she expected me to object. I shrugged my incomprehension. Her expression went through a number of agonised contortions, signalling a confusion of anger, frustration and fear. Eventually she stamped her foot, brandished two fists through the air and began to cry. With tears a much smaller, younger Grace Powers worked through her features. She really did want her mother. It was too much to carry, the mystery of Abby's going, the antecedents to its occurrence. If growing up meant the admission of bitten skin, fierce raw sores, then she wasn't ready, in all likelihood would never be ready. It ripped away the world's cover, its greensward, its slag, its scrub.

I didn't know what to do. I couldn't make it right, couldn't pull Abby out of a hat, no matter how much I might long for it. Like Grace I suspected something bad, without being able to formulate it. The one thing I was sure of was that I would be held somehow responsible, as would Grace, and, of course, Abby too. We were in an unknown territory, somewhere probably out of bounds. Not knowing was never a defence. We were at fault, worse than naughty. We had committed terrible wrong. Something had happened to our sister, who no one but us knew was our sister, and we would be blamed, all three. I was pretty sure that if our relationship was discovered, that we had named ourselves sisters, we would be punished. Our sisterhood was at stake. I don't know how I was aware of it, but aware of it I was. I knew they didn't want us together, and would seize on any reason to forbid it. I didn't know what they feared, but I knew they did, sensed it, felt it deep within me.

Even now I don't know what inspired that thought, what made me so fearful for me and my sisters. It was maybe just the fact that Abby was missing, that a part of us, a piece of our own body and mind was absent. Why it should have manifested as a certainty that they wanted to stop us, stop us falling in love with anyone, stop us marrying, stop us having babies, wanted to banish our language, our silence, I can't begin to understand, unless our genes carry the code of centuries, that the experience of those I would learn of later, deaf women such as Jane Poole and Eliza Cockerill was already part of me. Somewhere inside me I knew that life is variable and inconstant, and they wanted to refute it and say it wasn't so. I tried to tell Grace it was no good looking for help, Abby was our sister, our concern, but she was too scared to reason with and in no fit state to read my signs. Finally I took her roughly by the hand and pulled her from the tower.

I reasoned that we were being somewhat fantastical, or certainly I was. Abby had to be at the place where she had disappeared, more than likely lying in a ditch, conscious or unconscious, in need of her sisters. So with Grace's hand still firmly in mine I skirted the hill we had just descended and made our way back to where we had last seen her racing ahead, as excited as a young deer, before vanishing and set to work to find her.

Funnily enough, despite her disarranged state – she was blubbering even as I instructed her to look into every crevice, gully or pothole – it was Grace who discovered the hole into the earth. I was put out about that. I can admit it now. Now it makes sense. I wasn't annoyed that Grace should be the one to make such an incredible discovery, it was just that I had already taken on the role of Abby's protector, her guardian. It should have been down to me to discover the pit she had so fervently desired. It spoke of failure rather than success, of me not Grace. It was more than obvious I had failed Abby so many times already, her ripped translucent skin was evidence enough of that, but how many more times would I be destined to fall short of the mark. Already in our childish ways we were mapping out the future, a future I obviously didn't expect to hold any respite.

Grace appeared in front of me, her expression stern and disappointed, indicating that she had waved for my attention over and over, but I had chosen to ignore her. I shook my head. I even indicated my ears, my hearing, my failing. She shrugged. We didn't know what we were saying to each other, we were too young to be able to put it into words, but ideas were being formed, ideas that would be as fixed as a gouge on the landscape. She was asking how I could have abandoned her so easily, when she was so in need, so desirous of supervision, and I was making the case that I wasn't up to it, that I could take on and take off as I chose, not deliberately reliable or unreliable, but subject to deviation.

Grace took me by the hand. I took reluctant steps with her, as if I was as blind as I was deaf, seeing only shapes without definition or detail, everything blurred and not to be trusted. My reticence was unforgivable.

She led me to a slender cleft at the base of a hillock, a curling indentation like the whorl of an ear. She smiled and looked around, signalling pleasure and secrecy. I also looked all around, sharing her vigilance. As far as I could tell we weren't being watched. There was a row of buildings on the far horizon used to house cattle or sheep, though rather too tall to have been originally built for that purpose, but they were abandoned so not to be considered. Grace lifted her hand into the air, her index-finger raised pointing out the trick, and then she approached the cleft, manoeuvred into it sideways, ducked down, and like a baby re-entering the birth canal disappeared head first. It took seconds but seemed instantaneous, seemed like vanishing. I waited, perhaps defiantly renouncing magic, perhaps merely jealous of the miracle of it. Grace reappeared and impatiently signalled me to follow.

Though I was taller than Grace I was just as lean and navigated the hole in the hill, that ear-like fissure, with as much ease. In fact, the opening wasn't as narrow as it seemed, but was rather a sequence of curved obstacles, outcrops of rock, one in front of the other, hiding the ensuing tunnel in which I found myself. There had probably been a barrier of gravel and small rocks at one time, but weathering had disturbed them leaving an easily climbed low heap just past the entrance. After that there was a wide, tall tunnel that stretched ahead, going down into the hill with an easy gentle gradient.

Grace took hold of me again, wrapping her hand around my arm just below the elbow. Encouraged by her find she wanted to lead the way, convinced that this is what Abby had discovered. Seeking confinement, though, Abby would have gone deeper, no doubt until the tunnel terminated in rock, where she was probably curled up, contained by darkness. We had to go deeper, deeper and deeper, but I resisted. It wasn't safe to go stumbling ahead in the darkness. Where we were was all right, the light through the entrance sufficient for some considerable distance, the tunnel spacious enough for a horse, but after that it was black. – We guessed the tunnel had been constructed with horses in mind. Markings where rails had been could clearly be seen, and the rock between was worn smooth from the continual tramp of hooves. We had obviously discovered a way into a disused iron-ore mine.

Once again the fact that Abby was beyond calling was indisputable. Grace was right; if this really was where Abby had gone to earth then we had no choice but to follow, and the only way to ever follow her was to go exactly where she had gone, to follow in her footsteps, to look at what she had looked at and try to see what she had seen.

I took Grace's hand away from my arm and held her hand to hand, confirmed sisters. We began to descend the tunnel together. The temperature began to rise. At first progress was simple. The light was weak and diffuse, but enough to see the line of the tunnel, enough not to be disoriented by the incline which appeared regular, but when the dark began to become more complete felt subject to sudden downwards jolts. As the light failed I reached out and traced my hand along the tunnel wall. It was cold and moist to touch, as if the wall was drenched in sweat. Occasionally I stepped into ruts which were filled with water. I felt all of the time that I was going to strike my head against a ridge of rock, an outcrop, a decline in the tunnel's capacity, something hanging from the roof. The darkness became physical, solid. I held Grace's hand more tightly, and was sure she squeezed mine at the same time.

I don't know how long we had been descending, perhaps minutes, perhaps only seconds, when Grace stumbled over a rut and fell. Due to the tightness of our grip I kept hold of her, but she jerked me to the side so that I ended up on my knees in front of her. I reached out with my free hand to touch her. She was sprawled out. I could feel the heavy contractions of her chest. She was evidently sobbing. I couldn't hear her. My hearing aid wasn't working. Maybe it was wet, or had been damaged in the fall. I strained to hear. I crawled over her, coming closer, bringing my ear to her. Eventually I heard her sobs, her broken moans, help- lessly crying to go home. It sounded as if through water, bubbling in my ear, at first shapeless, meaningless, but then as if thrown into relief by sudden shafts of light, giving up meaning, a sob, a word, a word with a picture, a word with a desire. I – want – to – go – home.

I stroked her. I stroked her with my two hands, running them across her chest, down her side and across her back, outlining her shape, giving her substance and form in the darkness, confirming I was there and that it was going to be all right. Still the bubbles of her distress formed in my mind. At that moment I heard Abby's name. It was a dull note, repeated over and over though it was impossible to say from where it came. I was convinced it was coming from Grace. I rubbed her more vigorously, rubbed her to take away the pain of Abby's name; but then it came from somewhere else, somewhere in the dark, though I couldn't say from where. The darkness was everywhere, eluded shape and pattern. It was unmistakably Abby's name, though, unmistakably Abby. She was full of it, bursting with it. It was as rich and sonorous as laughter. I don't think I had ever heard her as excited as she was in that moment, and then I felt her hands clutch for me in the dark. As soon as she made contact her voice burst out in a great peal of excitement. I heard it, heard it as clearly as if I was not Grade II deaf at all.

Straight away I felt her hands covering me, rapidly form- ing my fallen outline in the dark. I felt her face close to mine, so close it was as if she were sniffing me, Grace and me, confirming it was indeed her sisters, and then she began to coax and encourage, her hands gently pulling, persuading me back to my feet. She lifted me and I lifted Grace and we stood bound together, not hand in hand, nor linked, but my arm wrapped around Grace, Grace's hand clutching my skirt, Abby's two palms resting on my shoulders, her face close to mine, her excited breaths against my cheek.

It was Abby who took the first steps, deciding the direction out of the darkness. We shuffled forward as if walking were a problem, though no bones had been broken. Grace hadn't been wailing in physical pain, just fear and the desire for home. Every second I expected to walk straight into a wall, or find the tunnel closing all around us at the face of some last unmined vein: but my fears were groundless. Abby never wavered. She knew exactly how to manoeuvre through that space. After all, she was in her element. Why should it have been such a surprise? Really, the only surprise was that she was willing to relinquish it for the sake of her sisters. I could see it in her expression as she brought us into the light, the disappointment, the reluctance. Already she was quite the subterranean creature, her face smeared red with ore. Even in the dull light that began to gather around us it was clear that her paleness had a new tincture, not robustness but stain. As the light increased it became obvious that her hands too were thick with the orange-red ore. I could only wonder at the thoroughness of it, and imagine her joyfully tracing the contours of her confinement, running her hands across the sodden walls then excitedly all over herself, though whether she realised the transfer or not I don't know. I tend to think she did, she carried it so much like war paint.

When we finally reached the entrance I had to promise that we would come back soon in order to get her to leave. In fact I had to explain it would still be there and that it couldn't be taken away. It was a difficult explanation.

Rock, earth, dug out, forever.

Hole, forever.

Forever.

I remember thinking she was kidding me. It never occurred to me that she might not live in time, that yesterday, today and tomorrow were indivisible; but in reality where was the change or the alteration that could have alerted her to the possibility of it? I should have seen the way they had taken time from her and known the gift one sister can give to another is to return it, accepting that as with many gifts there is a cost. In time things will end, will be drawn to a close, but time cannot distinguish between those things we would want to have terminated and those we would want to have survive. That is the chance we take. That is why we have to sign, because we know time is everything we have to contend with, my time, Grace's time, Abby's time; but time wasn't on her face, not then. She must have been sure she had found the door that went right through it, the door she had been looking for for so long, and it was her sister that told her it was time to go.

Grace was all for leaving her. She indicated her coloured face, her filthy clothes, suggesting she was safer where she was. What would Harold make of his red-skin child, other than to use it as another reason to disown her, claim she was unnatural, not a Sempie at all but an impostor, a deaf, red-skin cuckoo. When I frowned my disapproval Grace shrugged and said Abby would follow anyway, once she realised she was alone, there was no point fighting with her. I wasn't sure though. I believe she would have stayed there forever, and who would have come looking for her? It would have been left to later generations to dig her up, an artefact, a Grade III deaf girl, buried without apparent ritual or crime – her bones yielding no evidence, her skin long gone – sometime in the uncertain decade following the Second World War. What story would they invent to explain her, certainly not one that would do her justice, one that would tell of the look she had in her eyes, the look she had when she gazed at the horizon, a witness.

113

I promised we would come back and explore every gallery; up and down we would go until we had made the whole mine ours, hers.

I had her laughing, jumping, calling her name, shaking out a perfectly neat war dance in her ochre war paint.

Grace said we couldn't take her back looking like that. I had to agree. So, once again we washed her, this time in fresh water, not salt water, in the v shaped pool, though it was every bit as cold, and despite the fact that unlike salt water it didn't leave the skin taut and still unclean, it wasn't sufficient to remove all the redness from her. Grace said she was being stubborn, without even trying to explain how she might affect that trick. After that we climbed inside the segmented creature. Along the ridge of the tube there were occasional portholes large enough to allow us access. A shallow, rainbow streaked stream ran across the floor, but it was easy to stride along with our feet to either side. We ran first to the far end where the stream was at its narrowest, then down the whole length, until the water was too much and we would have had to wade into it. At that point we climbed out and found we were someway out into the pond. So the creature was an island in the middle of a flood, a boat, an elephantine saviour.

If it wasn't for the mine we might have found Abby inside the creature rather often after that, though it would never have become an entirely favoured place because the water stopped her lying down. She always knew asylum was a place in which she could lie down comfortably.

It was Grace who solved the mystery. The creature was the remains of the drainage system of a subsided and subsequently flooded iron-ore mine. Her father, Seamus, told her, but whether he expected her to remember is doubtful.

*

Why is that we pity the past but fear the future? Is that really reconcilable?

The past, the near past, the far past, the past we remember, the past we calculate, is invariably considered a more innocent time than the one we are in. We scoff at an Anglo Saxon world that only knew spaghetti in tins, detested garlic and, when pushed, drank sweet German wine, much preferring beer and gin. Our sophistication is global – though presumably there are tastes yet to be unearthed.

We trek every path from the Arctic to Antarctica. The globe is a toy, something to brag about, to encounter in a package deal if necessary, independently when at all possible. Technological superiority proves the case. The modern world is complex, refined, peopled by a global tribe. The old world was a grey world, a world of floral patterned embossed wall-paper, shampoo and set women, wife beating men. We've outgrown all that, all the fights that were the wrong fights, the emergencies and whims which were, in the clear light of hindsight, so trivial after all, and, it goes without saying, we've said goodbye to ridiculous fashions.

My hairdresser has had quality training. She knows all there is to know about hair, what makes it rich, what makes it take colour, its patterns of growth. She knows what the old world did not, that hair is a specialist subject worthy of study, and if one scrimps on study then the customer will recognise you are trying to palm them off with an inferior product. There is no one as worldly-wise as the modern customer, the expert, democratic consumer.

So why is it that the innocent world will not leave me alone? Why does it cry out for a vengeance that it feels I am adequate to give? Perhaps because progress has taught me that there is no straight line from innocence to knowing, but endless spirals, curvatures, loose ends.

Of course, my vanity knows no end, my infectious young hairdresser is well aware of that mundane fact.

What does progress mean to a deaf person, to me, to Grace, Abby: hearing or respect?

Chapter Eight

I went to see Agnes. She had the same worried, put upon look she always had, but she had more weight and was neater than I had ever known her, her clothes cheap but not unfashionable – a flowery dress and turquoise cardigan with mother-of-pearl buttons. Her hair, now dyed copper brown, had been set in a tight perm which made it appear as if it had shrunk around her head. Her skin was markedly more aged, patterned over with numerous fine lines. She had been a heavy smoker all her life, it was a smoker's face, the face I was destined to have; faces we had so rashly contributed to.

Straight away she told me he was out and didn't know how long he would be.

"No," I said. "I know, I saw him go. It's you I came to see."

"Me," she said, smiling faintly, nervously, "why would you want to see me? I'm sure I've got no interesting news."

I smiled. "Everyone keeps assuming what I'll be interested in, what I'm not interested in. I was keen to know there's still a meat van, a butcher."

"But you're in London now."

I shrugged.

"He told me, told me you'd been away, wondered if I knew, and he said you were in London now."

"Did he approve?"

She looked confused. "He doesn't mind."

"No."

"You don't want to know about the butcher's van. What would you want to know?"

"Everything."

"Why? I don't get what you're after."

"So I'm not shocked one day to find everything gone. Just to keep pace."

"But you're in London now. He told me."

"It doesn't mean I'm not interested."

"There's nothing to interest you here, there's nothing here, nothing for you, that's why you've gone, isn't it, because there's nothing here, that's why anybody goes, and who'd blame them."

"I'd be interested to know if there wasn't a butcher's van anymore."

"But that's just laughing at people. That's not real."

The colour momentarily drained from her face, and she eyed me with cold curiosity. It was unexpected, suggested depths I ignored to my own cost. Agnes was made up of shades, compromises, learnt strategies. I was in error. I actually felt a pang of fear. It was unmistakable. Agnes would not countenance games. The set of her face indicated it. She was signing a warning.

"No, I'm sorry," I insisted, "I am interested. I don't want to find I don't know here, don't know it at all."

Her expression changed, the transition imperceptible but real, and she looked sulky and beaten again. "There's nothing to interest you here."

I shrugged, signing my disagreement, not insisting on it, insinuating. Something like a smile passed her face, but it was as if smiling had become so unusual an act for her that she no longer knew how to fully affect the trick.

"Do you want to come in?" she asked, her tone matter of fact, neither encouraging nor discouraging.

I shrugged again, accepting if it was no inconvenience, no bother, and sat down, resuming my place in that new room, with the rose covered wallpaper and fitted carpet. Of course, she meant sit down, because I was already in, just crossing the threshold meant one was in. She didn't offer me tea. She wasn't prepared to go that far. She did offer me a cigarette, but it was an afterthought, after she had lit her own and taken a number of quick, deep drags.

"No, thanks," I said, "I'm trying to give up, think I should give up."

"I've thought of that," she said, taking long inhalations, relishing the pleasure for my sake, "but Harold likes a smoke, his Players, untipped, so there'd be no point."

"You do a lot for him."

"What do you smoke? What do they smoke in London?"

"I said you do a lot for him, a lot of what he wants."

"I bet it's not Players and Woodbines in London, and I suppose they're all tipped."

"Rothmans, I smoke Rothmans."

"Never heard of them," she said wistfully, disappointed.

"Don't suppose you had much choice then, back then, women had to buckle down."

"I just got on with it, Judith, that's what I've always done, got on with it. That's how I am."

"You're right, they're all tipped."

"Leave me one. I'd like to try a . . .?"

"Rothmans."

"Rothmans."

"Changing religion is more than just getting on with it."

"I don't know about that."

"I would say it is. Most people would say it is."

The colour left her face again, replaced by sternness. It didn't flash across her face, but was apparent in just a turn of her head, two tendencies lying side by side.

"My mother just got on with it as well," I said, "always proud they never drew the dole."

"I never changed religion."

"But going to mass, the children."

"I said I never changed religion. You don't just change religion. That would be a difficult thing. I didn't do a difficult thing."

"So, you're Catholic."

"Of course I'm Catholic, what do you think?"

"Good, a good Catholic?"

"Yes."

The lines tightened across her expression, her smoker's face contracting, the colour squeezed, becoming increasingly meagre, nevertheless I chanced it. It was what I was there for, to chance things, chance light and dark, hubris and a fall. The opposite would have been to accept decline, insignificance, charity. I could only suppose my own smoker's face, not yet properly reformed, was as ash-grey as hers.

"What does that mean?" I asked.

She shrugged, indicating incomprehension, incomprehension rather than refusal.

"Being good, I mean, what does that mean?"

She shrugged again, but lightly, partly amused, partly embarrassed.

"But good at what, Agnes, good at what?"

"Don't be silly. Is that how they go on in London?"

"I just wondered, that's all, wondered."

"He said you'd got a bit flighty."

*

I don't know when Abby gave up her belief in flight, but it happened. Of course, I was guilty of not recognising its possibility until it was too late and the likelihood was gone. I should have suspected the dream of it whenever I saw her gazing at the horizon, her features dazzled yet coy, as if it were a forbidden gem and she was criminal to ever contemplate it. In truth when she ran around, flapping her stumpy wings, I never really understood whether she believed in the air or the earth. I tried to decipher her though, how she defined herself, as if the calculation could produce something definitive: an insect, an albatross, a scout, a trickle of water. I never realised, not to be begin with, that she recognised herself as chameleon. She didn't have to be tied to

119

one thing, because inevitably the singular would desert her. Besides, she wasn't allowed to be one thing. Certainly by the time I'd worked that out her belief in flight was gone. In fact maybe it was the absence that signified the existence, that only when it was lost could I know it had ever been found.

There is so much we only recognise when it has ceased to exist, when something missing subtracts from us, so that our definitions reduce around us, ourselves robbed of shade, texture, line, temperament. Usually we complain about those things over which we have no power, berating acts out of season, ill-will, accident, ignoring completely those things we can control, because then we would have to act, assume responsibility, chance failure. Having said that, I don't think it was failure that made her give up her belief in flight, but certainly her expectations changed. That is in the nature of a chameleon, it is after all its instinct to survive. Without adaptation we are finished.

Some adaptation is a terrible admission to make, though, so terrible we usually refuse to acknowledge it. So, maybe she still gazed at the horizon, knew what desire compelled her attention, but drew a line under any possibility. Instead she would have told herself that the sky and the sea were two dimensional, a flat surface, one of her confined spaces, unsuited entirely to flight. Of course it never stopped her launching Poppy on single doll missions, as free and doomed as Icarus, her unkempt figure flying gracelessly against sea and sky, inevitably coming to ground in a minor eruption of coal blackened sand. Grace was quite put out by such a display of rough treatment of her gift, but would invariably run to reach Poppy first in order to launch her ever further afield, which sometimes created friction between them, though more often than not Abby demurred to Grace, the natural mother, the legitimate owner. Our games always were only as good as those we had seen.

Flight strikes me now as really quite imaginative, indeed

sophisticated. Of course, we had no sense that flight was also falling, falling a thing to defend.

*

I smiled at Agnes. She didn't return it but eyed me sceptically, suggesting that my smile was misplaced, that there was nothing worthy in being flighty. That deliberately dour look struck me as really quite funny, though I had not reckoned with laughter. I reached up and fiddled with my hearing aid. It was a mannerism. It is something I do. Very rarely am I altering anything, nor do I believe I am drawing attention to its existence, which I make no attempt to conceal; it is simply a pause in proceedings, a bridge from one circumstance to another. In this instance it stopped any laughter: it created laughter's opposite, which isn't a sound of any kind at all.

"He thought Abby was a bit flighty, didn't he?"

She pursed her lips and raised her eyebrows, clearly signing that she was on her guard and would reply only to what she wanted, what didn't aggravate her. My question was evidently sanctioned because she straight after shook her head and, without any emphasis, said: "I wouldn't say that."

"That she played games. He thought she played games."

"You don't know what they're thinking," she replied, then smiled, pleased by her comment. "No, you see, you really don't know what they're thinking."

"Did you love her?"

"You don't know what they're thinking," she repeated, mouthing it carelessly, as if she hadn't heard my question, or didn't choose to.

I repeated it, my voice rising, becoming brittle, which was stupid, betraying things about me I would sooner have had ignored: "Did you love her?"

"I brought her up," she flashed back.

"Is that the same?"

"Is this London talk? Do you have time for all this, then, because I don't think I do?"

"Why are we ashamed of it?"

"We're not ashamed. Don't be so full of yourself. We just have things to do. You see what happens when you go away?"

"Do you love Harold?"

"Don't be cheeky. Remember you're in my house."

"I know, I know. You can tell me to go if you want."

"When I'm good and ready."

"I mean it. I'm at an age, wondering, wondering about myself. Marriage and love."

"We got by."

"Is that enough?"

"More than a lot."

"But, still, does that make it enough? I think you've put up with a lot."

"Nobody knows that."

"But it's not secret, not brushed under the carpet."

"You don't know what you're putting up with, because you have to do it, that's all. That's all."

She eyed me closely, her expression nettled, yet at the same time curiously patient. She had decided to give me the benefit of the doubt, the younger woman seeking guidance, advice. Maybe it flattered her, though it undoubtedly surprised and disturbed her.

I smiled, a helpless, deprecating smile and said: "I always thought of you as a shy woman."

"I brought up four children."

"Why did he hit her?"

"I didn't like him hitting her."

"You didn't stop him."

"I made him go outside."

"I thought he chose to do that for you."

"I made him."

"Your father's deaf."

"Not like that. You wouldn't know. A bit like, well . . ., you wouldn't really know."

"But you do know."

"No, I do not know."

Her face was again that one drained of colour: a stark, impressive, hostile face. She seemed to be taunting me to say more, to pursue my insistence that she possessed knowledge, knew what I didn't, but at the same time was insinuating consequence.

I had said I considered her a shy woman, but that wasn't true. I had considered her lacking in any notion of volition, devoid of life, of the jeopardy that constitutes life. It was as if she had never entirely become grown-up, but nor had she retained anything of the child, rather was caught in some dulling transition. I blamed the combined influence of Harold and Martha. Who could have survived their joint ministrations, particularly if entry into their domain had been entirely voluntary? And yet, that same woman, a Shaughnessy, was effortlessly threatening me, effortlessly blunting my arrogance. I had clearly misread Agnes, but wasn't that the whole point of my being there, to read things correctly, pursue suspicion and give myself entirely to the final rash act. I was delighted by that colourless face. It spoke of opposition, deceit, strategy. I was shored up by it. It bruised me with the past, and defied the future. She could frighten me, that after all wasn't a difficult thing to achieve, but she couldn't decipher me, read my signs, know the prophecy I kept in mind for her.

I smiled, smiled broadly, though at the same time fingered my aid, and asked her about her mother, asked her lightly, her mother's dutiful visitor. "Your mother, how is she, he said she isn't well, wasn't well?"

She took a moment to answer, a moment to allow the colour to return to her face. She picked up her cigarettes, but before she could take one I offered her mine. She took one, examined it with her eyes, sniffed it, and then lit it and took a deep drag. "Nice," she said, "not bad at all. No, she hasn't been too good, nothing serious, the chest, but gets her down none the less, can't do for herself as well, or him, and that was never her way. You'd know that though, that it was never her way. I've had to go round, help out, a bit of washing, ironing, a spot of cooking, but I don't mind, not a bit. I've done that all my life, washing, ironing, cooking."

"I know, it can't have been easy."

"You seem very bothered by that, things being easy."

"Curious, interested, yes; bothered, why not."

"I told you, we got on with it, that's what people did, got on with it. That's what I did."

"Why did you stand by?"

"Because somebody had to."

*

That day with the rat, when she stood close to the door of the lean-to – for how long only Agnes really knows – wasn't the only time she chose to stand by. Only Agnes herself would ever be able to say how many times she decided to stand by, but one time in particular stands out, the Christmas she watched the ripples on the water.

It always surprised me that Harold and Agnes bought Abby Christmas presents, and for that matter birthday presents. I don't suppose Harold was much involved – the only present he had ever given was a chicken claw – but he watched, nevertheless, on Christmas morning when Abby trailed Joseph, Ruth and Dennis into his and Agnes' bedroom to show them the presents Father Christmas had brought, and managed to feign a modicum of interest. Abby always followed her brothers and sister, despite being the elder, something she had learnt was for the best soon after Joseph had started to walk. If she tried to lead him she got in the way, and that was something she never wanted to do, get in the way.

Of course, the fact that Joseph, Ruth and Dennis were

there could account for Harold's uncharacteristic patience, but that doesn't account for the fact that the same sense of truce existed on her birthdays – she was born under Pisces, the twelfth sign of the zodiac, the two tied fishes. There was obviously something regarding the occasions themselves that mellowed him. I don't suppose he was taken by Christmas spirit or fatherly tenderness, but rather custom – simply getting on with it.

I am sure that if I had brought up the question of Christmas and birthdays with Agnes she would have said, and with some pride, that they always bought Abby a present, always ensured she never went without, in much the same way she never went naked or barefoot. They were, after all, her parents, and they accepted the obligation, even if they didn't like it. Not that her presents amounted to much – though, nor did anyone's – a picture annual, mixed nuts and raisins, a tin of biscuits and a tangerine. It means that neither Harold nor Agnes were necessarily evil. If that had been the case there would not have been a single hazelnut. If that is accepted, then what does it make them?

It is too soon to say, and probably by the time I know, it will already be too late. Life leaks away, the expectation changes, the vendetta remains, the persuasion goes on begging, understanding wanting.

On the Christmas in question I don't know that Christmas Day itself was cold, but certainly the day after Boxing Day was. – In all honesty I can't remember whether Abby was seven or eight, so can't name the year, though in my mind I feel that such details are important; how else can the past exist but through accuracy. – Agnes had decided she needed to get Abby out of the house. She had spent the morning lying on a rag rug flicking through the pages of her annual, though it can't have meant a great deal to her as she couldn't follow a cartoon or read a bubble. Nevertheless, she must have been pleased because when she picked it up again after lunch she began to shout out her name. Harold, who had been drinking for most of Boxing Day, hadn't appeared until then. – He drank modestly on Christmas Day, limiting himself to four or five pints at lunchtime whilst Agnes prepared the pork, therefore felt he was owed the following day. – Joseph, Ruth and Dennis had had sense enough to play in the yard, but as they had made no sign of invitation Abby hadn't followed.

Harold began to swear. Abby had no notion of it. Agnes placed her palm against the side of Abby's face. She didn't stroke it or run her palm across her temple and head, but simply held it there, firmly, neither caressing nor hurting. For a moment it quietened her, the surprise of it shocking her into submission. No doubt she expected such a touch to be followed by a slap. When she realised the blow hadn't materialised she looked up and saw Agnes peering at her with an expression she had never witnessed before. With a minor movement of her head Agnes indicated for her to go out, and it was evident from the slight movement of Agnes' body that she intended going with her. As if to underline the point she helped Abby with her coat.

It was bitterly cold outside. The sun hadn't appeared all day. The frost and ice of the morning remained. Ruth was drawing pictures in it with a length of stick. Joseph and Dennis were in front of the house sliding. The yard was too rough and uneven. For a while Agnes simply looked at Abby as if presenting her with the choice of joining either her brothers or her sister. Abby didn't respond. It was obvious they didn't want her. Eventually she uttered her name very quietly, perhaps more subdued in using that syllable than she had ever been since discovering it. She wanted to show Agnes something.

I don't know how Abby came to the decision of which space she would show her mother, which confined environment she wanted to reveal, but she opted for the mine, to begin with the disused mine buildings and then the subterranean space itself. I suspect at that moment she simply considered it the most impressive, not to mention the most recent of her haunts. Agnes was to be admitted to the most magnificent of all Abby's domains. Nevertheless, despite the prize she knew she was suggesting, she was still surprised when Agnes agreed. She saw her mother look back at the door through which they had come, then turn and study Ruth for a while, then slightly cock her head to listen to the boys, then stare at the ground at her feet for some time, until finally, once again with the slightest of head movements, she signed for Abby to go wherever she wished.

Abby didn't rush off, of course, but sidled away, looking back to see if Agnes meant it, whether she really did intend to follow. She decided to go across-country, the frost attracting her, the joy of treading on untouched crystals. Much to her surprise when Ruth began to follow Agnes sent her back. Ruth didn't kick up any fuss, simply resumed her drawing, a sequence of circles, squares and spirals patterning the yard and pig-sheds. Abby wanted to shout out her name, shout it loud and musically, but somehow knew it was a bad thing to do, bad for Ruth who for some reason was not favoured.

For Agnes the frost rendered everything quiet, her footfalls crisp and, unaccountably, pleasing, even uplifting. For Abby the silence of hard winter was immaterial but its colour, basal greys, turquoise hints, a swirl, light filtered and struggling, had the same effect. She wanted to let her name burst free, but taking her cue from her mother conformed to the human tendency to control the urge to cry out. Still, as she witnessed the formation of incomplete footsteps behind her, the frost smudging rather than allowing neat imprints, her name rang inside her head – in no way aping hearing, more like a sensation of pain. She looked at her mother regularly, apprehensively, sure she had transgressed, been unfair to Ruth, but Agnes showed no disapproval, no disappointment, no anger. In fact Agnes' expression was imbued with satisfaction, albeit a solemn rather serious satisfaction, but that made it all the more believable. Abby was certain she wasn't being cajoled, or humoured. It inspired her to give more.

She brought Agnes in sight of the tower and the tumble-down sheds but didn't show her the stair, didn't take her up to reveal the extent of winter, the revelation the viewing tower could achieve. Maybe it was simply deferred, a promise of something to come, or perhaps she reasoned it wasn't hers to give. – Grace and I never did know whether she had discovered it before we did, whether her indifference to it when we took her there was because it was familiar or because it simply did not match the scale of the mine. – She stood on the crest of a frozen knoll and gazed down at it. There were thin white mists trailed along the banks that led up from the pond. The mist had frozen onto the trees and bushes making them so thick with frost it looked like snow. The funnel shaped gorge that ran to the pond was whiter than anywhere she had so far seen. The exposed ground, in patches completely devoid of vegetation, was frozen solid; it appeared granular but was unbreakable. She felt the intense cold through her shoes and her ears burnt with it. Still she stood for a while showing off one of her places, an appetiser to the underground galleries. In the mine she would be warm. In the mine she would show Agnes how she could be comfortable.

Agnes was undoubtedly aware of the existence of the old mine buildings but she was generous enough not to let Abby know. When Abby looked for a response she smiled appreciatively, agreeing it was interesting, approving what she understood to be a place where Abby played all those long hours she wasn't under anyone's feet. Agnes might even have suggested admiration for Abby's play world, disclosing as it did an imagination she hadn't before considered. Abby was delighted with her success, delighted her mother so clearly saw as she saw – though Abby's listening was of a different order. She decided that the mine workings, the sanctuary of cover and warmth, should be postponed further still. There was the pond before that.

Abby didn't take Agnes' hand but tentatively moved away, hesitantly looking back to check that Agnes hadn't grown bored or impatient with this after Christmas game. To her surprise it seemed she hadn't: she followed willingly, not offering encouragement, simply allowing herself to be led. Her expression became even more solemn, which if Abby had known of Hazel's prediction that her daughter would always be a Catholic at heart she might have taken as spiritual. There was that quality to it, of being impressed and satisfied, knowing something of grace.

As they made their way to the pond the frost deepened to either side. The trees and shrub spread out a network of silver-white filaments like connecting nerve fibres. Leaf litter sparkled, furred over with crystals. The pond was a grey, opaque sheet. When they reached the shore Agnes picked up a stone and threw it onto the ice. It bounced and then slid across the surface making zither music. The sound delighted her. She turned to Abby smiling. Abby made out that she had detected something of the weird, wire tightening sound, but Agnes was sceptical and her smile evaporated. Nevertheless Agnes threw stone after stone, seemingly determined to throw them ever farther distances. Some went completely awry, ending up in the bushes behind them, sometimes off to right or left. After a while she signed for Abby to copy her. She didn't give any of her stones but signalled that Abby collect her own and throw them. It hadn't crossed Abby's mind until her mother suggested it. Abby immediately set to work. At first it wasn't too difficult, there was some loose debris, but the supply was quickly exhausted and then she had to pry away stones frozen into the earth. Her hands smarted with the cold and the effort but she kept on. After all, her mother hadn't given up, so nor would she. Eventually though, Agnes had enough and the stone throwing came to a halt.

The end of the game created something of a problem. Up until the game Abby had been leading. She had brought Agnes to this shore. Agnes had initiated the game, though, and brought her into it. Whose was the next move? Was it time to take her mother to the mine, to the warmth, or was Agnes leading now? It was so cold the mine certainly made sense. Abby's face and hands ached with it, and she held the muscles along her torso and thighs rigid, guarding herself, trying to keep the cold at bay. Her mother's face shone with a distinct symmetry of white and red. Her breath was visible. Still Abby waited, uncertain whether she was through or she still had permission to lead.

She thought Agnes gave her a nod, something slight, almost indiscernible, but a nod, nevertheless. She couldn't decipher it. Did it allude to the present, the past or the future: stone throwing, tower or what came next? She waited. Agnes pursed her lips and then made her way to the water's edge, to the ice sheet. She stretched out her leg and tested it with her toes, pressing down, at first gently and then with increasing force. It didn't give. She turned to Abby as if looking for encouragement. Abby simply stared, but her name ran round her head, quietly, as if whispered numerously at once. Agnes stepped out completely onto the ice. It bore her weight without any sign of strain. She held her hands out like a dancer at the commencement of a performance, and then began to kick at the surface with her heel. She hardly scarred it, managing only a limited contusion of white crystal. She began to slide, at first heavily and carefully, keeping both feet on the surface, but eventually with greater freedom, taking short runs, propelling herself forward, even having the temerity to lift one leg and glide on a single shoe.

She beckoned Abby to join her, urging her with an impatience Abby found entirely novel. Abby couldn't have refused, even if she had felt so inclined, which she certainly didn't. Such an invitation was not to be gainsaid. At first she

130

was hopeless and struggled to keep any balance. As she picked herself up she expected her mother to be angry and disappointed, Agnes was so adept herself, so at liberty in this discovered element, but Agnes helped her. She took hold of Abby's hands with her own, took small backward steps, sliding her shoes across the surface and pulled Abby along. At first Abby's back was arched but slowly, very slowly, she lifted herself up, until she was fully upright. Agnes periodically released and grabbed her, the time between each growing ever longer, until Abby was moving by herself, not fluently nor with any great freedom – left to her own devices she arched her back, rounded her shoulders and kept her attention directly on the ice in front of her – but not hopelessly either, though likely to fall at any moment.

She kept sliding, scared to stop, scared to look up in case she should lose her balance and come crashing down. The name in her head ran rapidly, though she had no concept of whether she was scared or thrilled. She did know she was pleasing her mother. That had to be the case. Agnes had brought her to it, tutored her and let her go. Abby felt she had to keep going for her, despite the fact the cold was making her feet throb with pain.

When she did eventually look up she found she had strayed some way from the shore. Agnes was waving at her from the frozen water's edge. Abby didn't comprehend that signal at all. Her name welled up inside her head. The edge of the pond seemed so far away. She felt elastic. She couldn't keep her balance and fell onto her hands and knees. She gazed towards the shoreline. Agnes was still waving. Abby's hands ached with the cold, though when she pressed her fingers together, criss-crossing them, she couldn't feel them. She was sure her mother must be telling her to get up, get up and come back. She pulled herself up onto her knees, and then with some effort regained her feet, but she felt incapable of moving, the shore seemed just too far away to manage.

She stood there for some time incapable of movement, as if frozen with the environment. She was no longer able to gaze directly at the shoreline, her attention was too drawn to the ice sheet in front of her, but from the corner of her eye she could see that Agnes had stopped waving, though she remained exactly where she had been, keeping an eye on her. Abby lifted her head slightly higher, expanding her field of vision. The segmented creature, the bloated worm, wasn't too far away, certainly much closer than the shore. She thought she could make that. Its inner belly called to her. She didn't stop to consider how she intended to scale its back, which at that point in the pond was certainly raised enough from the surface to be a challenge.

She inched forward, her arms crossed over her chest, each palm resting on its opposite shoulder. She forgot about Agnes, forgot about trying to decipher what message was intended by her waving and then not waving. She only had thoughts to reach the drain. The mine was banished from her mind.

She was still some ten feet from the tube when she saw a white line pattern through the ice, a stronger white than the surface. She stopped. The whole surface was veined and streaked with a variety of shades, in patches grey, almost colourless, in other places still pure white. More fractures appeared. Water spread around the soles of her shoes. She instinctively lifted her feet away, treading on the surface. With each step the water was deeper. She panicked and began to jump and hop on the surface. Fracture lines appeared all around her, and the ice broke into smaller insufficient fragments. She plunged into the blackness. There were ripples on the water. She thrashed her arms and grabbed at the ice sheet, but it broke in her hands. As she struggled on the surface she tried to look towards the shore, but in the chaos of her fight she didn't manage to see Agnes, though she was pretty sure she was looking at the place she had last seen her, waving and then not waving.

It was already dark when they came looking for her. Of course, it was dark early, just after four. Harold brought a paraffin-lamp. They thought she had to be dead. Harold walked down the spine of the drain looking for her body, swinging the lamp from its wire handle in large arcs towards the pond, lighting up the ice and frost in a glittering display. He had a broken branch in his other hand and periodically poked at the water. Agnes watched from the shoreline, her expression solemn and sombre as she had been when she accompanied Abby to the pond earlier. She recognised that Harold never hesitated long enough to indicate he had found anything. She waited with a sense of overwhelming expectation, already rehearsing in her mind the moment of discovery. Eventually Harold threw the branch towards the pond where it landed without breaking the surface, and then marched back down the length of the drain. He went up to Agnes, where she remained rooted to the spot. He roughly told her that Abby was inside the drain making disgusting sounds, not at all recognising the name she was uttering. He strode off and for a second day became hopelessly drunk. It was left to Agnes to crawl along the spine of the drain and find a portal to reach her, which in the dark wasn't easy, Harold having taken the lamp with him, in the end having only Abby's voice to guide her.

I don't know how Abby didn't die. She was ill afterwards, but never critically. She remained in bed for a number of days and Agnes brought her soup, tins of condensed tomato or oxtail, and sometimes her own home-made broth. She placed the bowl with a spoon already in it on a small bedside table and left Abby to it. Abby couldn't decipher her mother's guarded look, the brief half-glances she gave her as she walked in and as she placed the bowl down, though Abby recognised it was similar to the look she had revealed on the day they went skating together, though not identical. Each time Agnes lay down the soup Abby was determined to leave it, but hunger invariably got the better of her and she

133

eventually lifted herself up and slowly swallowed the by then tepid offering. Her sheets evidenced each meal, sipping soup recumbent being a skill she never quite mastered.

For those days she was in bed she didn't exhibit any sign of fever, any obvious discomfort or pain. If anything she was simply morose. She lay with her eyes wide open and stared blankly at the ceiling, but what she was witnessing remained secret. She certainly made no attempt to describe her escape to Agnes, remaining remarkably quiet whenever Agnes brought in her soup. Her survival was something Agnes would have to mull over and accept as wonderful.

If Agnes had waited longer than simply watching the ripples break across the frozen surface she would have seen that when Abby calmed, when the intense cold modified into dull numbing ache, when she gave herself to the certainty of drowning, she found that her feet could reach the bottom. If she bobbed up and down she could bounce in the water. So that's what she did. She bobbed along the length of the segmented creature, breaking the fragile ice where it met the rust encrusted pipe, until she reached a point where it sank deeply enough into the pond to be scaled. She discovered that leaving the water was the worst moment. The cold was so intense she nearly passed out. Somehow she managed to crawl inside the drain then along the inner tube until she reached a point where she could balance on its side above the stream that still flowed along the floor despite the freezing conditions. Of course there was nothing to warm her so she simply wrapped into herself as best she could and waited. Once again, as Grace and I thought so often, it might have been presumed she was dying; she was so numb, so devoid of any life giving warmth, how could it have been any other way? She couldn't have done any more herself. All she had left was to wait, though she can't possibly have known for what. If Agnes and Harold hadn't assumed they should claim her body she certainly would have died. How else could Agnes peek at her but with wonder?

They never did give up the obligation of Christmas, though they were always unforgiving. The following year when Abby ate all her biscuits, because the tin was on the end of her bed, they beat her. Harold was particularly severe as the tin contained a number of chocolate biscuits which, to his mind being luxuries, greatly amplified the crime. Of course he had lived with rationing for many years. Abby never seemed to learn her lesson though. The year after that saw her receive yet another beating when she tore up the wrapping of her present to find that it was part of it. Inside the envelope she so inexpertly and wantonly ripped open and tore to shreds was a paper doll dressed in only fringed white knickers, her cut-out clothes, all outlined with thick black easy to follow scissors lines, were on the envelope itself. Not a single costume could be saved. That year it was Agnes who proved the more severe, who seemed to take great exception to the paper doll going naked. In truth the doll went unclothed but not naked. She berated Abby, struck her, slapped her around the head and dismissed her as the most stupid girl on the planet. Of course Abby was attending school by then and should have known better.

*

Despite the fact that Agnes had smoked heavily for so long she was not an accomplished smoker – her eyes contracted and gave her a crimped, reptilian look, emphasising the damage it was doing, the ageing, the making ugly – nevertheless, she smoked with a real air of satisfaction. I know that was obviously as a result of me. She was indulging herself for my benefit, for me, against me. It infuriated me. What achievement was she so smugly enjoying? Dealing with me, making of me an outsider, a misfit? I wanted to slap her across the face.

I froze at the possibility.

I saw the scene. A shrieking young woman, her noise diluted for herself, unaware of the spectacle she was. The elder of the two, nursing her smarting cheek, the rough, discoloured skin puckered, saying it was all right, no need to fuss, it was all over.

Of course, Agnes would understand the sign. She would peer at me from her bruising and more than likely smile, the smile denoting comprehension, vigilance and the certainty of retaliation.

It was her language.

Why was I literate with their language?

A wave of revulsion surged through me. I had to be free of their signs. I had to eradicate their lexis.

I stood up and uttered: "I should be going. I don't want to detain you."

She smiled and replied: "It's no bother. I would have told you if you'd outstayed your welcome, if I'd had things to do."

"Your mother. She must keep you busy."

"She's not on death's door, a bit chesty, can't catch her breath, a bit hoarse, but not dying."

I shrugged and made my own way to the door. As I reached for the handle I turned and asked: "Did she ever tell you she loved you?"

She looked momentarily incensed, but quickly controlled herself. She inhaled deeply, burning the cigarette down to the tip, her face contracting as she did and then stubbed it out, smiled and said: "I said, she's chesty, not dying. No need for that."

I smiled back. No, no need for that.

"What kind of life has your mother had?"

She shrugged. "Why would she say?"

"She's done things, that's all, good things."

"I think so."

"Of course."

"She wouldn't look for thanks."

"No, I know."

"But she'd have it. That's why I do my bit. No need to be la-di-dah about it. But you'll grow out of that, maybe."

136

"Do you think?"

She smiled again. "Kids don't give you time."

"I don't have kids."

She raised an eyebrow.

I pulled the door open. "Do you think Abby would do her bit?"

"I said, you don't know what they're thinking."

"That's right, you did. Don't know what they're thinking."

"And do they?"

I smiled and nodded my leave taking. As I went out she called to me. I could only just hear her voice. I could have ignored it. She had already had the last word. Nevertheless I turned, let her know my aid was up to scratch.

"You were going to leave me, you know, whatever they're called."

"Rothmans."

"Rothmans."

I stepped back, leaving the door open, took the pack from my pocket and offered it.

"Just one," she said, "maybe two, just for a change."

"Take it. I've bought bulk, duty-free, and as I said, I should be giving up. Maybe Harold will want to try."

"Players, untipped, not particular, but, well."

"I know."

"He's spoken about packing up, but, well."

"Willpower."

"It's chilly with the door open."

"I'm sorry."

She nodded and averted her eyes. So, I had the last word and it was what she wanted to hear.

She was formidable. I had learnt that, at least.

Chapter Nine

My kind and vivacious hairdresser offered to do my nails, insisted on it, in fact. Something a bit flashy, she said, taking up my permanently stained fingers, which I don't believe she would have if the tarnish wasn't past tense: at least my fingers no longer smell, have a purity of being well looked after and respected. Strange the disrespect we pile on ourselves when young. Is it over-confidence, ignorance or disgust? The trouble is, at some point everything ceases to be ours to change around.

My lovely hairdresser, more blonde than usual, certainly down the right side of her head anyway, commenced to do my nails with neat strokes of deep crimson, the fine fibres of the brush covering the nail in numerous distinct clean lines. She worked with incredible concentration, her expression that of an old master, not wanting a single fibre of the brush to deviate and so treacherously despoil perfection.

As I watched the colour form I began to cry, big slow drops that pooled along the lower lid, but then inevitably overflowed and trickled down my cheek. It was stupid I know, but it's such little things that speak to us about how much we have lost, how much we failed to gain, how little would have made it well.

When she was through with one hand she stood up and, as always, looked at me in the mirror. How must life be for her addressing people in the mirror everyday, seeing herself? It must be one endless performance. Presumably it is so second nature that whenever she speaks, mirror or no mirror, she can see herself in her mind's eye as she must be. She must know every nuance of herself. Such self-aware-ness bound to get her down at times. How could anybody stand themselves so much?

Seeing my tears, my evident grief, she expressed the most natural and exquisite concern.

I said the nails were beautiful.

She frowned at me sceptically, yet warmly, with her crisp, talking to a child look, which presumably says something about the half-crazy, demented way I come across to her.

I insisted. The nails were lovely. They reminded me of when I was younger, I said, when women of my age wore wigs, false eyelashes, velvet chokers with cameo brooches, and painted their nails, pink, purple and orange with lipstick and eye-shadow to match.

She smiled and said what anyone would in such a situa-tion, that she bet I was a wild one.

I gazed straight at myself in the mirror and smiled, though I wasn't looking at myself at all, rather right through me.

She suggested it would be better if she did the other hand as well.

I agreed, saying I had no desire at all to be a lopsided freak, making no consideration at all of the fact that half of her head was almost all blonde whilst the other was virtually all black.

Luckily I have never been a nail biter and could carry it off.

*

Despite Abby's obvious enthusiasm for life, the way so many different and distinct things made her call out her name, associating herself with each one, making a compact, we always suspected she was dying, she was so pale and disarranged. How could we have been surprised then, when she chose burial; the calmness of her pleasure was un-expected, though. She was simply content to be in the dark, sitting or standing immaterial. In the mine she felt continuous with it, her mind free to explore any shape it chose. It was Grace who recognised that skill in her. It was the second time we found her there. As was so often the case she said enough to lead us to her, but there was something different, the frequency of the note making up her name had a new music to it. Grace called to me, loud enough to be a whisper: She likes finding herself here. Grace was right, of course, she was finding herself, finding the contours that made her an insect, an albatross, a scout, a trickle of water.

Grace didn't like it. The dark scared her. The dark underlined the problem we had in finding Abby. Her name came so distantly, and at such a low volume, it seemed as if she was farther away from us than she ever had been before, and then suddenly she would be there, someone to stumble over, to collide with. Worst of all was the fact that she would run off. She had no fear at all.

Grace said it would be full of ghouls and ghosts. It was obvious. That's where such things would find a natural home, underground, hidden, removed from prying eyes. After dark they would emerge into the outer world and wreak their revenge for being forced out of sight.

In the daylight we told stories, Grace and I, of those subterranean creatures. At first they were monsters. We described heavy footed, troll-like ogres who liked nothing better than to gnaw the bones of unsuspecting children, particularly those who couldn't hear its ponderous tread, though they might feel its vibration through their spine; but by that time it was already too late. At different times of the year witches would search the shafts for lost birds, mice and rats, and, naturally, hidden children, which they would take away to boil up into disgusting potions: and there were always ghosts, the sick spirits of the unfortunate buried, though we never thought of them as miners, those who might have met an untimely end, but always someone inadvertently finding themselves in the grave, not buried alive, just unhappily dead.

To begin with we didn't say anymore. The point was

simply to justify fear, and no doubt enjoy it as well, but before long we found we had to put an alternate flesh onto the bones. It wasn't enough to talk of monsters, ghouls and ghosts, there had to be something else. Grace said that if we went deep enough there would almost certainly be a dragon's den, and if there was a den, then there had to be a captive. The creatures of the mine became beautiful as well as hideous. Everything had to have its opposite. That is how the world was constructed, in opposition, negative and positive. Pretty soon we were the beautiful things. That was Grace's idea, her contribution to the game. If she had to find herself underground, then at the very least she had to be a princess.

It was also Grace who demanded light. It must have been the fifth time we had been forced to climb through the breach in the ground to find Abby. Grace wasn't in any mood for games. It didn't matter that I signed for the utmost care and vigilance before we went inside, signalling the possibility of all manner of fantastic creature below, she didn't want to play. She complained bitterly about Abby's compulsion for burial. She went so far as to suggest that if Abby wanted to bury herself alive then that was her business, but she didn't see why we had to join her. I said it was because we were sisters and that's what sisters did. I know she was ready to snap that we weren't real sisters at all, so I ran ahead and plunged into the mine without listening. Grace shouted along the shaft after me that she would only ever come again with light. I heard the word light which Abby can't have, nevertheless it was Abby who brought the paraffin-lamp from the pig-shed the next time we went below ground, holding it above her head to reveal that hitherto hidden world, though she didn't need it herself. The light was for Grace, for me.

We never recognised the risk we ran taking the lamp in there. How could we?

When I picture Abby now moving dreamily, gracefully

along the shaft, like a fish in a tank, carelessly but generously eyeing everything around her, yet fixing on no point in particular, so that everything remained outside of time and space, it strikes me that she wasn't a party to our games, but engaged in something altogether more serious. If she had discovered food and water in there I don't suppose she would have ever returned to the surface. I thought there was something innocent and sweet in her infatuation, but now it weighs on me. Now I want to strike it from memory. Now I want them to suffer who could nurture in her a rejection of sunlight, of sky, of open space.

I suppose it is only ever possible to play when you feel half good about yourself. You can't play when you're soaked through to the skin, when you're freezing with the cold, when you're frightened, when the world only treats you with hostility.

So, if she wasn't playing what was she doing? What did she see as she took in the blood-red veins, the splintered haematite, the clusters of crystals, the shifting surfaces, dull and drab and then bright, sparkling, telling a strange narrative of abandonment and richness? It's impossible to say. I have no way of knowing whether her love of rock dwarfed her love of the sea, but for a time it must at least have equalled it. She was obviously an elemental child, a child needing an element, a density with which to augment herself.

There was something transparently beautiful in her appreciation, and yet at the same time impossible to describe. The only thing we could do was to join her in the quiet incantation of her name, which was no small thing, because, of course, language doesn't just allow you to do, but also to be.

Did Grace and I ever cease playing, girls' parts, women's lines: Little Bo Peep; Mary, Mary; Old Mother Hubbard? I don't suppose we did.

It was Grace who turned the mine into a real adventure.

She questioned her father about it. At first he simply warned her to keep well away, saying mines were dangerous places, not to be interfered with. When she pressed him he became quite angry and warned her that he would punish her if he discovered she had been anywhere near one. She began to cry.

Whether Seamus was motivated by heartfelt concern for his daughter, or rather was convinced that she didn't have the mental capacity to understand is impossible to say. Presumably there were elements of both tendencies in his initial response. However, why it should have been on this issue that he chose to relent rather than any other is even more difficult to explain. Up until her questions about the mines Seamus had denied continually that Grace had an obviously enquiring, hungry mind. It just couldn't be. Deafness was incompatible with religious experience and only religious experience was the authentic outcome of thought. Nevertheless, he chose this question as the one to answer. He brought home maps from the local library, having made a point of going there during his school day. He spread them out on the sitting-room floor and commanded her to join him. He took hold of her hand, prised the index-finger out of her cluster of fingers, held it firmly and guided it from one named, disused mine to another, forming clear arcs and ellipses. After that he made patterns to overlay the map, making a tracery of imagined shafts, galleries and passages. He still warned her to steer clear, but now detailed the dangers of subsidence, collapse, becoming trapped.

Grace never admitted her knowledge to Seamus, her participation in Abby's discovery, but did stay clear for a few days, and in her most animated, grown-up voice insisted we did the same. After those few days of absence she brought us the maps so we could investigate the names together. Of course, we weren't good readers. We weren't taught to read, only to speak: but we didn't speak together, we signed. So it was slow and painstaking work deciphering the words, but we stuck at it and then we signed them, signed mines, signed them for Abby, translating them for her, marking the air with their image, places of sanctuary, concealment, burial. We never gave much thought to the history that produced them. They were like natural wonders. Of course most of the mines weren't nameable. We didn't have a sign for Yearton, Scallow, Pelham, but had no problem with Black Moor and Stone. Abby started to chant her name when Grace pointed at her, meaning there was a mine called Yew. She didn't understand when Grace added tree. She thought it was another. And then Grace shouted out with delight that there really was one named for Abby, a mine called Abbey. Just after that she looked downcast, even apprehensive and said there was a mine called Salt. There was a mine for me too. Grace didn't hesitate in suggesting that my family must have owned a mine. – Years later I would find out that it was really Salter, but on the map it definitely said Salt. – Try as she might she couldn't find one named Grace, though there was Florence, Hilda and Marigold, named after the daughters of the owners – Seamus told her that when she went back with more questions. That piece of information only served to confirm what Grace had said. If mines were named for families there must have been a mine in the Salt family. It was one small step to say if there was an Abbey, then it was hers, hers at some point in time. It didn't matter that she was Abby, Abigail. Grace set out to prove it.

Grace managed to turn her envy into sister love and was ambitious on our account, wanting our success, confirmation of our claims. Clearly having to accept the fact that his Godless child was demonstrating beyond all scepticism that she was educable, Seamus listened to her repeated questions with increasing confusion. He struggled with his own opinion, which he had never questioned before. He still refused to consider that his deaf child could ever fully know the truth of God, but maybe there were grades of insight as there were grades of deafness. Certainly she could never aspire to the whole extent of God's grace, but possibly a lesser grace, knowledge of God's lordship. He refined his sense of sin. His deaf child wasn't a stone weight he had to carry, but a stone he was also expected to carve. She was a labour. She had to be educated. The questions about the mines started a new phase in Grace's life. Seamus began to take an interest in her, which meant she was subject to rules and discipline. Eileen could no longer keep her out of the way, Seamus made her his business.

Grace wasn't aware of her new status in her father's life, but simply accepted that he now bombarded her with questions each evening about what she had done, and more importantly what she had learnt, and set her small tests that resulted in his displeasure for failure. Years later Eileen chose to explain it, absolving Seamus of any fault on the grounds that he was a deeply religious man. For Grace the familiar was what it was. She couldn't decipher the fact that she found herself asking with increasing regularity, and in an ever deflated voice: Have I been a good girl? The familiar is what we know, and erases what we knew. Memory is a dream of ourselves, which we can't always believe. What we remember is gone and can never be retrieved. Memory is a struggle against oblivion, against the entire world dying because of our oversight. So much rests on it.

I can't afford to forget, yet I can't live with the memory. Someone had to die.

Grace said that the men worked in the mines at the foot of the fells whilst the women looked after sheep and cows on the hills. Seamus told her the byres on the hill were once home to these people. The men would trudge down from the high ground before dawn and the women would set to in the fields. He rebuked her with the history, evoking its harshness. She would have been up before dawn, tending sheep, and been grateful to do it. There was no indulging children then. She should count her lucky stars, because she must

145

have them, being fortunate enough not to have lived at that time.

She wanted to know whether the Sempies or Salts ever owned a mine.

He almost smiled and said the Sempies probably thought they did, but the Salts were never like that.

It was evidence enough for Grace. The Sempies probably owned a mine, whilst I was disinherited. Of course, I was a Sempie too, my mother Flora, a Sempie, so I wasn't disheartened. Nevertheless, we insisted, as guileless, loving, trustworthy sisters, that Abby's was the first claim. It was important to us that she was the rightful owner, ignoring completely the fact that the mines were finished anyway, exhausted, empty vaults beneath the earth's surface. She had already claimed it as a special place, her prize, but we wanted to make it real, make it true. We determined to prove categorically that the mine was hers, not realising she had already decided it was, hers in the only way that mattered, through belief.

I questioned my mother, Flora, a Sempie, about her family. I asked her who the first was. She shrugged at that thought. They didn't keep family records. She could tell me who she remembered. She could go as far back as her great-grandparents, Arthur and Belle. She didn't remember them well, just a vague impression of strictness and darkness. Belle, whose name before Sempie is lost, always dressed in black, with a white apron and a bonnet. She had long grey, lifeless hair which she tied up under the bonnet into a dry, brittle knot. There were only three children as far as she knew, Martha's father, Wilfred, her own grandfather, Jim and Hilda. I started at the name Hilda, the daughter's name, the mines being named for the daughters. My mother pulled a face and said there was something wrong with Hilda, but it was never mentioned. She was pretty sure Hilda was taken away somewhere. Her grandfather Jim was the best of the bunch. Her own father, Dan, favoured him. They never missed a day's work, never drew the dole, even when times were hard and times were always hard. How could I be expected to understand a time when times were always hard, she asked disparagingly, when there might not be enough food for the table, though the Sempies were better off than lots of others, but then the Sempies worked for all they had. Apparently Arthur had been shrewd enough to acquire a bit of land, which Wilfred after him had been gradually expanding, a bit here and a bit there, which might have amounted to a great deal but for the fact he died of influenza before the war, then both his sons were killed. No one knew what happened to the land after that. It didn't appear that Martha had sold anything. It was generally considered lost, a tragedy, adding to the tragedy of all those hardworking men dying so young. So, the Sempies might never have been rich, but they had been landlords, on Martha's side anyway. Jim wasn't cut out that way.

So what did they do?

It seemed they worked hard, though not fixing themselves to anything in particular.

What about the mines?

Naturally, that was only to be expected, as it was for my father, until they paid him off, but he went straight onto permanent nights in the paper-mill.

There was no glamour or heroism. It didn't seem that the Sempies had come from anywhere. We were always here. We hadn't exchanged countries like the Shaughnessys. It seemed a drab history, apart from Hilda who had to be taken away, and the fact that Arthur had acquired a bit of land, which Wilfred was managing very well until he died of influenza and his boys were shot before they could take it on. Presumably the mine was on the land. Why else was it called Hilda? Arthur was my great-great-grandfather. He must have acquired the mine and named it for his daughter, before she was taken away, or in memory, named for the daughter who was gone.

We went back to the maps. Everything fell into place. Hilda Mine was Abby's mine. She had found the way into her own mine. Perhaps it was ownership drove her there, natural ownership guiding her.

Of course she was only a Sempie because Martha said.

We refused to consider that the mine would actually be Martha's and then Harold's. Hilda was Abby's. If anything, they were keeping it from her. We determined we should explore every inch of it, try to unearth something, Wilfred's or Arthur's name engraved into stone, the Sempie name, Sempie somewhere underground. A mine called Hilda, Hilda Sempie.

We said: You are a Sempie, your name, Sempie.

Abby repeated it, delighted with it, thrilled with identity.

It was probably ownership, the knowledge that the mine was hers, each spade of spoil extracted in her name, that tempted her to obsession. She had never been obsessive before, simply enthusiastic. There had always been too much to inspire her before for her ever to settle to one thing. She had had time for it all, the lichen crowned angel, the sea, the whole disorganised, scrappy domain, but for a while they were all abandoned in favour of time underground. Each day we found her there. She didn't wait for us. It was as if delay like that would jeopardise her finding herself there. Nor did she have any need for light, which Grace insisted on. Indeed, it's likely she preferred the dark and found the light an intrusion. Maybe that's why she chose not to wait for us.

I can only guess at the pleasure she felt during that period before discovery, feeling her way around the most perfect confinement she had ever discovered, one she owned, named for her, but I am certain it was immense. She had an understanding of pleasure, or rather had a talent for it. She knew from the very beginning that it was within her gift. When she called her name she was pronouncing the pleasure at her disposal, pronouncing the vastidity of which she was capable. She could create the whole world with her state of mind.

It infuriated Grace that Abby chose to bury herself every day. I'm pretty sure she suffered from mild claustrophobia, which was never declared but was clear in her face. She hated the mine, feared it, and was resentful of the fact there wasn't one named Grace. She would pointlessly call Abby's name, shouting at the top of her voice, knowing full well that it meant nothing to Abby. She had no intention of being summonsed. Invariably we found her drifting along a passage, quietly muttering her name, projecting pleasure onto the intractable seams, and then Grace's fit of temper would subside and she would eye Abby as if she was more spirit than body, able to occupy elements hidden to us.

The day came though when Abby vanished, even to us.

We went to the mine as usual, going through the routine we always did – Grace angrily calling Abby's name – but when we searched the passage she wasn't there. We had no doubts she had been there. Not only was it the place where she always was, there was evidence of her breakfast, a half eaten slice of bread and jam. She was often messy with her food but never wasteful. Besides, bread and jam was a particular favourite. Grace began to whine and said we should go home and tell, but that was impossible. I knew it, knew that couldn't be. It would have betrayed Abby. I wasn't old enough to define betrayal but I knew it, knew the trust that existed beneath ground, in that confinement separate to Agnes, Harold and Martha. I told Grace to hush and impressed on her the fact that it was down to us to find her. We were sisters, after all, sisters of a special kind, which had to stand for something.

We went deeper than we ever had before. Instinctively we knew that is what Abby would have done. The only surprise was that she hadn't sought out those depths before. It was in her nature to go deep into things, the deeper the better. The fear we had was that she might deliberately want to lose herself. We recognised that she was infatuated with the mine. She went there everyday. She didn't share it with anywhere else anymore. The old haunts were abandoned. Even the sea, which still seemed to me her natural home, no longer enticed her. It stood to reason she might want to stay there forever. There was, however, the nagging evidence of her breakfast. Why had she so uncharacteristically discarded it? It couldn't have been that she was full. She was never full. She had a big appetite. She had either decided with a sudden fit of pleasure and enthusiasm to go deeper, or she had been disturbed. We had made up so many stories about those passages it didn't seem unlikely, despite the fact the only evidence we had so far was that they were dead. Without needing to signal it to each other we entertained the possibility she had been abducted, but by what or whom we didn't dare consider.

Was that still a game, a scary story we shared, or did we already believe in a hostile world?

When does knowing bring a game to an end?

Is this a game, in which case I am only a player?

Is the truth of the matter that someone intrudes on our games and insists on making them real, despite our protestations that we want to remain naïve, shy of life, immune?

Yes, evidently, this is a game, because from the very outset there were always going to be winners and losers.

We rushed along the passage, only pausing when we came up against a choice of direction, or even a dead-end. We signalled rapidly, not stopping to consider, conscious that speed might be everything. What we didn't think about was the fact that we were becoming hopelessly lost ourselves. It was Grace who first became aware of it. She suddenly stopped and backed against the passage wall, letting the paraffin-lamp drop to her side. There were large shadows on the walls and roof. She didn't say or sign anything, but by the look of panic shaping itself on her face I knew what she was thinking. Once she allowed herself to consider the possibility all of her suppressed fear came flooding to the surface. Within seconds she was in tears, sobbing that she wanted her mother. The torment in her expression was awful, made all the more twisted by the fact it was lit from below.

I tried to put my hands on her shoulders – a gesture I had seen somewhere, though I don't recall where, that seemed to denote the need for courage, though now I know how mistaken I was – but she refused it. Fear overtook everything and she just stood there sobbing, wanting her mother. I tried to bring Abby back to mind, but Grace had locked everything out other than her own panic. I tried again and again to touch her, as if by laying hands on her I could absorb her terror into me, but it threatened to degenerate into a fight, so I gave it up.

In the end it was a voice louder than her own which quietened her. We heard it along the passage from where we had come. I couldn't make out any words, just the fact of the voice, and then the fact that someone was running towards us. Grace stopped crying. We were frozen. Even if we had been able to run it was too late. We weren't going to escape from whomever it was descending on us.

A moment later a man snatched the lamp out of Grace's hand and extinguished it. He flashed a torch into our faces, one after the other in rapid succession, and then shouted aloud that we could have had us all killed.

He became silent and peered at us intently in the light of his torch, no longer aimed directly into our faces but above us towards the passage roof, its beam nevertheless clearly illuminating us. He had a pointed, sharp face like a bird's, a small hawk, with a hawk's intensity of vision, despite wearing small silver framed glasses. He considered us for some time and then appeared to come to a decision, his face becoming even more pinched, his thin lips pressing tightly together. He began to nod his head and mutter something, certainly inaudible to us. A half-hearted smile passed across his lips and he pointed to his right ear with his index-finger then wagged it in front of our faces evidently indicating deficiency. We didn't respond, but he seemed quite satisfied by his deduction. After that he held up three fingers and tilted his head, posing us a question. He knew we were three, evidently, three sisters, and wanted to know where the third was. Grace began to sob again. He tumbled his hand through the air, sending shafts of light and shadow in all directions, presumably asking whether she was lost. Again we didn't answer, though Grace continued to sob, albeit very quietly compared to earlier. He flashed his torch back along the passage from where he had come and ushered us along. We didn't move. A flash of temper crossed his face. Once again he indicated the path he wanted us to take. It seemed better not to argue so we began to make our way in the direction he suggested, following the light of his torch, whilst he remained a step or two behind. In that way, using his torch as a guide he led us back to the surface. It didn't feel like rescue but eviction. Once we were in daylight he indicated that we go outside and wait. He would go and find the other. He kept his eye on us until we were outside and out of sight.

So, Mr Drake found Abby somewhere in the dark. We never did find out what she had discovered, but there was obviously something, something that changed her love of being underground. We assumed she'd had a fright. She wouldn't let us touch her when she appeared, but snapped like a little dog, her face full of wonder. As far as I know she never went back to the mine. Maybe Mr Drake had somehow let her understand that it was his domain, not hers, or perhaps he had impressed on her the dangers of subterranean worlds, as Grace's father had wanted to do with Grace – certainly he gave us a vivid and angry lecture on the likelihood of a paraffin-lamp causing an explosion – but maybe it was altogether more sinister than that. I would prefer to think Abby returned to her natural element, which was always really the coast, because the mine, even if it was named for her, would from then on be marked by the possibility of intrusion.

Chapter Ten

I try to imitate Abby's talent for pleasure, the way she could impose herself on the most seemingly insignificant of things – a cluster of frost on bracken, the colour of sea water, the smell of saline, a flotsam of sponges – but my attempts tend towards lesser thrills altogether, and so often things that do me harm. Though I would say, my darling, vivacious hairdresser does me little or no disservice, not knowingly, anyway, and I would certainly list her as a pleasure. I let her insist I keep colouring my hair, that supposed pale russet-brown which we both know is metallic copper and altogether unnatural. I enjoy the indulgence. I take pleasure – yes pleasure, not disputing the word – when in the middle of relating some exploit or drama with her latest boyfriend, she looks wistfully at me, breaks off and like a reproving parent suggests to me, no tells me, to consider another style. I look patiently at my exposed face, the hair, copper bright, swept right back, smile and shake my head.

No, you lively, wonderful child, I have no inkling to hide myself, and it isn't necessarily lack of stamina, though at my age that can't be discounted, just something I have to do, reveal that face for all its crimes and misdemeanours, though I would say it is remarkably free of the evidence of my former habitual pleasures, namely Rothmans and London Gin. I can lie to myself that my yellow, mahogany tint is either natural colour, or a deficiency in applying makeup. Natural is simply a register of lifestyle. The child, young girl, born with a certain colour, certain style, can't hope to survive. So confidence gives way to doubt, joie de vivre to helplessness, pleasure becomes cigs and gin.

Yes, ciggies and gin – and not just gin, my tastes growing in sophistication year by year, and quantity as well, what need is there to deny it now – were my pleasure, somewhat tawdry I would agree. Urban pleasure, pleasure that goes with a comfort in streets, which maybe isn't pleasure at all, but a delightful, exquisite fatalism. In all but reality I have become a Londoner, feel at home there, if not exactly ecstatically at peace.

In the city I hear an undifferentiated hum, a pleasing confluence of enmeshed sound, a chorus of wordless song denoting reason and desire, soul and body. I am one kind of natural object among others. I am never lonely in London, though sometimes sad, weighed down by voices speaking within voices, speaking of possession, occupation, ownership. Ownership disturbs me. I would eradicate it if I could, yet would protect the territory of my own slice of it to my dying breath. The rules of the game force us into some very crazy situations.

I love my little corner of Camden Town. I am self-sufficient these days. The days of the midwife and the nun are long gone. My space is my own. I say it with pride. I am privileged in the crowd. I have my walls, my taste – which is commented upon – and time; time to go to my hairdresser and keep alive this pleasure seeker, Judith Salt.

It is so different here, watching the waves, though only hearing a murmur because I have removed my hearing aid, which seems the right thing to do, though I don't have the energy to work out why. Sometimes we have to accept our instincts without question. – I have questioned myself enough over the years, so much so that I am a positive interrogator, but still don't understand why anger makes me cry. – In Abby's places, inland or coastal, everything seems so finished, yet incomplete. It reveals its history without explaining it. It's as if history were abandoned, thrown up, because it wouldn't work out.

There are weathered posts for gates abandoned in the middle of fields, maybe a rut or escarpment indicating an old track, which might or might not be man-made. Decrepit sheds, drainage channels and spoil create a cryptic landscape. Stone and brick underline human activity, but the purpose, the product, the result is forgotten, as if amnesia were necessary because human kind can't stand too much memory, too much awareness of the labour endured in its name.

The past is a forgotten country, a despised destination, a mistake.

I try to say I am through with it. After all, it never gave me pleasure, but no matter my little corner of city life, the terrible sea calls to me, calls from depth and weight, a name, her name, her pleasure, pleasure maker.

*

In a true love-story the object of love has to be somehow forbidden, I know that, but then if Donald and I, despite ourselves, managed a true love story who was the one forbidden? Was it me, because I was the one with the difference, the one who could turn off a great portion of the world with a flick of a switch? – The first time I ever wore a hearing aid I didn't like it at all, the re-acquaintance with the sound of life, hush having become such a peaceful norm. – Or was it him, with his fleshy skin with its buried, dormant freckles, firm yet liable to sag, who was really out of bounds? Or was it a part of both of us, the body we produced, the baby that made it prohibited? Donald certainly didn't know what to make of the baby. At first I thought it was because he wanted to be grown-up but still a boy at the same time and couldn't appreciate that the two were irreconcilable, but maybe that was generous.

He insisted we keep to our routines and patterns, so we still went to pubs and restaurants around Camden, Donald more convinced than ever that it was because of him we were able to do it. My reluctance, now I knew I was pregnant, only served to confirm his view of things. If not for him we would have festered together, under the same roof as the nun and the midwife.

I assumed there was something entirely natural about it all. How could a baby be a reality to a man? It could only be speculation, particularly as he had no real experience. His brother had two children, a girl and a boy, and Donald was Godfather to the second, though he didn't seem to take it too seriously, birthday and Christmas presents, nothing over and above the usual. He never really spoke about them, and certainly didn't express any desire to see them. There was something stale in that, something I presumed Calvinist, without needing to understand it. I suppose I thought reality would change everything and that a living, feeling child would breathe away the sterility. Donald's silence was simply wonder, time to think.

That didn't explain the amount he was drinking, though – I admit, I still joined him with more than an occasional gin – nor did it account for the determination he had to be out in those pubs and restaurants. Common sense should have suggested that he obviously didn't want to be alone with me, but how could I have worked that out when there was no sense to it? If he had been uncertain about the baby then surely he would have wanted the opportunity to talk about it.

The truth is, he wasn't really uncertain about the baby, not a baby, just this baby, our baby.

I realised that the night we went to Hampstead. It was a few weeks to Christmas, only a matter of weeks before I would return to the shore for Abby's birthday, born under Pisces – three sisters, born in the same village, in the same year, one under Aquarius, Judith Salt, the elder, then Abby, and finally Grace, the prettiest, a spring and summer child, born under Gemini, the third sign of the zodiac, denoted II, meaning, disturbingly perhaps, two children – having just celebrated my twenty-fifth year.

Donald suggested Hampstead – for a change, he said; he would take the car. I wasn't sure. He was straight away annoyed. It was only Hampstead, for God's sake, he declared, just up the road. It had nothing to do with the distance, but Donald driving, but he was too impatient with me for me to be able to suggest that. I just shrugged: neither acceptance, nor refusal. He said I had to snap out of it. I shrugged again. He was inventing me, creating me to suit his own purpose. I might as well have been a doll, and then he could have told stories about me to his heart's content, without the problem of contradiction, of reality. Of course, he told good stories. The nun and the midwife liked them.

It was obvious we were going to go. He was in that mood. Anything less would have been taken as a criticism or, depending on how far he wanted to take it, a betrayal. I was to be flaunted, though no one would care, no one would look, only him, guarding me, extolling me.

Despite the fact the pub was packed and noisy we managed to get a small table to ourselves. It was impossible to talk so we didn't try – I couldn't have heard in such an atmosphere, anyway. In fact, the noise was painful so I turned off my aid. I should have taken it out, but he wouldn't have liked that, not the mood he was in. So I left it, pointless as it was, for him. We just looked around, watching other people's parties, other people's pleasure – people already celebrating Christmas. He drank quite a bit, though I didn't realise just how much. He must have been having them at the bar. He would signal with his empty glass, I would shake my head and off he would go. Having no ability to speak I guess all he could do was drink.

During one of his visits to the bar – I don't know how many times he had been by then – a young man approached and asked me something. Naturally, I couldn't hear a word. He had a pleasant face, something appealing in his eyes, its outline sadly spoiled by a thick bush of hair that hung onto his forehead and cheeks. I just looked at him. He tried again.

Eventually I reached to adjust my hearing aid. It was absurd not, absurd simply enjoying his attention, absurd and wrong. He could have been asking anything. He straight off made signs of apology and indicated that he was only wondering whether the chair was free. He was shouting, trying to make himself heard. He was shouting when Donald returned, his drink already half gone. Donald stiffened and demanded to know why the other was shouting. He was shouting about someone shouting. I could hear all that. I was sorry I could.

The young man shrugged and moved away. I watched him go. He stood over a table where a group of boys were sitting. He was the only one standing. He had obviously only wanted a chair and had assumed I was on my own.

I stood up and told Donald I felt sick. In answer to his sceptical frown I pursed my lips, signalling that the cause was obvious.

We didn't speak either going to the car or once we were in it. I wanted to suggest he shouldn't drive, we could easily have taken a tube or bus or even a taxi, but I knew it would have been taken as criticism and I didn't feel able to chance that.

He actually drove carefully, his over-caution underlining the fact he shouldn't have been doing it at all. In fact he was going so slowly that some kids rounded a traffic island on the wrong side of the road to pass him. I don't know what infuriated him the most, the temerity, the danger or being overtaken. He was straight after them, and caught them at the next lights. I was hoping they'd go right through, but they didn't. Their lawlessness only went so far. I guess when he got out of the car and strolled up to theirs he expected them to make off. If they had everyone might have saved face. They could have laughed. He could say he had frightened the life out of them. And I . . . There was nothing in it for me.

They didn't make off though. They got out of their car.

There were four of them, just kids, seventeen, maybe eighteen years old. He started threatening them, telling them what he would do to them if he ever caught them pulling a trick like that again. They burst out laughing. Of course he wouldn't catch them again, not in a city of six million. They weren't amused though, weren't laughing because a joke had tickled their fancy. They were laughing in cold-blood, relishing an opportunity that had come their way. They really were lawless. The rules dictated they provide a few obscenities, maybe a few threats and then make off, scarper as fast as they could, but no, they were happy with this, loving it.

They approached Donald, chins protruding, lips pursed, leering, and then without any preamble one of them started hitting him. Again there was no let out. The boy was hitting him hard, brutally, smashing his fist into his face and kicking him. The others kicked him as the opportunity allowed. I began to scream and jumped out of the car as well. One of them came straight for me. Donald started shouting, shouting at me, telling me to get away, get back in the car, but it was too late. I had stumbled into existence as well; I wasn't to be allowed to back out.

I stood my ground. What else was there to do? It was obvious he was coming to hit me. He came right up. I saw his arm go back. Before he could do anything I struck, slapping him in the centre of his face. I caught him with the edge of my palm. It took him by surprise, but incensed him. I hit him again in the same place. Bubbles of blood appeared at his nostrils. At the sight I began to scream. Having drawn blood I was terrified.

I screamed with all the strength I could muster, declaring aloud: I am deaf and I am pregnant. I screamed it over and over, trying to defend myself with it, trying to settle the world with its terrible reason.

I don't know whether the complaint had any affect. By then other cars had stopped and the kids took off anyway.

As their car sped away I was sobbing, still repeating the reality that only a small behind ear device offered. I am deaf and I am pregnant.

Eventually I quietened down, refusing any assistance that was offered. I went up to Donald. He was sitting on the ground, conscious, his knees up, his head hanging between. Drops of blood splashed slowly onto the pavement in front of him from his nose. I knelt down beside him wanting him to accept my concern, wanting him to want me. I spoke his name, trying to shape my feeling for him in the word, as if experimenting with it.

He cocked his head towards me. He growled bitterly: Why the hell did you say that?

I didn't reply. What could I say to him? It was true, I said it because it was true.

He jumped to his feet. He stood over me, his face twisted with distaste. He asked the same question: Why the hell did you say that?

I shook my head slightly, inquisitively, at a loss. I told him I thought they were killing him.

I was sure he was going to shout again, make another complaint, but instead he slapped me. As soon as he had done it he looked horrified. He moaned aloud, hesitated for a moment, obviously in two minds as to what he should do next, and then quickly made his way back to the car.

I thought he intended to drive off, but he waited. I got to my feet and followed. I sat down beside him without uttering a word. He immediately started the engine and drove me back to Camden. I got out of the car still without either of us speaking. As soon as I slammed the door he drove off.

He came to see me the next day, early, before he was due at work. He apologised, but his voice remained angry so there was a complete mismatch between words and meaning. It was either a lie or there was something more complex going through his mind than simply saying sorry. I would have queried that rough, raging apology, except his top lip was swollen and he spluttered his anger, reducing it somehow, for me, making it absurd, making him absurd. The man who had nine hours earlier struck me was making a demanding apology and seemed ridiculous. It was all I could do to stop myself laughing, though I couldn't suppress a smile. To layer absurdity on absurdity he took that smile as a gesture of consolation, took it as the response he wanted: an indulgence towards his shamefaced penitence. So, I realised, it was all about him, the slapping and the being sorry, his story. I shook my head. It didn't matter. He would take anything I did in his own way. He said he couldn't stand it, blurting the words out, assailing me with them. My being pregnant, I queried? No, deafness. Deafness? He couldn't stand my being deaf, I queried again, uncertain then whether I wanted to laugh or cry? He shouted aloud, at the ceiling – at the sky, I suppose, sun or moon, immaterial – no, no, no, using it, abusing it, playing it for deranged young thugs.

I told him quietly, without any fuss, that it was my choice. He blustered without managing a single word. He looked ever more absurd, his lip swollen beneath his nostril which was pulled slightly out of shape. The more I looked the more I realised that the whole of one side of his face was misshapen. One eye was deeper inside the orbit than the other, the flesh around it plump and mottled. In another day or so he was going to be black and blue. Strangely, he didn't provoke my sympathy, but then, that wasn't what he had come for. He would say he despised sympathy. He had come to explain himself, without explanation, other than the inference that his rage conveyed that his was a complex world-view.

I don't think the radiologist saw himself as anything less than a rebel, an individualist, an artist maybe. He was the one who had broken with his Presbyterian background, the elder brother staying put, though deep down it was all pretence and lies. He could never fully relinquish it. He

Chapter Eleven

I went to see Mr Drake. He lived in the same small terraced house he always had. Even houses on the same row differ enormously in terms of grandeur and design. Mr Drake's was smaller than most. He examined me on the doorstep, his entire poult face involved, eyeing me, sniffing me, listening for something, guarding, all of his expression pulled into it, giving him a suspicious, yet hurt air.

"Am I not welcome? I was once. We were friends. You said we were friends."

He looked around me, weighing something up, almost as if he hadn't understood a word I had said and was bemused by his lack of understanding.

He smoothed his hand over his thin, neatly cut grey hair, moved his silver glasses for no apparent reason and then said: "The Shed's gone, long gone."

"There's a meat van, but nothing else."

"I don't know about that."

"Don't know there's a meat van?"

"Don't know there's nothing else."

I smiled. "You always liked to tease, Mr Drake, that's what I always think about you, that you liked to tease."

"A bit of fun does no harm."

I shook my head. "Do you still like to tease?"

"I don't know about that."

I shrugged, and in a lowering voice – which I meant to be teasing, but whether alluring, I can't say – said: "For a man who has seen so much, suddenly you don't know very much."

I believe he was going to treat me to the same refrain, but thought better of it. Instead he got straight to the point, his voice soft yet sharp, quiet but not without its own warning. "What do you want anyway?"

"To talk, catch up, you know, find out what's new."

"Nothing's new. Nothing's going on. I do my own thing. I'm retired now, got the time."

"And you gave up The Shed?"

"No, not really. The Shed gave up me. I still watch, all of the time, matter of fact, but just for my own amusement, just for myself."

"Do I still need a ticket?"

"I said, I told you," he began irritably, and then laughed instead, quietly, correcting himself. "Oh, I see, you're teasing me. Very good. Yes, very good. No, no, you don't need a ticket, but the proprietor reserves the right to eject anyone found misbehaving."

"Did you ever?"

"Boys sometimes, bit rowdy, high spirits, nothing serious. Always came back. Made it up, sort of style."

"Of course."

He led the way indoors, carefully as was his manner, everything lithe but with intent. The living-room was small and cluttered, every surface covered in magazines and knick-knacks, porcelain dogs, horses, ducks and other farm-yard creatures, all manner of vases and jugs, picture ash-trays, plastic and pot, with beach scenes and rudimentary maps. Mr Drake was a hoarder.

He moved some magazines and a pile of clothes and made somewhere for me to sit. I commented on his collection. He gave a brief smile and said he liked to pick up little things, odds and ends he found in town. Besides, a lot of it was his mother's. It was still her house, after all. I suggested he must be a seasoned traveller these days, there was so much beach memorabilia. He frowned and said that people, other people, friends, brought him things, always thought of him on their

164

travels. People were always gallivanting off these days, he said, day trips to Bowness, Morecambe, Blackpool, and God only knew where. I smiled, acknowledging his popularity. Of course, I knew he was lying and he bought everything himself. He knew people, but he didn't have friends, and the only family I was aware of was his mother. He had never left her. She died of heart-failure just a few years previously. Her photographs were everywhere.

"You must miss her."

"Of course I do," he replied quietly, "she was a saint, in her own way."

"The last years must have been hard."

"Why?"

"Well, I was told she needed a great deal of care."

"She was like a feather, and could take her own weight. She never gave up on that. Always managed her own weight. There we are, dear, I'd say, holding her close, so much easier on the spine, down you go, gently does it, and there we are, and shout when you're finished."

"Didn't you mind?" I asked.

"Do you think I should mind," he snapped, "mind popping my mother on the toilet, mind wiping her bottom? Is that what I should mind? Did she ever mind?"

"No, I don't suppose she did."

"No, I don't suppose she did," he repeated, echoing my sentence exactly. "People have such minds, you know."

"I never meant . . ."

"Never meant what? Hah, nothing to say. And yet you felt free to say it, free to be hurtful."

He turned away and began to pick around the room, pointlessly moving bits of clutter from one place to another as if tidying, a smile apparent across his sharp features. He looked triumphant. He had wrong-footed me and he knew it. There was nothing for it but to apologise. He greeted that with a derisory smile. Nothing was said for a moment or two then he shook his head, dispensed with his fussing and sat down opposite me, quite close, leaning forward, his head bowed slightly. He spoke quietly. "It doesn't matter. I know you, Judith Salt, know what you mean. Just a way of talking. But, you'd think it was wrong to care, the attitude of some. I never wanted a medal, but I didn't want anything else either. You're right though, she was frail, frail but strong. Maybe she went on too long, but not long enough for me. It's a quiet, closed world, the one we live in."

I smiled, coaxing him: "You showed us the world Mr Drake, showed us the only other world we knew for such a long time."

"Made up, but fun."

"And you still, you said?"

He smiled broadly, like a mischievous child: "All of the time. The greats, *Oliver Twist, David Copperfield, Wuthering Heights, War and Peace, Love.* I could watch them all the time. It doesn't have to be Sunday or Christmas. I watch in the mornings."

The Shed was a makeshift cinema. Mr Drake ran it as a sideline, fitting film showings around his shift pattern in the brick factory where he worked as tea-boy, post-boy and ran any other general errands they could think of. He had acquired what he considered a classical education courtesy of films, albeit limited and not always accurate. He said that if a film started with the image of a book with turning pages you knew you were on to a winner, though he was never tempted by the books themselves.

The Shed itself was more or less just that, a small wood frame and panel construction, daubed with creosote, which would hold at most twenty people. He acquired his films from someone he described as a fellow enthusiast who worked in the large cinema in town, The Queens. Presumably he acquired his rolls of cinema tickets from the same source. Mr Drake sat at the entrance with his small cash-box, doling them out and tearing them at the same time. The only heating came from a small oil-burner so people brought

166

flasks of tea and soup. You could smoke in the Shed. Its popularity waned as people acquired their Defiant televisions, paid off on a two weekly Co-op card, but it never closed. If no one turned up Mr Drake would show the film anyway. I don't know that it ever formally closed. As Mr Drake said, The Shed gave up on him. My last recollections of it are of a decrepit, damp blackened shell, beyond repair.

My first memories are of magic. Our first film was free of charge, though he insisted we have a ticket and he tear it as they did in all the movie palaces. I have no idea what that first film was called. It was about some kids and a horse, someone stealing it and the kids rescuing it. All I remember is an image of the kids looking over a fence, three faces looking straight ahead in my direction and talking in the strangest of accents. I wanted to look over my shoulder to see what they were looking at, though I knew that was stupid and never actually did it. I told myself that behind me there was only Mr Drake and his projector. I never quite got rid of that strange sensation though, and never really worked out whether I liked it or not.

I could never tell whether Abby had taken to the pictures or not. She could never really settle, but fidgeted on her chair, flopping from side to side, looking all around, very rarely just at the screen. There must have been something that took her fancy, though, she certainly uttered her name often enough. It wasn't her usual declaration of existence though, but an awkward, troubled announcement, as if she were shy of herself, which she certainly wasn't.

After that first film Mr Drake offered each of us a boiled sweet, one red, one green and one orange. Grace and I both said bags red, but Abby wasn't at all sure. I can still see her, her whole figure and face curling at the same time, again as if she were shy and didn't know how to take it. Grace took the orange one and dangled it in front of Abby's face. Abby began to shake and eventually hit it out of her hand.

Mr Drake asked if Abby was all right. There was no

displeasure or sympathy in his expression, just enquiry. Grace said she couldn't hear, that she wouldn't have heard any of the film, not like us, and maybe that had upset her, though it never had before. We could hear; we had our Medresco hearing aids by then.

After that Mr Drake added special silent features – Buster Keaton, Charlie Chaplin, Mack Sennett – for us, he said, though Grace said the other films were so loud we could hear most of what went on. Abby watched with curiosity and confusion. Sometimes she laughed, but sometimes she laughed when she was scared, even when she was hurt. Harold could never understand or tolerate that. He hated her laughter more than anything. He would growl and demand of Agnes to explain what Abby was laughing at. He knew there was nothing funny, and he knew she wasn't laughing in that way, but he just couldn't fathom what it meant. So, as much as he tried to beat language into her, he tried to beat laughter out.

"Yes, made up, but fun," I agreed, methodically, without warmth. Both of our voices had reduced to whispers. "Where did you get our films from, for The Shed, I mean?"

"I knew someone in the trade. Like minded. On loan from the big places, a couple of nights, a few pound in his pocket."

"The silent ones, the ones for us."

"Stock."

"Like minded?" I smiled.

"I meant to be kind, wanted to be kind."

"Of course," I agreed. "I know what you wanted."

"Do you think she enjoyed them? I never knew, could never tell. She was a bit of a funny one."

"Yes, when you say it affectionately, like that."

"Oh, yes."

"Yes."

"I like to think she might have enjoyed them."

I could have told him that she had a talent for pleasure, that it was her gift to see into its true nature. She was in equilibrium with the world around her. Its still objects filled her with their shapes, movement drew patterns in her mind, and colour and its complement were like inner light. She had a knack for it, a system of naming, and an appetite, but whether she needed slapstick and jokes, I don't know. I remember she laughed appreciatively at Charlie Chaplin in *The Circus*, particularly when he went through the hall of mirrors and when he battled across a tightrope hampered by falling trousers and a clinging monkey, but then his face was so sad with disappointed love she wouldn't have missed that. So, I decided to pass on her enjoyment: besides I was more interested in his enjoyment.

"Tell me," I whispered, as if inviting him to confess a guilty past, "why did you go inside the mine called Hilda?"

"Local history, an interest, just an interest."

"We might have killed ourselves."

"Young fools."

"Unknowing."

"Lucky I discovered you."

I flashed him an intent look, my eyes fixed on his. He flinched at it, flinched as if he had barely avoided being hit.

"Something crossed my field of vision," I explained. "Strange, unaccountable really."

"What?"

"Oh, I don't know. A trick of light disorients me. I think I see things. Not like a mad-woman, you understand, though you never know, more, I get deceived by things." He shrugged but didn't comment. I went on: "I'm easily deceived, yet I am in everything suspicious. How can that be?"

"Why, why are you suspicious? Has something happened to you?"

"So much is illogical, doesn't really stand up to much examination, but you know that, being a movie watcher."

"I just watch, I don't make anything of them. I'm not like that. I don't pretend to make anything of them."

"You must be quite at home in the dark." He moved back

slightly, his sharp chin lifted, signalling effrontery, suspicion. I smiled and followed him with my eyes. "In a village language is like shadows in a cave where meaning flickers, cryptic and ominous, on grey walls, then falters."

"What are you talking about?"

"Then there was lightness, lightness and sound."

"I don't know what you're saying."

"What did you do to her underground?"

"I saved her," he said, his voice trembling, though whether with anger, heroism or defiance, I couldn't say. For good measure he repeated it, no louder, his voice scarcely registering more than a whisper, but with obvious greater force: "I saved her."

*

We penetrate so feebly the mystery of this life, that the stars in the night sky might as well be wallpaper for a doll's house.

I often think that, sitting in the hairdresser's chair, watching everything in reflection, everything as absurd as Chaplin in the hall of mirrors, that I might be in a doll's house, moved about by unseen fingers, made pliant in my pleasure seeker's throne.

At times it is all so unreal the business of having my hair pulled back, held tightly between the first two fingers in small bunches and then trimmed, the scissors dancing around my head like a large egg laying insect.

My instinct tells me I shouldn't be there, my desire counters with quite the opposite, and the strange internal war of who and what I am carries on in its oh so secret chamber, with myself an involuntary witness.

At those moments time in the salon rotates like one of Mr Drake's reels, liable at any moment to run off the spool, leaving only the sound of missing life, which I would be fortunate to hear at the best of times.

Life then is always around the corner somewhere.

I recall, one day, my hairdresser was skipping with fun,

admiring things in the looking glass, not necessarily herself, but things which she herself brought to mind. Being full of charity, which is after all her virtue, she wanted me to be part of it, and opted for the only route available: disclosure. She would permit me to know the scandalous behaviour that so amused her, but even as she began to tell me of her escapade with a young man, best friend of her current boyfriend, I had drifted away. She was simply a constellation in glass, her blond and black hair destinations in some far-flung firmament.

It didn't take her long to realise that I hadn't heard a word, but she took no offence, merely inquired whether I was all right, the incident with my nails still obviously on her mind.

I looked at her, though away from what, I can't recall – I couldn't have at the time – and she looked so lovely, brimming with hospitality and care, I had to explain myself, my drifting, my absence.

I said, when the stars are taken away, when clear night is overtaken by cloud, rain heavy cloud, do they cease to exist? Does the sea exist in Camden Town? Do tigers really survive in the wild? Does anything exist outside our sense of it? I am deaf to so much, you see, blind to so much I want to see, and I think I have spent a lifetime wanting to be touched, but somehow never affected the trick. Is that banal?

To my utter amazement, my beautiful, efficient, effervescent hairdresser began to cry. Really, she is so special, so burdened with charity.

I wanted to go on and say it is so pointless worrying about death when we haven't even worked out where life came from, the tragedy being that it will be over before we even realise it has begun, but she looked altogether too beautiful to bother with such things.

Abby would have understood, eyeing us peaceably from her place of seclusion. Her beauty was of a different order, though whether one or the other is given to longevity, I really can't say.

It is rare to see a star in London, recognise the pattern on the walls of the doll's house.

It is only when I am faced with the northern sky, with Orion, Ursa Major, Ursa Minor, Cassiopeia, Pleiades, and the rest whose names elude me, that I realise I miss it, at all other times, I get by, thankfully.

Yes, we penetrate so feebly the mystery of this life, that the stars in the night sky really are wallpaper for a doll's house.

*

He enjoyed telling us that if we had been born in Germany we would have been gassed.

As I said, he was always a tease.

I told him again. "You were always such a tease."

He warmed to it as if it were a compliment fit to make him blush. Besides, he was pleased I seemed to be back on solid ground. He visibly relaxed. He said: "I was never spiteful." I agreed with him. He warmed to that too, repeating it, re-creating himself in imagination, the projectionist, one of a certain kind, who was never spiteful.

"It gave you pleasure," I suggested.

He seized on that. "Yes, and no," he mused. "I hope it gave everyone pleasure."

Once again I had to agree with him. "Of course, I'm certain."

Not spite, but pleasure, pleasure in control, as if it were in his gift to sanction life: a charity, an indulgence, a weakness. It also implied what sort of people they were, the community he came from, a community who didn't gas people.

"It wasn't true, what you said."

"What was that?"

I smiled. If I said no more would he ever question his charity, or his community, because I was pretty sure he would never question his views on Germany? "That if we'd been born in Germany we would have been gassed."

"Of course it was true. They gassed all people like you."

172

"No."

"A people devoid of pity."

"No."

"I don't see why you should defend them."

"No, I'm not, not really. The truth is bad enough, but they didn't gas deaf people when it didn't run in the family. They tried to put a stop to that, sterilisation, gassing, but not the others."

"Like I told you, if you'd been born in Germany you'd have been gassed."

"No!"

"All right, sterilised, then, sterilised."

"No," I said, finding myself in the ridiculous position of losing my cool over the truth of Nazi German crimes. "There was no deafness in the Sempie line."

"Who said that, Martha Sempie? Well, ask her about her Aunt Hilda and see what she says."

"She hates deafness," I said, involuntarily, speaking before I'd thought.

"She certainly didn't find much wrong with Aidan Shaughnessy, and I don't recall he was much a one for music."

"What do you mean?"

He leaned forward again and smiled, for the first time without hesitation. "The other one, the bad one, she'd have been gassed, I'll tell you that for nothing."

I returned his smile, grimly, but determinedly: "You always liked to tease."

"That's right, don't mind a word of me."

"You saved her."

"Saved you all, all three, young fools."

"Why do you think she never went back into the mine?"

"She must have got a fright."

"That's what I think."

"But she could never say. Sad, that, in a way."

"You're wrong again, Mr Drake, we could never get her to shut up."

He sat back and simply gazed at me, all expression slowly seeping out of his face. I said I would see myself out. He made no reply, not that I heard anyway.

Chapter Twelve

For many years we received all of our education from Mrs
Gunn, a peripatetic teacher who came to the village three
times a week. She was a woman of endless complaints and
misery who, as far as we could tell, seemed thoroughly to
enjoy her desperation. She peered at the world as if it were a
place of intrigue and corruption, its many obstacles personal
and disgusting. She moaned about manure and mud on the
roads, stating that all farmers should be fined and made to
clean it up, that the pollution was deliberate and malicious,
she knew, she came from that stock. It was dangerous for her
Austin, she insisted, which would slide right off the road on
a whim, talking of the car as if it were yet another disobedient child: her personal experience, the claim by which she
measured everything, having taught her that all children
were disobedient; deafness, blindness, limbless, notwith-
standing. Sub-normality was no guarantor of goodness.
Of course she was right about that. I might even say I
was grateful to her for that judgement.

I was the first to come under her instruction, not because I
was the eldest, simply because my parents put up no
opposition: my father, coming from the Salts, had no opposition to anything, and my mother, from the easy Sempie
line, saw no harm in it. We were already sisters when Grace
joined me. Seamus had to be threatened with action from the
school-inspector before he would relent. He didn't quote
Aristotle who maintained that the deaf could not be educated, or St Augustine who claimed that deafness was a sign
of God's anger at the parents, but he was insistent that it was

futile to even try to educate the girl – a point of view he held as both a parent and teacher himself. The fact that Grace was as quick-witted as any child her age was simply ignored. He was certain she couldn't have an aptitude for true intelligence, which was a relationship with God – and, unlike Abby, I don't ever recall that Grace was much given to God, not in anything but a mechanical way.

Later, it was Seamus who insisted Grace attend school – at first the local village school – when her interest in the mines opened his eyes to the fact that although his deaf offspring may never learn the revelation of Christ's ministry, she undoubtedly had a thirst for knowledge. Martha, on the other hand, would never countenance a school, least of all a special school, a step that had been pressed on her ever since the audiology tests proved conclusively that Abby couldn't hear. She maintained that if you put deaf-mutes together they would breed, forming their own deaf-mute race. No Sempie, as long as she could help it, was going to put their name to such an ancestry. As regards Mrs Gunn's lessons she was simply dismissive. There was no need to waste the woman's time, the child was fit for nothing and never would be. It was Agnes who finally brought the sisters together, educationally speaking – Martha having forced her to defy the school-inspector for years – not out of any conviction, simply for the relief of getting Abby out of the way. As she explained to the matriarch, Martha couldn't know what it was like day in day out, to which, thrusting her fist through the air, Martha had to agree.

Mrs Gunn would come and collect us, house to house, and then take us to the Reading Rooms, a nineteenth century village hall used for Parish Council meetings, Sunday School groups, baby clinics and, for two afternoons a week, the travelling library, the meagre stock of books changed by three or four every fortnight by the visiting librarian. Mrs Gunn would plod along, her centre of gravity heavy as if she were stepping through mud, her head lowered, her face framed with thick grey hair shaped like a bonnet or German soldier's helmet, never acknowledging us until we reached our destination where she told us to sit around a large mahogany desk which was so high for us, perched on our small fold-away Sunday School chairs, it came up to our shoulders.

The Reading Rooms were two wood panelled rooms, separated by a wood and glass sliding partition, both rooms decorated with sombre portraits of stern faced men, and in one an award to a drama group dating back to 1928, though no one we knew could ever recall a drama group, nor in the case of my parents really knew what one was. Each room was as equally dark, damp and cold as the other. Sometimes she would light a paraffin-heater, though more usually we simply kept on our coats.

Her first task, standing in front of us, her face outwardly severe, yet not concealing an inner sadness, her lips puffed and rounded downwards, was to ensure that our hearing aids, our large Medresco aids were switched on and working. – What styling advice would my vibrant, life loving, life affirming hairdresser give if faced with a wire dangling from my ear to my pinafore pocket?

In the early days we were uncomfortable, Grace and I, with our aids, both of us since our illnesses having become accustomed to a muted, hushed world, but the discomfort didn't last long. As Mrs Gunn never tired of telling us, we lived in a hearing world, hearing was normal, hearing was correct. It was the world we began in. We had learnt speech and sound. The hearing aid may not have been lovely to look at, but I wouldn't deny its beauty. Abby hated it though. I can't imagine what sensation she felt – could it really have been a remote sound, the dreadful, indecipherable sound of life? – but she couldn't bear it. It cut through her like pain. The first time it was inserted she ripped it out, but Harold struck her, glaring at Agnes as if Abby's ingratitude proved the wilfulness of her lack of hearing. Every time it was replaced she repeatedly pulled it out, only to receive ever heavier blows from Harold. The nurse suggested it would simply take time, but Harold insisted she was stubborn by nature. Between coaxing and punishment the hearing aid remained in place. In class she inevitably sat to attention as if the thing were delivering her an electric shock. Over time Grace and I taught her to be patient. Our lessons with Mrs Gunn weren't long or arduous, in fact were concluded pretty quickly, then she could dispense with it, with sound – if sound it was.

It is impossible to know what the pain was Abby felt, what that suggestion of sound was doing to her. We can all be hurt by meaning, by what the signifier intends, but with her it was as if an element of existence itself was crippling her, running through her like electricity, scattering her nerves and displaying her like a spray of lights, yet failing entirely to reveal her, in fact leaving her more in the dark than ever. She could only respond with tantrums, something she had learnt from Martha and Harold, hitting out as best she could. No one had ever offered another way. There was no suggestion that light has many forms, one perhaps more suitable than another. There was a mantra, *you live in a hearing world*, a mantra that for her didn't apply. So, they were wrong, except they were in no position to be wrong, so naturally, she had to be wrong, wrong in all she did, despite her agony, despite her vision, and certainly in the face of her beauty. She had to be wrong. You must talk, Mrs Gunn demanded, talk is the world you must live in, even if it is not the world you want to live in.

Behind the panelled walls of the Reading Rooms Mrs Gunn displayed an angry eloquence, willingly exposing to us, who were inexpert in hearing, the fatalism of her misery. You must do as you are told girls, she commanded, that's all that counts. The child, she announced, the two year old, the three year old, uses gesture, and though this may be its mental salvation it is also the greatest threat to its future mental life – without words there is no thinking, without words there is no world. So, you must do as you are told, girls, and that is speak. And you must learn to speak correctly and well, just like everyone else.

The first time we were given this speech – which afterwards was repeated endlessly – Grace put her hand up to ask a question, only to find herself slapped across the face. I never did learn what that question was going to be, though I assume it would have been simply a request to go to the toilet, which I also assume would have been refused.

Mrs Gunn taught us our prayers. We were expected to end each lesson with the Lord's Prayer. I didn't see God, I saw sky. I didn't know what to make of it. As Mrs Gunn began in her slightly high pitched, twining voice, Our Father, who art in heaven, I saw sky.

I worshipped sky.

I pictured, tame sky, violent sky, blue sky, turquoise sky, yet always a sky without the sun. The sun was an infringement, a light source that had to remain hidden, discrete, something to itself. And from sky I had to make explanations, discover correspondences.

It was a moment of revelation and inspiration.

I didn't know what I wanted to do with my thoughts, but I recognised I was undertaking a challenge. I was thinking about my narrow world, searching for meaning, even if it was only a dictionary of pictograms.

One day when prayers were over I took Abby by the hand and led her to her favourite place. She had taken to secreting herself in the mine by that time, but to my mind her element was still air and water. On the coast I saw her, a dolphin, a mermaid, a bird, her body limber and unconstrained, one with its choices, wind or wave, and I wanted to say I too had access to a portion of that magic, that worship I had always known she was engaged in, those looks she impressed upon the horizon, as if she saw through it and beyond it and somehow encircled a reality that came back and contained it. She had a sense of devotion as subtle and intense as that. I knew why she was enthralled, yet at the same time shy of the plate of Sir Galahad and the Grail.

I stood close to the water's edge, the white foaming surf stopping just short of my feet, making arcs across the damp, coal blackened sands.

I signed.

God is sky.

Everything that is so big, bigger than me, that I don't understand or need to understand, is sky.

Sky is, tip to tip, and round, and up and down, and everywhere: is God.

Grace began to sulk and say she didn't understand the game.

Abby threw Poppy through the air, gifting her with it, with sky, though the fall was painful and sent Grace scurrying after her, despite being at the stage of saying she was just a doll and wasn't it time Abby started to grow up: but then, nothing was just anything to Abby, because she had the ability to see possibility, the other side, the life that went on unbidden but vigorous behind everything. She knew sky before I signed it. She had dwelt there which was more than I would ever be able to achieve. She had dwelt in all the corners of our segregated existence, discovering its secret passages, its points of access.

Wind is fabric, pinafore, sheets, hung from a break in sky, a hole in sky. The sheet holds the body, her, me, flapping at our ears, the sheets of sky.

Rain is finger-tips, tapping the stem of a flower.

Spindrift is muslin, a bandage.

Time is a wax crayon, a purple line on white paper, never at the edge.

Life is a moth.

Death is a smile.

Birth is a scream.

Grace objected. She said it was a silly kid's game. Still, when I took Abby's hand and we began to dance around, trying to make shapes of ourselves, she joined in and she was the first to laugh, throwing out a question with her exquisite, quizzical face – what did it all mean? I didn't answer: Abby just hummed her name. So we simply danced on, signing that we were witches round a pot, though why we should have thought such a thing I don't know, and then we all broke into skittish laughter, though all we heard was a certain percentage of joy.

Laughter is a waterfall landing in a bowl of rock, intensely white, never taking final shape.

We were witches because we were special sisters and nobody liked that, and made out that such sisters were odd, but such sisters owe each other and don't forget, which is a special kind of magic, a spell.

*

I went back to see Martha. It had been raining hard, not finger-tips on a flower stem, but arrowheads, weapons, and the yard was stinking, a quagmire of mud and bird shit. I stepped lightly across it, cursing the filth splashing onto my extravagant, multi-coloured shoes, dulling the impression of lime-green and yellow, the impression of aquarium water, but grateful the sole and heel were ridiculously high. – I am sure my effervescent hairdresser would have approved unreservedly of such a fashionable choice. The shoes were certainly not lost on the matriarch who, when she answered my knock, peered at them with a scarcely concealed grin and a look that suggested I hadn't really thought that one through, which somehow left me feeling at a disadvantage. Funny that Wellingtons or hiking boots would have rendered me far more comfortable under her gaze, but then I of all people should know of the semiotic advantages and disadvantages of life.

"Oh, it's you," she said, finally looking me in the face, as if she hadn't immediately recognised me. "I expected you'd have been long gone."

"Expected or hoped?"

"You're nothing to me, why would I be bothered?"

"I was Abby's friend, more than friend, closer."

"Of course you were, you're one of her kind."

"Does it not amount to anything?"

The trace of a smile crossed her face, but she suppressed it, opting instead to treat me to a vague, inquiring look, suggestive of the fact that she really was in the dark. She began again, her tone confidential, even to a point sympathetic. "Look, what are you after, what do you want from me?"

"Can I come in?"

"No, not this time."

"Are you busy?"

"I don't choose to have you, not this time, not with those filthy shoes."

Involuntarily I looked down at her feet. She was wearing battered, mud stained brogues, which presumably had once been tan but were now more or less bleached of colour. She burst out laughing. I began to object, but quickly corrected myself, having no real sense of what I was complaining about.

In my mind I recognised I had made a mistake coming back to her so soon after rain. Her yard was her defence, its stinking pools her barricades. She had lived in the midst of this stink all of her life, claiming it as a world to itself – swine and poultry, breeding, feeding, fattening, selling and killing. A simple, unsentimental existence devoid of any subtlety of thought. Except intolerance.

"I guess, I just need to know why you hate her," I asked.

She looked mildly sickened by the question. The corners of her mouth turned downwards, but only momentarily. She said: "You know, you talk funnier now than you used to, and you were always a bit bothered her way."

"I've never had any trouble with speech."

"Is that a fact, well, from where I'm standing it sounds a load of gobbledegook, and that's more or less how I recall you."

"No, that isn't right."

"Are you telling me, or asking me, because believe me, you can't tell me, can't tell me a damn thing. Now are you through pestering me, or do I have to send for your mother?"

"I'm not a child."

"And what's that to me? Go on, get out of it, or I'll get your mother, what use she might be."

"Just tell me, hating her, why?"

"Because she spoke funny, just like you, will that do you?"

"So you did hate her?"

She hesitated for just a few seconds and then, forcefully enunciating each syllable, declared: "I lavished her with affection."

"But she let you down?" She flashed me a questioning look. "By not listening." She scowled and gave the impression that she might actually lash out at me for being so impertinent. "But she did listen," I went on. "She heard everything, all you had to tell her, your secrets."

"Don't be clever with me, or I'll cross this threshold and show you."

"The way you showed her?"

"Don't think I'm too old either."

"I don't, not for a second. I mean it, though. You didn't see what a talent she had. You missed it, missed it completely."

"She was an idiot, born an imbecile, God help her, though listening to you I'm not so sure she was as bad as you."

"And how bad was your Aunt Hilda?"

She eyed me blankly for a moment, evidently struggling with the contrary desires to hit me, slam the door in my face or find out what I had discovered. Eventually she uttered: "I called her auntie, not aunt. Who says aunt round here? You've heard it all wrong again."

"Auntie Hilda, Auntie."

She smiled: "You've heard it all wrong, I said, all wrong."

"Is that why you hated her, because it was in the family and you just couldn't stomach that?"

"Don't be stupid, it was that filthy family!"

"The Shaughnessys."

"I told him not to marry her."

"But you hated the Shaughnessys long before that. Why?"

She glared at me briefly, then all of her anger seemed suddenly to evaporate away, and with a final triumphant look she closed the door on me, saying: "I really must talk to your mother."

I stood in the filth of her yard, moving my beautifully tasteless multi-coloured shoes through the sludge and slurry and laughed.

Hate had to be as powerful as love. I had been given the injunction.

*

Mrs Gunn's persistent trials and torments were tedious. I suppose we had a sneaking awareness that we were on the list of those things that made her life so unbearable; and yet, at times her persistence to educate us smacked of enthusiasm, albeit one coloured by her limitless capacity to see obstacles at every turn. For weeks on end she would try to fill us with language, barking sound after sound at us as if we were vessels just needing an adequate supply of something to achieve the brim. At the culmination of one particularly protracted effort she produced her liquids and then her solids.

Having ensured that we were in working order, our hearing aids switched on and functioning, followed by a short speech and introductory prayer, she placed her liquids on the table – her features worsened by the expression of pleasure – a sequence of five bottles produced from a basket she had brought with a striped linen tea-towel covering.

As she placed each bottle down she announced a vowel,

uncharacteristically for her opening her mouth wide and articulating her lips, allowing her expression to register something other than disappointment, though as to what those new gestures meant we couldn't begin to comprehend.

A,e,i,o,u, soft vowels, formed with ferocity.

She then repeated the display with small packets of grease-proof paper, also laying each one down with an accompanying soft vowel.

Once she had her bottles and packets ready she began. She pronounced a hard *a* over and over, and made us in turn sip from the first bottle, repeating *ah, ah, ah* directly into each of our faces as we took it, calling as loud as her natural reserve would allow.

The bottle was filled with malt vinegar. As we screwed up our faces she called: vin-e-gar, ah, ah!

She picked up the third bottle.

Milk, ilk, i, i, i.

Soup, tomato soup, toe-m-ah-toe soup, upe, u, u, u.

Oxo, oh, ox-oh, oh.

Tea, eeh, eeh.

She made long screeching eehs, as if imitating an old door grinding on its hinges. I felt Abby stiffen with excitement beside me. As she took the cold liquid onto her lips she began to shiver – though whether she heard her name or merely recognised its shape, I don't know. The cold, tarry tea dribbled along her lips and then trickled down her chin. She began to lap with her tongue, all around her lips and chin, making them shiny with spittle, eager to drink in her name.

Mrs Gunn carried on as if she were completely unaware of the excitement she was stimulating. She opened the grease-proof packages and proceeded to go through the same process, offering us in turn a morsel of each.

Spam, am, am, ah, ah.

Pickle, pick-ul, ick, i, i, i.

Cheese, ease, eeh, eeh, eeh.

Abby took the morsel eagerly onto her tongue and began to chomp on it with an open mouth, spitting it everywhere, her saliva turning pink with it. At the same time as she munched she began to recite the syllable, her mouth opening and closing with the regularity of a bellows. Mrs Gunn nodded in approval, strangely indifferent to the mess Abby was creating and then joined in, making a chorus of Abby's name. As Abby grew ever louder Mrs Gunn kept on nodding her approval and repeating her, in fact, responded to her like for like. Yes, she nodded, her name, her name on her lips, in her mouth. Yes, her name. E, e, e.

Suddenly Abby pushed back her chair and stood up, calling her name as loudly as she could, though with momentary catches in her throat which sounded like laughter of sorts. Mrs Gunn demanded that she sit back down and started calling her a little savage, but it was too late. Abby had been nourished on her own name and didn't know how to deal with that except through ecstasy. She set off skipping around the room, flailing her arms through the air, twisting her head and body, a motion that was so musical it looked as if she were turning in saline water, but not drowning, dancing.

Mrs Gunn kept on demanding that she return to her seat, but it was impossible. She was in a different element, transported by her name, her reality constructed from far more beautiful material than we had at our disposal. For a time she was an aquatic creature, a mermaid set free, and it didn't matter that she was incontinent, the urine rushing down her leg, leaving a tell-tale path of her dance. It was the liberty a mermaid possessed.

In the end Mrs Gunn could take no more and angrily stomped from the room banging the door behind her.

If Grace and I had had more sense we would have supervised Abby's dance, guided her to her preferred element, though what we would have done if she had insisted on giving herself to the waves I can't begin to imagine.

Certainly the Reading Rooms were not the right place for her. When Mrs Gunn returned with Harold we recognised that we had let her down. He beat her all around the rooms, beating the dancing out of her, beating the thrill of it out of her, beating her until she returned to an element we all shared, but what he couldn't do was beat her name out of her. After that she was always in tea and cheese in a funny, mysterious way.

Once upon a time I only ever ate a red cheese called simply red cheese, and only ever drank Co-op 99 tea, but nowadays I partake of all sorts, cheeses made from cow's, ewe's and goat's milk, and one in particular, which I find very mystifying, tinged with the flavour of coffee, and I drink teas flavoured with bergamot, lemon, cranberry, raspberry and elderflower, nevertheless every time I eat cheese or drink tea, no matter how exotic or mundane, I think of Abby and the dance that could not halt, no amount of shouting from Mrs Gunn, and her name that could not be dismissed, no amount of beating from Harold.

Her beauty is so everyday.

Chapter Thirteen

It was shortly after this affair that we were transferred to the village school. Whether it was as a direct consequence I am not sure. Certainly it was also the time when Seamus was taking a much closer interest in Grace's education, and had become convinced she should be tried in an ordinary school, in which he was fully supported by the school-inspector. I don't think he ever believed she could aspire to the full revelation of God, but he evidently accepted that she could acquire something. Mrs Gunn kept on for a few weeks after the dance, but made no reference to liquid or solid, only the Holy Ghost, keeping to what she felt was the safe ground of prayer, and then without warning we were transferred.

The village school consisted of one class. On the first morning we were greeted with silence. There should have been something reassuring about that, the sensitivity not to attempt to speak knowing that the three awkward sisters might not be able to hear, but we knew immediately that there was no such intent. It was as if we had intruded on an illegal game, all eyes angry and alert. Even the teacher, whom we had been told was called Mr Miller, had the same expression, with the additional hint of impatience or bewilderment, perhaps both. – The school-inspector had collected us and dropped us at the yard gate and, not bothering to come in himself, simply told us that Mr Miller knew we were coming.

Mr Miller waved his hand, indicating that we find a seat, and continued writing numbers on the blackboard. We didn't move. We didn't know what to do with Abby. Grace took her hand. Abby hummed her name. I tapped her on the arm, eager to stop her glee, her appreciation of Grace's worry. I looked around the room, hoping the other kids would make a space for us, three seats together, a small segregated group. Of course they recognised our reluctance and relished our discomfort.

Eventually Mr Miller shouted at us to stop dawdling, sit down and stop wrecking his class. I took Abby's other hand and led her to a desk in the second row. Her hum grew in volume, though remained just a musical vibration. The desks were close together but separate, nevertheless the boy beside Abby, who was probably two years younger, snatched up his book and screwed up his face as she sat down. As I looked around for a place for myself he moaned to the teacher that Abby was dribbling. A shudder of revulsion ran through the class. Mr Miller turned from the board again and demanded that Grace and I sit; he had had just about enough of our disruption. We took two desks at the back, Grace in the centre, whilst I was on the end, beneath a recessed window. As in the Reading Rooms the windows were high in the walls, only allowing for light, and that partial, but not vision. Having settled myself I looked towards Abby. The boy beside her was staring at me. His flat face had a glimmering, avid expression. We exchanged ruthless looks, each determined to outdo the other. That tiny battle was brought to an end when Mr Miller smashed a chipped, yellow, twelve inch wooden ruler against his desk, obviously the sign for attention, causing the boy to spin back into place, and commanded us to get on with it. Having given his instruction he sat down.

The other kids began to write. I wanted to see what Grace was doing, but was too nervous to look along the row. Abby was rocking very gently, soothing herself. I looked past her towards Mr Miller, uncertain whether I should speak up or not. He simply gazed into space, distracted. His face was lean, the skin tough, coloured dull crimson, with small purple veins around his nostrils, his hair swept back in an oiled quiff. He looked bored and listless. I was scared of doing nothing, but scared of him, scared of that face, of that expression, too scared to speak.

Suddenly, without any noticeable shift in his expression, he looked directly at me. He stood and came up to me. He stunk of cigarettes. He held his head back, aloft, demanding that I speak up. Please sir, I mumbled, I don't know what to do. For the briefest of seconds there was a noticeable relaxation in his expression, a suggestion even that he might smile, but then he turned abruptly away and marched back to his desk, shouting that there was an exercise book inside the desk and sums on the board which, to underline the point, he struck with the ruler. When he resumed his seat he glared at me, then Grace, and demanded that we get on with it. He didn't say anything to Abby, presumably having already decided that she was no mathematician.

From the very first break the bullying began, in the main instigated by the flat faced kid with the avid expression. The school-yard was on two levels, surrounded by a wall surmounted by painted, decorative metal-work. The other kids ran all around it, making as much noise as they could. We stood together as if we didn't have any idea how to play, as if play were alien. Maybe they thought we were rejecting it and took exception. Maybe the sisters drew attention to their distinctness, and that wasn't to be tolerated. Anyway, it didn't take long for the imp face kid to approach, followed by three other boys, all bigger. We didn't know any names then. We hadn't been told, hadn't heard a register. They were just boys with different faces, but like expressions. He started grinning and called Abby dummy. He sang it, elongating the two syllables, producing questionable music. The other boys joined in, chanting the two syllables, in the same crude sing-song, dum-my, dum-my.

So, they called Abby names, and funnily enough they hurt. I don't think she read any meaning in their mouths, on their

190

lips, but she recognised displeasure: after all, she had seen Harold look at her, and the matriarch, had seen what expression displeasure took. Grace was about to respond – I could see it welling in her, her inability to stand by; it was unmistakable, she always was a wonderful signer – but before she said anything, the boys burst out laughing and ran away. I sensed it was fortunate that Abby had been hurt, her expression clearly registering the fact, otherwise they would have had to go on, on and on, until they had found a way through, a weakness, a victory.

I guess the real anxiety for Abby was the wall and the metal decoration. All of her places had been taken away, banished to the other side of that barrier. She sidled into the shadow close to the porch steps, and leaned against the school building, but she knew she wasn't hidden. There was no magic like that, at all. Shortly after, Mr Miller came onto the steps. He looked down at us for a moment without any alteration in his expression and then put a whistle to his lips and blew. Very quickly two straight lines of children, one of boys and one of girls, formed in front of him. Once they had settled down into orderly formation he stepped aside and nodded for them to march in. When they had all gone he again turned to us. He pursed his lips, gently shook his head and then signed for us to follow. I doubt whether his silence was for our benefit.

At lunch the sing-song began again, but this time they came closer, bringing their faces right up to Abby's. She twisted, hunching herself awkwardly against their insult. It was too much for Grace who stepped up to them and started to shout, demanding that they leave her alone. The little boy grinned, but was at a loss, cautious of Grace's temper. He simply nudged the other boys, getting them to laugh at her foolhardy bravery. I stepped beside Grace and signed for them to clear off, refusing to speak, to use their language. I was taller than any of the boys. At that point Mr Miller appeared on the steps. Grace fell silent, but no one moved.

He marched down to us and demanded to know why Grace had been shouting. No one responded. He grabbed hold of Abby just above the elbows and, firmly but not violently, began to shake her, insisting she tell him why Grace was shouting. Although he didn't shake her as I had seen Harold shake her still he managed to shake some wee right out of her. It dribbled down her legs and soaked into her small white socks. As soon as he realised it he pushed her away as if she had urinated over his hands, then pointed her towards the toilets which were at the far end of the yard away from the school. When she didn't move he turned to Grace and me and ordered us to see to her. As we walked her, hand in hand to the toilets, he marched back inside, leaving a refrain of dummy singing behind him.

At the end of the day they were waiting at the school gates. Abby wet herself again as we walked towards them. They formed a line barring our exit. We came up to them and stopped. They started singing pissy pants, pissy pants, over and over, using the same elongated syllables as they had earlier. For a while we simply gazed at each other, the boys singing, the sisters more or less silent – except for a faint hum from Abby, a faint meaningless hum, neither name, enthusiasm, nor vision, a sound signifying so little – no one knowing quite what to do next. I believe they were pleased when one of the girls, our age, similar in stature to Grace, not as pretty but almost, a girl we had heard called Maria, came up and told them to leave us alone. They laughed at her and called her pissy pants too, but they went, alternatively singing dummy and pissy pants as they did.

I don't know whether we failed Maria at that point, sisters closing ranks, sisters not having the words to allow for friendship, even though we knew the sign for love. If we had taught Maria the sign for love would she have been receptive, signalled it as we sometimes did, behind the lids of our desks, when Mr Miller's back was turned, love and don't worry, love and laughter. I think she was capable of learning the sign and could have loved Abby just the same as we did: I saw something of it in the way she looked at her over the next few weeks, trying to work something out, make sense of something, though, whether in Abby or in herself I never really fathomed. All she had to do was accept it, accept what everyone else by their actions told her was impossible but, of course, to agree to a sign as powerful as love means standing up to things that are not at all predictable. Love is never predictable. We knew that and we were only kids trying it out, trying it out in a preliminary yet perfect way. As far as Maria was concerned, even though she couldn't begin to calculate how savage the fight might be, I guess she decided she couldn't take the risk, even if risk, like everything, is relative, which in the end is sequestered and ridiculed by time, which only time reveals.

She looked at Abby's wet legs, screwed up her face and ran off without another word.

Over the next few weeks, at first by accident, but then, I am sure, by design, Abby discovered a place of concealment. Funnily enough it was thanks to Jimmy, the flat faced, imp-like boy. It was within days of our arrival when he produced a peashooter and from behind the cover of his desk pelted Abby with tiny missiles. At first she hunched against them and simply moaned her name, but then one struck her hard on the temple and she leapt to her feet and slammed the desk lid down across his arms. Jimmy cried out loud, but she did it again and again. Within seconds of her retaliation Mr Miller dragged her away, pulled her through the classroom door, threw her into a stationary cupboard and locked the door behind her. Grace lifted her desk lid and signed relief. When Mr Miller returned he appeared genuinely shaken. He glared at Grace and me and told us that the school-board would be informed, his expression implying that we were at fault.

After that, much to the increasing pleasure of the class, Abby was regularly consigned to the stationary cupboard.

Sometimes she wet herself in there, but that was only because of the amount of time she was left. Grace and I both knew her game, could see the twinkle of success in her eyes. Of course it wasn't good for her learning, but her natural look returned, the one she had when she scanned the horizon or pored over the pages of the Book of Wonders. The stationary cupboard was her new place, completely her own, debarred even to her sisters.

It was during these weeks at school that she started her rituals. Neither Grace nor I had ever been a party to that aspect of her and were at a loss to comprehend it. It began simply enough at first with her tapping her left shoulder with her right palm three times on entering the classroom, whilst at the same time pronouncing her name. As the weeks progressed though, her rituals became ever more complex, small bows and hand movements before sitting, and again when she was told to stand. Grace and I were bemused and troubled. She was using signs, but they were beyond our scope.

Eventually it was Grace who fathomed them, always being the most expert on signs. At the same time as she had started in the village school Seamus had allowed Grace to return to mass, which she hadn't done since before her illness, an experience she only vaguely remembered. She said that there was a great deal of excitement in the family, particularly from her mother who dressed up for the occasion as if she were attending a wedding or christening. As she watched Abby conduct her rituals she was struck by the fact that there was a similarity between Abby's signs and the signs she made in church: signing the cross, bowing to the tabernacle and clasping her hands in prayer. She was sure Abby was going through a religious period. To prove the point she brought a picture of the Madonna for her, which she had been given during one of her lessons of instruction – Seamus had ordained that Grace complete her first Holy Communion – tapping herself on the shoulder three times as she handed it over. Abby eyed it carefully, and then turned to the small, unadorned cross on the wall behind Mr Miller, which evinced a smile of satisfaction from Grace, certain that her suspicion had been proven right. Abby then secreted it away inside her desk. After that she regularly lifted the lid to view her acquisition, eyeing it secretly, guarding it jealously.

Of course, Abby's behaviour never went unnoticed. Mr Miller shook his head and screwed up his face in a quizzical, put upon look he reserved for us – though uncharacteristically he opted not to investigate whatever was inside the desk to which Abby was so infatuated. The usual punishment for being caught lifting a desk lid uninvited was at the very least a slap across the head, sometimes the ruler across the knuckles. Grace and I were regularly slapped, our need to sign being so great.

More disturbingly Jimmy recognised that Abby had a treasure. Grace warned Abby to keep her picture with her, but for some reason she wouldn't hear of it: she had decided that the Madonna had her own place of concealment, perhaps needed it, as she needed it, so that their two imaginations could be free, her faith preserved.

At first I didn't believe it. I told myself that Abby had never shown any tendency towards things holy. Looking back, of course, that was absurd. She lay down beneath the angel, she loved the book of angels, and she turned so many things into acts of worship, even the incompleteness of silence, which she hosted like a crowd. There was always evidence of that need in her to perform ritual, repetition, step and mime. The absurdity was that it took me so long to see. It was glaringly obvious that she was mimicking something, some convoluted prayer that sang through her silence, an adoration and affirmation, even under the terrible gaze of Mr Miller and Jimmy. In the classroom she needed her inner sacred world more than ever. She was possessed of such spirit that thrived on it. Her hum was endurance, its sound, unbeknownst to her, salvation.

Jimmy stole her hidden image, though, scribbled all over it, and then bandied it in her face, mocking her with it. By the time Mr Miller came into the yard she had seized so tightly onto Jimmy's hair that Mr Miller had to strike her repeatedly across the knuckles to get her to release him, and even then two clumps came away in her hands. Mr Miller pulled her away, striking her as he dragged her, and flung her in the stationary cupboard where she remained grieving for the rest of the day. I fully expected to find Jimmy and the others waiting for us at the gates, though when they weren't felt more disturbed than if they had.

Jimmy's mother complained and even started a petition against having us in the school, which even the matriarch, who remained convinced school was the wrong place for Abby, signed. Mr Miller defended himself on the grounds that he had been forced to have us by a misguided inspector. Jimmy's mother assured him she wouldn't let the matter drop. She was the only parent we ever saw cross the threshold into Mr Miller's classroom. He was obviously uncomfortable with his authority being breached in that way and afterwards eyed us with evident contempt.

Abby's rituals became even more fixed after that, an exact dance performed on entering the classroom and before sitting, a dance of hands, arms and expression.

I saw her look up at the recessed windows and smile one day as she took her seat. I signed to Grace that she was wrong. Abby had not devoted herself to a single God, she worshipped sky, and all the natural elements that contained her. Then Abby began to sing and willingly accepted banishment to the cupboard where she increasingly passed the whole day.

She was never exempt, though, from cross-country or the ensuing game Mr Miller called bull-charge. The girls weren't expected to run the course but had to be there to cheer or curse the boys home. The boys ran with sticks that they had to pretend were guns. In Mr Miller's cross-country winning was everything, for which cheating, however rough, was allowed. He said we had entered the war ill prepared, which was unforgivable, but it would be different next time if teachers like him did their jobs properly. It was a regular theme of his that the Russians, being brain-washed fanatics, would prove a much rougher opponent than the Germans, and that it had been a mistake to have ever been allied with them. On the back wall of the classroom he had a pre-war map, made of thick canvas, threading at the edges, on which the British Empire was coloured in red. He never once admitted that the world was not as depicted on that map, but would regularly have us recite the names of the countries of the empire, the countries in red, after him.

There were sixteen boys in the class, and nineteen girls, including us sisters. The first eight boys home were applauded as they finished the last stretch, crossing the yard from the gate to the toilets, but the last eight had to do the bull-charge, which meant crossing the yard where the girls and any of the first eight boys who were quick enough were waiting determined to stop them. The boys had to duck and weave their way through the waiting mob, our job to tackle them to a halt.

We were all guilty of the most terrible enthusiasm imaginable, and that is certainly guilt. Grace and I grabbed those losing boys as if they had personally and purposely let us down, laughing as we caught their neck and arms and dragged them down. At the end of it the boys sometimes had tears in their eyes, though no one openly cried: it was common knowledge, the way such things always are in a classroom, that Mr Miller caned any boy who cried. Of course, sometimes the boys sent us flying, Abby always ending up on her backside, her expression bewildered but generally amused. I can't help but think that she was also enthusiastic for the game, despite her inevitable tumbles, she wet herself regularly enough.

Our time in Mr Miller's classroom didn't last long, just a few months. I don't know what the final straw was, but it was obvious when Abby smashed up the medical head and torso that Mr Miller was beside himself with rage. He thrashed her mercilessly before throwing her into the cupboard, and was still banging on the door hours later threatening her with more if she didn't keep quiet. – It was strange for her to cry once she was concealed, but her buttocks and the backs of her legs were marked for weeks after that beating, and of course Harold added to it later that night certain from that evidence alone that she must have been particularly bad.

Certainly Mr Miller had seemed pretty pleased with himself as he stripped the anatomical layers from one side of the model, taking out the eyeball, jaw, tongue, ear, part of the brain, trachea, lung, heart, liver, spleen and intestine, getting us to say the words after him, then draw them as neatly as we could, fully labelled, in our exercise books. Abby refused the lesson, drawing criss-crossing lines all over her paper, which perhaps was her interpretation of soul. How she sneaked back into the classroom and managed to wreck the reassembled model I can't say. Her sisters were obviously at fault, but she could be sly when the fancy took her. The human parts were scattered all around and she had obviously stamped on most of them, the dirt from her boots clearly visible on any number of organs. When Mr Miller caught her she was actually jumping on the head.

He said it was positive proof that she was crazy and though I would obviously disagree with that, and hold that she must have had adequate reason for her attack, she never did explain it, other than to moan her name in the stationary cupboard for the rest of the day.

I suppose everyone realised our time would shortly be up at Mr Miller's, certainly Maria must have guessed.

It was only a few days after the incident with the model when we discovered the boys and some of the girls waiting for us, barring the school gate. We must have recognised straight away that there was something different about this group because we didn't hesitate but ran back through the yard, Grace and I dragging Abby, having taken a hand each, then through a gate in the back wall beside the toilets which let onto a play-field used for rugby and football matches, which after a few days of heavy rain was saturated. We ran across the waterlogged ground making for a wood on the other side. By the time we reached it we were covered in mud. The smell of sodden and dead vegetation was all around, choking our nostrils with the stink of decay.

The gang wasn't far behind us, and gaining all of the time, after all they participated in regular cross-country, Jimmy, certainly, always in the first eight. We made our way as quickly as we could through the wood, the trees thickening around us, the canopy growing more dense. By this time we were running out of stamina. I signed to Grace that we had no choice but to hide. The trouble was Abby was exhilarated, the brisk dash having stirred her sense of adventure. We went someway farther, the woodland breaking into thickets of shrub and brush where pools of light flooded through gaps in the leaf cover. In one particularly wide break made up of gorse scrub and rhododendron bushes we decided we couldn't go any further. Grace signed for Abby to crawl into a thicket of bushes, which she was only too pleased to do. Grace crawled after her. I pushed my way through a cluster of rhododendron and azalea, and then stood awkwardly in the centre, the branches spread all around me like numerous arms holding me captive.

We waited for quite some time, the longer the wait the more perilous it seemed. How could I contact Grace and decide when to make another break? Were they waiting, hunting like scenting dogs? I expected boys called out when they were following a trail, but we were in no fit state to hear. Certainly neither my nor Grace's hearing, even with a Medresco aid, was up to detecting foraging kids intent on running us to ground. I was scared of shivering, scared of sounds that escaped me.

Eventually I did hear someone call out, heard the faint outline of our names. It grew louder. It was Maria, Maria telling us everything was all right, they'd gone. She called again and again, repeating that everything was all right, the boys had given up; it was all right to come out.

Certainly my first thought was to go to her, there was something so frustrated in her voice, and yet I just couldn't move. I was stuck in that clump of rhododendron and azalea, scared of sound, the human voice, nature, life. Grace had no hesitation. She was only too relieved to know it was over. I heard her call to Maria. I guessed from the amount I heard that she had stood up, was probably waving her hands, beckoning Maria with that beautiful excitement Grace possessed. It was then that Maria's voice rose to the tops of the trees saying, over here, they're over here.

By the time I deserted my sanctuary Grace was sobbing, nursing herself, and Abby was lying on the ground, curled up, but with eyes wide open, staring straight ahead, which must have been a vision of long grasses and clusters of evergreen leaves, though she offered no sign of recognition of any such things.

I thought Grace might chase me away, but she opened her arms and held me, and cried, and I understood without her needing to explain that it was for Abby, because she had been beaten so often, and although this wasn't much, no more than a few slaps, it was all too much: Grace was her witness and it hurt.

The last straw was when Abby shit on the classroom floor. After that Mr Miller refused to have her back. He was in a particularly foul mood because it was cross-country day, but snowing too hard to attempt it. It was unheard of that the weather stopped the cross-country, but even Mr Miller had to accept that the snow was just too heavy to go ahead. Because it should have been cross-country Abby wasn't banished to the cupboard, but remained at her desk gazing up at the line of windows which revealed a narrow world of grey snow laden cloud. After lunch Abby began to wriggle. Grace put up her hand and suggested Abby needed the toilet. Mr Miller gazed first at Grace, then Abby, then back at Grace and shook his head. A few minutes later Grace tried again. He slammed his fist down onto the desk and demanded that Grace get on with her work. Grace lowered her head. Ten minutes or so later she tried again, this time causing Mr Miller to thrust back his chair and snatch at his ruler. Before he could take a step towards anyone Abby stood up. She squirmed over her seat for a moment, and then sidled out of her place. As she did she lifted her pinafore. A stream of black faeces trailed down her leg. She danced around for a few seconds, and then rushed from the classroom, leaving behind the smell of her distress and a few splashes of the reason. Mr Miller ordered Grace and me to fetch a bucket and mop from the cleaner's cupboard and sort out the mess, then he sat back down and gazed into space as he had done on the first day we had entered his school.

At first Abby ran to the toilet at the bottom of the yard, but already it was too late. She stood against a white-washed wall staring up at the metal grills below the ceiling, imagining the snowfall on the other side. Shortly after that, making no attempt to clean herself, she ran home. She stood in the yard for the rest of the afternoon, too afraid or too ashamed to present herself to Agnes, the snow coming down ever more heavily as she waited. She hadn't moved when Grace and I found her. We took her into one of the pig-sheds and cleaned her as best we could from a water-trough. I think she was hallucinating, seeing whatever fabulous visions she had access to: she was certainly unaware of the water as it ran across her, or the diluted stain, or the smell and sight of pigs. In fact there was a look of strange, careless pleasure on her face. Of course she was ill for a couple of weeks after that, so perhaps it was nothing of the sort, and as so often, I am simply being fanciful.

Grace and I spent another couple of days in the village

school, until a letter was sent to our homes stating that it was felt better we attend a special school, arrangements for which would be made soon.

*

The sentence, I am suspicious of light, came into my head, but that is ridiculous. Maybe I am suspicious of the shadows and colour effects of light. I have spent too many days along poorly lit corridors with magnolia walls and insubstantial windows looking out onto grim courtyards, too many days in dingy confinement, for it to be any other way.

Perhaps it would be better to say, I am troubled by light, troubled by its associations, the impression of its being good, troubled, for instance, by the fact that sunlight suddenly flooding a length of sterile corridor is seen as a pouring of joy: but joy, of course, as with everything, is indecipherable from its complement, all opposites being part of the same thing. So, if I am deprived light it is darkness that signals the absence, it is light I perceive. The sustained differentiation of opposites is not about opposition at all but unity. The fight then is always for something, something that exists in absence, not simply against something.

To be simply against something, is to be for nothing.

The real world can drive you mad, though, and sometimes I have the suspicion that that must be the case. I have been locked up for so long, thought about a killing for so long, how could it be otherwise? It drives me to say I am suspicious of light, as if the word suspicious had meaning in such a crazy sentence.

It has to be for something.

I am suspicious of light because it is never an end in itself, but dazzles and therefore obscures its source, so light is in fact dark.

And the world rolls over.

And I try again with my hand-full of signs, wanting to escape my knowledge of narrow corridors, of confinement

202

and killing, but what then am I left with? Just a woman of sixty who takes shallow delight in having her hair washed and dried.

I want to correct myself. I am not suspicious at all, but I relish light, relish sunlight on steel, on glass, on concrete, its tranquil shadow, its unviewable ray, sunlight on faces, on the London crowd, my thoughts fluttering like wings, signing worthwhile pleasure, condign punishment, and I speak, coaxingly and coyly to my efflorescent hairdresser, words to the effect, it is a lovely day.

I am in contact with a human being, with my world.

The trouble is they are surfaces, exterior actions. In my deepest thoughts it is as if only I have an interior life, which is signed by sky, sea and stone, and the other life, in a stubborn limited manner, a way devoid of imagination, or even deep rooted ill-will, collides with it.

Sometimes though, as with the matriarch, when the hate was palpable, as sometimes the hurt was palpable in Abby, there is the utter realisation of another human being, but why that should only exist in hate and pain is incongruous, maybe even inexcusable.

So, I am suspicious of light, of dark, of the air through which we dive believing in flight, however supernatural, magical or physical, a flight which will inevitably dissolve in itself anyway.

Chapter Fourteen

I waited at the end of the street wanting to see Harold alone. It was a dreary overcast evening, with no moonlight, but luckily no rain either, though liable to showers. Certainly it was dark enough to feel hidden, to consider that a mask was in place, the human agent freed up for any possibilities. I knew Agnes was still indoors because I had made a tour of their pig meat estate, their property by seizure, setting a number of dogs yelping, and had seen her through the lighted kitchen window. My mother had told me that Hazel remained unwell, finding trouble catching her breath, her chest tightening and causing her to panic, and Agnes had been spending more and more time there, so I just had to wait for her to go. It was important for me to see them severally, keep them guessing, refuse them any opportunity of ganging up: and besides, Agnes was more formidable than I had ever given her credit for. Before she had been least in my thoughts, but since speaking to her had really come to the fore.

The smell of pig manure stayed with me as I sidled up and down the street, pausing now and again to look at my watch as if I were waiting for someone – which indeed I was – wanting to deflect any unwanted attention. Nobody questions someone who has obviously been stood-up; nobody would want to be involved.

Comic, tragic, sordid, waiting is, and fearful, I signed, speaking in my head, my nerves tangled, visible to me, like strings tied in rows, my mind playing tricks, off on flights of nonsense.

I walked away a few yards, crunching my feet, seeing if I could locate such a remote sound, in an attempt to calm down.

As I was coming back a young girl came towards the houses from the opposite direction, from the village, whereas I was on the lane to St Bridget's. Inevitably I thought of Abby and, as there can be no separation from her, no point at which she ends and becomes me, or I end and find other, I thought of me; and, naturally, by the same law there could be no separation between the girl and me. So, when she looked along the lane and saw me, she knew, recognised the prediction of herself in the meaning of my being there. I felt a great surge of loyalty flow from me, wanting to bind with her, inform her that the like existed, the possibility, the frankness. I am sure she must have felt it: why else should she have looked so knowingly at me, unperturbed by the unashamed directness of her interest, and so calm?

As she stood on the step, waiting for the door to open, still patiently looking at me, she really was Abby. It was unmistakable. The look was her look, earnest, amused, wicked and a-wing, and I was unmistakably myself, the two of us together in that moment transcending the barriers that break us up into individuals and nations.

At that moment I had the satisfaction of waiting to see Harold, of being his judgement.

A moment later, following a quick frame of yellow light and a momentarily opened door, she was gone, and with her went a certain yearning, the pity ascribed to false peace. Perhaps the shouting, the hair pulling, the beating, the hands where they had no right to be had started already. Peace is the break between what is normal.

Finally Agnes came out and hurried off towards the village. It was time. I wasn't going to hesitate for a minute. I went straight up to the door, Agnes having only just that second disappeared from view.

Harold answered impatiently, obviously assuming Agnes had forgotten something – presumably a key – then quickly corrected himself on seeing me. They obviously shared a marriage turned habit and irritant, though it was impossible to discount style with them.

He stepped right out into the street before speaking and looked up and down as if my being there might be a joke, a put up job.

He stepped up behind me and uttered close to my ear: "Did you pass her?"

I shook my head.

"But you must have," he went on, "she's only just gone, just this second, gone."

I turned, slightly inclining my head towards him, assuming a playful, mildly impertinent tone. "I know, I waited, saw her, watched her go. She must have been late, she went off at quite a step."

"It's Hazel."

"I know, finds a tightening across her chest when she breathes. It doesn't sound that good."

"It's nothing, it'll fix, the way things do. It's Aidan, Aidan she goes for."

"Because Aidan can't cook."

"I don't know about that, don't know what he can do."

"You don't know?"

"No," he replied sharply, "why the hell should I?"

"You could ask?"

He considered for a moment, then relaxed and asked: "Why would I be interested?"

"Because it's your wife's family."

"I didn't marry them."

"She married yours."

"What the hell's that supposed to mean? Anyway, why keep going on about her?"

"I'm not, I'm going on about you."

It was obvious by his failure to reply that my response

206

pleased him. He stepped back up to the top step and looked down at me, a stupid grin shaping itself on his lips.

"What does she go for, if not to cook?"

"How the hell do I know? Christ are you coming in or not?"

"Have I been asked?" I responded in the same testy tone.

He slammed the door back causing it to smash against the wall, keeping his hand on it to forestall any rebound, then dropped his arm leaving a passage for me to go in. As soon as I crossed the threshold the door slammed behind me and I felt his hands roughly grabbing me around the torso, his mouth searching for mine, in an ugly exercise of passion.

"Not so quick, God, not so quick!"

He let me go, pushing me away without violence. "I thought you wanted it," he said, quite matter-of-fact, a business deal he had miscalculated.

"I didn't say I didn't."

"Look," he said firmly, warning me, "don't piss me about."

Again I replied like for like: "No, you look, Agnes might be home any minute."

"You watched her go," he mocked.

"And I don't want to watch her come back."

He grimaced and fell away, shuffling into the sitting-room proper, taking up what I assumed was his usual seat by the electric fire. "She'll be ages yet," he called back.

"You don't even know what she does."

"Don't I though," he said, smiling lewdly.

"No, you don't."

"Please yourself."

"Have you always been so willing to be unfaithful to her?" I asked, sidling into the room behind him, standing behind a three seated settee.

"What do I do now, butter you up?"

"Please yourself."

"You're no beauty, but you'll pass."

"Thanks."

He grinned: "Straight people, straight," he said, signing it with his right hand. "Or have you forgotten?"

"I haven't forgotten anything. I keep every detail locked up, precious, like china, dainty bits of porcelain, easily broken or snapped, but all there, certainly all there."

"Well, take us as we are, or go back to London."

"Us?"

"Whoever," he snapped, confused.

"It's you who interest me."

He looked at me through slightly narrowed eyes, whether distrustful of me per se, or of what I seemed to be promising I couldn't tell. "What, what interests you?" he asked.

"All sorts."

"I said she'll be ages."

"I know, but other things as well."

"What other things?"

"Your kids, for instance."

"What about them?"

"Do you see them?"

"Of course I do."

"All of them."

"Of course, all of them."

"You never mention them."

"To say what?"

"What they're up to?"

"Up to?"

"What they do?"

"They do things in the brick factory, hot things, heavy things, make tea, that sort of fashion."

"All of them?"

"Look," he said, standing up, his arm stretched across the top of the mantle-piece, "whatever way you want to put it, all of them. Joe's married, one kid, nice kid, should grow up all right; Ruth's married, no kids, not yet. And Dennis, Dennis is Dennis. Now, I think I've had enough."

"All right, not deaf you mean."

"Not anything."

"But then there was Hilda, your Great Aunt Hilda, Hilda who had to be taken away. So you shouldn't be too sure. We never know what we have in our families, do we."

"I said I've had enough of this."

"Oh come on, it's just a little game, we'll get to the serious stuff."

"Don't piss me off, I've said."

"I don't think you'll be disappointed." He started to come towards me. "But not here, I said. I'm not doing anything here, is that clear?"

He grinned again: "I've got the pig-sheds out back."

"And have you used them before?" The grin evaporated from his face. He was about to speak, but I put up my hand forbidding it, my index-finger raised, in perspective pressed against his bulbous lips. "What about the old mine tower? I know you're not comfortable with heights, but it was always cosy there? I presume it's still there."

He eyed me coldly for a moment then slowly nodded, and in a voice full of suspicion said: "The tower wouldn't bother me. It's still there."

I smiled, slowly rounded the settee, walked up to him, put my palms against his cheeks one after the other, then kissed him once, on the outside of the lips, then again spreading my tongue along them, then past them, demanding a response. Within seconds we were kissing and panting, his hands groping all over me, across my breasts, around my waist, and then pulling at buttons and zips.

I pulled away, straightening myself as I did, and said: "I'm sorry, really, I couldn't do it here, but tomorrow, I'll wait. When Agnes goes."

He nodded. I kissed him again, twice, briefly, like promises, then backed away smiling, saying: "I'll bring a blanket, so we won't be cold. I don't want to be cold." From the door I called back, again assuming that playful, impertinent tone of earlier. "There's one thing intrigues me about you." He simply cocked his head in question. "Do you never wonder who you are?"

So, how far would I go to find the light, that thing I was to become so suspicious of and troubled by? Did it matter, if in the end I was able to kill him? Wasn't there a transcendental beauty to that?

Maybe.

*

We were collected each morning in a small bus together with nine other special school kids from the surrounding villages.

On the first day it felt like a holiday. Not only had we escaped the village school and Mr Miller, but also we were going on a journey. Only Grace had ever been on a bus before, her mother regularly taking her with her when she went shopping in town. Abby felt it too. She told everyone on the bus her name, groaning its syllable as loud as she could. It began straight away when the driver had to get out and turn a handle to start the engine, and the whole bus began to shake and made enough noise that Grace and I could hear. Abby couldn't help but shout. Grace was quite embarrassed by her display. She signed for her to be quiet, but there was no hope of that. A boy on another bench – there were four rows of wooden benches – signed to Grace that it was all right. His signs were very small compared to ours, those that Aidan, Peter and Paul had taught Grace and Grace had taught us. He was a pretty boy, with a light, luminous expression with deep blue eyes and straight blond hair combed in a neat quiff. I thought he was shy and liked Grace. I hoped he liked her. They were as pretty as each other. I told her straight off that he liked her. Grace frowned in her quirky, grown-up child's way. She didn't sign another thing to Abby.

Later we discovered that the boy was called Phillip and he was sorry he had signed to her.

The special school was to our eyes a grandiose place, a sandstone building at the end of a rough track with two wings with triangular frontage, and roofs that seemed to go in all directions. There were two short lawns, then trees all around. Later, we learnt that there was a small yard to the rear where we could play that was in permanent shadow.

The driver took us to the office of Mr Archibald, the master, as he called him. – The driver, Mr McBride, a short, casual man, we always considered friendly, though he never did anything but smile at us as we boarded his bus. – Mr Archibald, a plump, bald, round faced man, stood up and peered down at us through thick rimmed, circular spectacles. He neither smiled nor frowned. He spoke to Mr McBride, but we heard neither part of the conversation. As Mr McBride left he waved. Grace began to wave back, but Mr Archibald reached for her hand and pushed it down, then pressed it gently against her thigh and held it there, his five fingers spread across it. When he released his hold he gave a brief, negligible smile then told us to follow.

He led us through the school's wood-panelled entrance hall, along a corridor to Miss Sowerby's class, the deaf unit. Phillip was in the front row. He blushed as we walked in. Grace gave him a discreet greeting. Miss Sowerby was standing on a wooden platform at the front of the class before a board perched onto the front of a blackboard covered with small pictures of everyday objects, a cane pointer in her hand. She was a thin woman, with straight features, her hair parted to either side and curled at the fringes. She looked at Grace disapprovingly. Grace blushed more deeply than Phillip. She called Grace to her. Grace stepped up to the platform. Miss Sowerby pointed to one of the pictures, one of a ball, and asked Grace to say it. Grace signed ball. Mrs Sowerby put down her cane, walked to the edge of the platform, bent over Grace, pushed Grace's hands to her sides and held them, as Mr Archibald had done, and mouthed at her: ball, b-all. Grace repeated the word. Miss

Sowerby stood up, and with a look of satisfaction spread across her face announced: Rarely write, never gesticulate, always speak.

Rarely write, never gesticulate, always speak, she repeated, and then demanded that the class say it with her, calling out in an agitated voice: Say it, say it. The response was mumbled, broken and incoherent, nevertheless Miss Sowerby looked pleased. She turned to me and Abby, who were still standing just beyond the classroom door with Mr Archibald, and invited us to say it. Abby told her her name, assuming that that was what was needed, a name to identify her. I mumbled the response she wanted, but Abby's name was stronger. Miss Sowerby looked crestfallen.

Mr Archibald stepped up onto the platform beside Miss Sowerby, stroking Grace on the head as he went past her, to which show of sympathy Miss Sowerby screwed up her face in derision. He removed the picture poster from the front of the blackboard, picked up a piece of chalk and wrote, Abigail Sempie, after which he turned to Abby and said: Your name, Abigail Sempie. Ab-i-gail Semp-ie, Semp-ie, ie, ie, ie.

Abby was victorious and, like me, assumed he had understood that she was saying her name. She greeted the recognition with a great answering rendition of who she was.

Mr Archibald smiled, whilst Miss Sowerby looked on expressionless.

He turned back to the board and wrote the name Judith Salt beneath Abby's, then turned to me and said: Your name, Ju-dith Salt, S-alt, S-alt.

Judith Salt, my name, I agreed.

He wrote Grace Powers below Judith Salt.

Grace claimed her name before him, which to my surprise pleased him more than offended him. He smiled broadly and agreed with her, nodding his head and repeating, Grace Powers, good, Grace Powers, your name, good. You speak fairly well then, I didn't realise.

The naming was too much for Abby who straight away

wet herself. It had recently become one of her personal signs, though it covered a multitude of meanings. Miss Sowerby gazed at the pool of urine forming around her boots and, as if speaking to it, said she hadn't been told.

Mr Archibald tutted a few times, shook his head, and made to step from the platform, but then corrected himself, evidently remembering something he had overlooked. He made a small speech, which I presume was something he had learnt off by heart and was able to deliver whenever circumstances demanded, such as to new children, visiting dignitaries and school governors. The breath of life, he recited, resides in the voice, transmitting enlightenment through it. The voice is the interpreter of our hearts and expresses its affections and desires. The voice is a living emanation of that spirit that God breathed into man when he created him a living soul.

His speech concluded he again tutted and shook his head then stepped from the platform and taking Abby's hand led her away. When they had gone Miss Sowerby told us to sit, warning us to be sure to have our hearing aids turned on at all times. She replaced the picture board, covering the two lower names but not Abby's, Abigail Sempie remaining like a title over the everyday objects, then again picked up her cane pointer and indicated a brush, then mouthed at the class, b-rush, b-russsh. Having repeated the word twice with great gymnastics of her thin lips, she turned to Grace and told her it would be better if she sat on her hands for the rest of the lesson. Grace blushed as she placed her hands, palm down on the seat beneath her buttocks, and strangely enough, I saw that Phillip did too.

We had been right through the pictures when Mr Archibald brought Abby back. She was dressed in a clean pinafore, with clean socks and slippers instead of boots. The pinafore was too small for her and she obviously didn't like it because she was quiet for the rest of the day, obstinately quiet, though both Grace and I told her it looked fine.

213

At break we ran off into the woods with Phillip. He signalled it as soon as we were in the yard. It was like being part of an escape troop following him, the careful way he kept looking back, kept checking we were still with him. He really was as lovely as Grace. It was inevitable they would tend towards each other but, funnily enough, Grace never claimed him as a brother: there was no repeat of our momentous meeting on the shoreline. I think it was sufficient for all three of us, the sisters, to realise we weren't alone, that there were others of the same generation. Martha was right to be hostile; we couldn't help but love each other. Phillip was so full of remorse it was silly. He hadn't realised that Grace didn't know it was forbidden to sign. It was all right on the bus, he explained, because even though Mr McBride could see you in his mirror he didn't seem to care. He told us that lots of kids, those with parents who could hear, couldn't sign but the other kids shared them. We didn't need to ask why. Signing was easier.

As Phillip was describing special school to us Abby lay down sideways against a tree, twisted in that shape she adopted when she believed she had insect qualities, her knees up and crooked, her arms held up to her chest, her hands dangling from pendant wrists, her eyes sunken but searching out undergrowth, confinement, a narrow world.

Seeing her press herself ever harder against the tree Phillip broke off speaking to us and went and knelt down in front of her, despite the fact the woodland floor was damp. He asked her what her name was. Grace said her name was Abby. He smiled, touched Abby's lips with his fingertips, and said, of course, it was a pretty name and she should be proud of such a name. There was something lovely about the fact that he realised she had been saying her name, announcing it with great sociability to the whole class, which was so much her way. He repeated it a number of times, drawing it in the air, a name to be proud of, a pretty name, Abby, her name, traced in space, in flight.

He said it was better not to leave Abby alone with Mr Archibald.

He sprang up, burst out laughing and said all the kids knew that, not to be alone with Mr Archibald. He looked down at Abby, her gaze gone to those far away places only she could access, and said you sometimes had to be careful of the kids who didn't talk because, even when they could hear they liked to sign and they got you into trouble. Grace said she thought all the kids couldn't hear. Phillip laughed at her and said there were all sorts in Ingwall, all sorts, kids in carts, mad kids, strange kids, deaf, dumb and blind kids.

And we're all special, Grace said, and laughed, which was very like Phillip's.

When we returned to the classroom Abby was very ritualistic, though her language had changed. It seemed to me she had lost patience with her former signs and adopted ones more rigorous, more severe, involving her entire body: there was a great deal of head shaking and touching of different body parts, no longer just the shoulder but the cheeks, the ears, the top of the head, then the neck and the torso, and finally the thighs, both inside and out.

Miss Sowerby watched her go through her dance with the same expressionless look of earlier, then she stepped from her platform and went and stood over her, eyeing her with a look I couldn't comprehend, but certainly was neither anger nor sympathy, but a merging of the two making something new, something too complex to define.

Grace thought Abby was going to get into trouble, or worse, wet herself and be taken out once again by Mr Archibald, so she signed for her to sit.

Miss Sowerby rounded on her instantly, saying she could see her in the reflection of her glasses, and what had she said, never gesticulate, always speak. As it was Grace's second offence in one day she would have to spend the rest of the lesson with her hands tied behind her back. Grace blushed and as her wrists were knotted together struggled against the tears which were burning her eyes.

Abby took the restraint of her sister very badly. She banged in and out of her seat, sitting then springing to her feet whilst at the same time thumping on her desk. I didn't understand the performance at the time, the sign she was creating, but I have seen apes with eyes almost as beautiful as hers describe their cages in very much the same way – Donald took me to the zoo in Regent's Park a couple of times, despite the fact that on both occasions I cried for the gorillas, monkeys and polar bears. Miss Sowerby once again strolled from her platform and stood over her, watching her with the same complicated look as before, but this time suddenly reached out and slapped her across the head. In response Abby called her name, as if she were trying to make contact with someone in the woods, and began to laugh: it was unmistakable, though not something she was prone to.

Miss Sowerby shook her head and, speaking aloud that Abby would have to be removed, went out of the classroom, returning a few minutes later with Mr Archibald. As Abby was led out Miss Sowerby lowered her head refusing to look.

I don't think either of my sisters were quite the same after that.

In the ensuing lesson we had to painstakingly repeat the sounds Miss Sowerby made, deaf children searching for the right place to put the tongue, the right vibration, our hands in turn on Miss Sowerby's throat then our own – Grace released temporarily – comparing, copying, trying to get it right, taaa, daaa, teee, deee, over and over. At the end Grace asked whether she had been a good girl, and Miss Sowerby conceded that she had. Grace blushed with pleasure. Phillip pressed his lips together, but I think he was pleased as well.

Abby was brought back to us halfway through the lesson, but she refused to participate, preferring to quietly hum her name to herself, defying the classroom with identity. From then on she was marked out by the fact she didn't want or need to please. She didn't care what anyone thought about her name, about her, about her acts: she proclaimed herself with a new obstinacy, a new stubbornness, an individuality that even her sisters struggled to breach, though we weren't ever banished entirely.

Grace and I would have claimed that we didn't want to please either and that our commitment to ourselves was such that we would never be anything we didn't like, but that was never really the case. We couldn't help but want to please. Grace's refrain at the end of every lesson became, have I been a good girl, and it was a refrain she took home to Seamus, desperate for approval, for sanction, which certainly Miss Sowerby gave, albeit sadly, though I doubt Seamus ever truly did. It didn't matter that Phillip would tell her over the years that she was better than those she asked; even when Ingwall was long past Grace was still requesting of a grown-up world, of which her deafness somehow deprived her, whether she had been a good girl.

I don't claim to be very different. I still want to please now. When my hairdresser suggests I grow my hair it gives me great pains to stand my ground and proclaim myself. How many other instances are there when the desire to make someone else happy prevails and another few cells of being are lost, and the translation into something I never liked takes place?

Grace and I survived in Ingwall, despite the slaps, the blows, the ridicule, being turned into infants, on occasion eating with our hands tied behind our backs because we had been caught signing – in possession of sign, we called it, though I don't know who was the first to say that, my guess being Phillip – but Abby never compromised and so it had to come to an end.

Despite the fact that we were sisters, three, deaf, having discovered each other, they separated us.

Chapter Fifteen

I waited in the lane, again assuming my abandoned pose. I wanted to see Agnes but wasn't going to chance being alone with her indoors; besides Harold might not go out, so the chance wouldn't arise. Of course, if she guessed I had come from Harold all the better.

As I waited the cloud blew over, leaving scattered fragments and a three-quarter moon. I was pleased of the moonlight, yet conscious it revealed me, revealed my charade of waiting. I wandered farther than before towards St Bridget's, and then fearing I might miss her hurried back, only to then repeat the performance.

As I progressed towards St Bridget's I visualised a lichen crowned angel and thought of Abby crouched in supplication, the angel's charge. She was capable of devotion, of signing love, despite the fact that she learnt she didn't want or need to please. The love offered the angel was given without reservation, no strings attached, the love entered into in silence, which is always an act of trust.

I don't know how many times I made that tentative move towards St Bridget's, Abby's angel in my mind, before Agnes appeared. I know it seemed an age, but waiting is like that, uncertain, liable to tricks, liable to setbacks and sudden progression. I was patient though, despite my gravitation towards the angel, which was, after all, just cover. I had waited for this for so long, time was immaterial.

As soon as I saw her I set off, wanting to catch her well before she reached her door. I didn't want Harold to hear us, to be able to piece together his own time sequence and wonder. It didn't matter if I looked flushed and flustered, that was to the good.

As soon as she was aware of me she stopped and eyed me all the way, until I was right in front of her. She seemed both hostile and amused. She spoke first, which I found surprising. "I expected you to be long gone."

I smiled. "You're not the first to say that, but I never said. I still have things to do."

"You can't have much here, there isn't much."

"Oh, I don't know." She shrugged and made to move on. "How is Hazel? He said that's where you were, that you might be a while."

"Harold, you were talking to Harold?"

"He said you'd be a while."

She eyed me sharply, suggesting, maybe, that she wasn't going to fall for that, or that she already had, then gave a brief, bored smile and said: "Fanciful." She made to continue again.

"So, how is she? You didn't say."

"I told you before, she's not on her death-bed, just chesty."

"Yes, you did, not on her death-bed, I hadn't forgotten."

"So, it's cold and late, and he likes a bit of supper, nothing too much, cheese on toast, fried egg, nothing fancy, but something, so I'll get on."

"Do you ever think about your death-bed, Agnes?" She didn't reply, but looked at me steadily, trying to read what I was saying. "I do, I think about it a lot." She shrugged, as if she didn't understand, or was deliberately making light of it, deliberately smiling at my morbid train of thought. I smiled in return, a small, insignificant but fatalistic smile. "We used to be weighed down with the thought, what if? What if there hadn't been scarlet fever, influenza, measles? What if Mr Drake had been right and we'd found ourselves in such a country?" She shrugged her incomprehension. "Of course, you don't know what Mr Drake said, or what he ever did, do you?" Again she shrugged, giving it the appearance of listfulness, boredom, but I knew she was listening, taking it all in, trying to decipher my pregnant signs. "What would Harold have done if he'd known about Mr Drake?" Still she made no reply. "Do you really not know?" Again she made no reply, her expression now completely blank. I smiled as before. "I think I want to ask your advice again. You see I'm trying to work things out, for myself I mean."

"Advice?"

"Why not. You've been married a long time. Advice to a young woman."

"I've never given anyone advice."

"How does marriage work, Agnes? Is it just impulse and obedience?" She walked on, past me. "I just don't understand how you did it, how you do it, cheese on toast and the rest."

She rounded on me, glared, and looked as if she were about to hit out, but settled for saying: "I've just about heard enough from you."

"I just mean," I went on reasonably, "how did you manage, Martha hating your own family so much? How do you live with that?"

"You just do!"

"Impulse, obedience?"

She was about to reply, but thought better of it. She considered for a moment, and then very calmly suggested: "Not very real, talk like that."

"I think you survived, but didn't realise that mothers are supposed to do more than survive, they're supposed to protect their young."

She took a step towards me. "Don't you dare question me as a mother."

"What, you always made sure there were birthday and Christmas presents?"

"And do you think that was easy? Are you so flush down there that you think the past was easy?"

"Why did you send her away?"

"For the best."

"Or was it Martha sent her away?"

"Don't be so stupid. It was all down to the school. They said it was for the best. We had to go along with what they said."

"Why did Martha hate your family so much?"

"They're Catholics, that's all."

"She said she couldn't care less about that."

"Well, that's not true."

"I've heard she was quite fond of your father."

"Well, that's not true either." She shrugged and half-smiled. "She's her own worst enemy, really. Never been to our house, never made up with my Auntie Nora, stubborn, set in her ways, that generation."

"What was it between Nora and Martha?"

"None of your damned business," she replied emphatically and immediately walked on.

I called after her: "There's something I really don't understand. Please." She turned and eyed me impatiently. "Your father, Aidan, he was lovely with Grace, taught her to sign, taught her really well, Aidan, Peter and Paul, but mainly Aidan, and later he helped me, with sign I mean, but he wouldn't go anywhere near Abby. Why was that?"

She looked at me for a few moments more, and then turned away without any reply.

"Do you think he'll tell me?" I called.

"Don't go anywhere near him," she called without turning back.

"We converse in the same language."

She turned fiercely and called along the street: "I don't want him bothered, not whilst she's ill like this."

"It was Mr Drake said she was fond of Aidan."

"Well, who'd be stupid enough to believe him?"

"So you did know?"

She began to walk back towards me, though stopped still at some distance. "All I know is he'll be wanting some supper and I'm late and he won't like that, so I suggest you go now, go right away, back to London, and stop raking up things that couldn't be helped."

"Could it not be helped, Agnes?"

"I told you, it was the school who sent her away, the school's fault."

"He will be annoyed," I suggested and smiled. "He told me you're like clockwork, said exactly what time you'd be back. To be honest I think you were a bit ahead of time though."

"Not clockwork exactly, but that's how they get, wanting things done at a set time."

"Comforting, a routine."

"They find it."

"And you're always back in good time to do his bit of supper."

"That's right."

I smiled broadly. "You're very good, doing all that."

"You do what you have to."

"Yes, thank you, that's sound advice, thank you. I'll make sure I do that. And you saying you never give advice."

I turned and went on my way. I never heard her footsteps behind me at all, advancing or retreating, or looked back to see if I could read her intent.

I would see her again tomorrow night, alone, without fear of interruption.

I just had to wait, wait and read the signs.

*

The essential feature of language is time, which includes both tense and aspect, the ability to say where I was, where I am and where I intend to be. Time then is awareness and aspiration. In pursuit of time I have investigated the past. I wanted to know what the weather was like on the day we found Abby in the pig-yard covered in shit and snow. Did the meteorological office agree that it was indeed snowing

222

and I hadn't embellished the event, given it a certain story telling veneer?

In fact they couldn't say, not on the phone, and suggested I might be better exploring local archives, the information I wanted being so particularly local. The advice was sound, of course. There was so much else that fell into the same category. Was the brick-works as large as I maintain? When did they demolish some of the large sheds and chimneys? When did St Bridget's become a place of partial use? Who really owned the mines?

The grammar of history is chronology: presumably if we existed we had to be part of that grammar. The day they took Abby had to exist, had to have a pattern of cloud, a temperature, a quantity of light and dark.

I sign it as absence, but as I said, absence is knowledge of its opposite: so Abby's no longer being there was part of her belonging. Her figure was always there, then, always existed for us, curled, patient and strong, beneath the negligent gaze of an angel, a crowned angel, who I would say failed entirely to be her guardian, though perhaps Abby never imposed that duty on it. She was never demanding like that.

Language doesn't do it though, isn't enough, just seems like a make-do, a surface to put on things, so little of it seems accurate, just a habit, a routine. A sign though is different: a sign is deliberate, meant, accurate. A sign is not given lightly.

I can still see the look on Aidan's face when Grace told him she was ashamed to sign. At first he looked ashamed himself, as if he had been found wanting and was really quite used to the feeling, then he looked hurt, but finally indignant. It was unexpected: older generations seemed to demur so much to the younger, as if it was only natural that what they had accepted was naïve and false, but not this time. He admonished Grace, wagging his finger at her, the index-finger of his left hand, and told her she should never forget it was her language. For Grace the question *have I been good girl* was too strong to fight, though, and yet she was one of the best fighters among us, feisty and impulsive, but ultimately scared of embarrassment.

Language allows for culture: shame, guilt, anxiety, taboo.

We were educated in the Ewing system – not that we knew we were taught in any system – and had to accept it was right. If they said language was like gravy that had to be poured over children to make it stick then that was the truth. When they said we would never be able to work with direct access to the public, on public transport, as rent collectors, metre readers, postmen, librarians, waitresses, then they knew best.

All those months and years we spent in the woods, signing with Phillip, and out of school signing with Aidan, Peter and Paul, were acts of informal dissidence in a situation where dissidence was hopeless.

We didn't know to say: sign has prefix, suffix and plural.

Couldn't say: I think in sign, I dream sign.

I am not inferior, stupid, ashamed, nor do I lack anything. Sign is not an absence: my memory is sign: my memory is retrievable and can be verified by local records. Yes, of course it was snowing when they made Abby shit herself. Of course the brick-works went through periods of growth and recession.

My memory is composed of tense and aspect.

I remember they took Abby.

They took her away, away from us, from her sisters, from herself, when she was only ten. We couldn't complete our games. They have remained unfinished. In memory of her going I played all sorts, but Grace was unsure, so they became harsh reminders, pretending I was one of Pizarro's conquistadors discovering all over again the Book of Marvels, and nursing poor Poppy who was left behind, watching the tide come in all on her own. I didn't realise that when they took Abby they also took the greater part of Grace, of me, that when you remove one sister, the other sisters must suffer, be reduced, occupy a narrower world. It seems unforgivable that they took our games.

They never had any sense that things ended, that things that existed in time weren't forever. They mindlessly swiped away her childhood, treating it to their own pointless vandalism, without ever thinking that there was no retrieving it, no second chance. One day we would want to play skipping and the next day the desire was gone, at best played out years later in a parody of ourselves, just for a second wiping away time and the rule-book, but in reality the thing is irredeemable. We don't skip, we don't play hop-scotch, don't play pirates, knights templar, ladies, queens, princesses.

It's not that Abby never came back, because she did, but by then the games were no longer ours to play.

I suppose I should have been pleased they took her away; somewhere residential, Miss Sowerby explained, hoping I think that we could explain it to her, somewhere more suitable to her particular needs. It was selfish of me to want to keep her, but she was the one with the vision, the one who understood the horizon, the face of angels and the world of insects. I thought I would be nothing without her, cease to exist, answering the world out of habit and consent.

I had failed her completely, though. I never stopped Mr Archibald cleaning her up when she became excited and forgot herself, or stopped Mr Drake from insisting on sharing his silent films with her, or stopped Harold from beating her whilst Agnes stood by.

Maybe, after all, she wanted to go. Why else would she have gone to the matriarch as she did, which was unheard of, if it wasn't for the fact that Martha insisted she shouldn't be taken, citing her usual complaint that if you put deaf-mutes together under the same roof then they were bound to breed and produce a deaf-mute race.

Martha sent a message that simply said: Come and get her. Harold grimaced at the injunction and thought to himself he would go when he was good and ready. Still, he didn't take off his boots. Shortly after, the same boy – presumably someone Martha had called from the street – brought a second message: Come and get her or I'll kill her. Harold thought that was interesting. Was she serious? He scowled at the boy who waited on the step, having obviously been instructed by the matriarch to witness that her instruction was obeyed. Harold reading the fear and uncertainty in the boy's features growled, lifted his fist and gestured that he might club the offensive brat. The boy cringed and shrank away, pleading as he did that she had said. Harold swore at him but immediately set on his way, pushing him aside as he went.

When he reached the farm Abby was screaming. Her face was raw with the exertion. It was the first time she had been back there since Martha had rescinded her claim on her. It was a mystery to everyone why she had chosen that moment to return. The matriarch said she had gone completely mad.

The child is crazy, she screamed, possessed, a witch.

Harold seized hold of Abby by the shoulder and demanded that she shut up. She shrugged him off and screamed directly at him, glaring right into his face as if cursing him. He lifted his arm into the air, his left arm across his chest and above his right shoulder and threatened to smash it into her face. She immediately thrust her face forward and screamed ever louder. His hand came down like a catapult and struck her across the jaw. She was silenced for no more than a second, and then began the same concerted noise. Harold responded by grabbing her and smacking her repeatedly. At first she fought back, scratching, kicking and biting, the two of them flailing at each other, but then she ran out of fight and tried to cover herself. Harold kept on, until he was overcome by silence.

After he had finally stopped hitting her he held her for a few seconds then threw her down. He was breathless and stood still for a moment and then snarled aloud that it wasn't as if the stupid bitch could hear her own commotion. He immediately reached down, grabbed her by the collar and began dragging her away. As he was leaving he heard the matriarch's voice, slow and hushed now, saying that Abby was a child of the devil and needed sorting. Harold turned, glared at her and reminded her that she had said she would kill her. She didn't reply. He went on and also reminded her that she was the one standing in the way of sending Abby away, something that even the authorities considered the right thing.

Harold had been home no more than a few minutes when the boy returned again with a note that said: Get rid of her, whatever.

Abby was in her element when they came for her. She knew, of course. Why else would she have fled to her most natural domain, the conjunction of water, air and earth, the round world stretching out as far as the eye could see? They sent for us to tell them where they could find her. In my memory I can't say that the two who asked were frightening in any way, or seemed to wish her any harm. From that point of view it isn't surprising that Grace told them she would be either with the angel or by the sea.

She was dancing, flying close to the waves when we reached her. I could sense her bewilderment that her sisters had brought strangers to such a sacred place. Grace began to sob. What else was there for Abby to do but shout her name above everything, deflecting everything with the scale of who she was? I think she would have torn the faces of the two who had come for her, so insensitive were they in interrupting her, had it not been for Mr McBride who whispered to her, words she could never have heard, but somehow sensed. I was surprised when she allowed him to touch her, but then he only took her hand, and by then we were all changing, even her. How else could it be that she left Poppy, prostrate on the sand, the waves liable to claim her.

Maybe Poppy was intended to be set free, though, given to depth, to the caverns beneath the sea, a mermaid, careless and a-wing, Poppy, Poppy, Poppy.

I am sure that conversation put his mind at rest. Perhaps it was only coincidence, after all, that I should appear so persistently on his regular shopping trips. Besides he must have been fairly sure I wouldn't be around for much longer. I presumed he wouldn't be so guarded the next time.

The next meeting was two days later. He had just come out of the greengrocer, carrying a straw handbag, unperturbed by its femininity.

After a few initial comments about the coldness, but the clearness, and thank God the dryness of the day, I said: "The buses must be full of kids, so many people driving these days."

"The buses are empty," he replied, shrugging his indifference.

"But on Saturdays, I know you're a Saturday shopper as well, there must be loads of kids on a Saturday."

"I don't mind kids."

"I know, I know that, I know you like kids, but do they not torment you, call you names, some of those school lads are big lads."

"Of course not."

"Funny, I thought they would."

He made to walk on, but couldn't resist asking: "Why, why would they?"

"Because they'll know what you're like, with kids I mean, messing with kids. Everybody knows. Agnes told me that everybody knows, knows what you're like."

He glared at me fiercely, the little colour he had draining from his pinched face, but quickly controlled himself, then eyed me with a look of accelerating spite and said: "Agnes said nothing of the sort, did she? See, I know that isn't true."

"Were you never scared of Harold finding out? Harold has a flaming temper."

He grinned with increasing viciousness, then mused, repeating Harold's name as if he couldn't quite bring to mind the person I meant, and then declared: "I don't remember Harold much caring for her. You have a filthy mind, really, a filthy mind that can't work out that I was her friend, and all I did was show her pictures. Maybe you're a touch jealous, is that it, a touch envious?"

"I know I was never your type," I smiled wistfully.

"Gangly, plain, mouthy," he said, with unexcited triumph.

"Exactly, able to speak."

"Though not very well."

"No, not very well."

He pouted his lips, the smile still apparent, tilted back his head somewhat and made to move on, evidently quite pleased with the situation as he read it, and yet, strangely, he didn't let it go but asked: "You'll be heading off soon, I expect. Done your time."

"No, Mr Drake," I replied formally, "I'm not finished here. I have unfinished business."

"I'd have thought you'd spent enough time."

"I'm such a glutton for pleasure."

He eyed me with a look of deliberate sympathy, a look that would have enraged Donald, and said: "You should stop bothering people, no one is quite what they were." He said something more, but as he had turned his head away I missed it. As was so often the case, I was lip-reading. I never did hear half so well as I made out. He turned back, smiled again, and indicated his intention to go.

I said: "She really did tell us everything, everything."

He shook his head doubtfully, his look combining pity and scorn, together producing victory. "She never said a damned word, Harold told me, not a damned word, never."

"She was fluent."

He continued shaking his head, a note of temper entering the gesture. "Just shut up," he snapped. "Shut up."

He walked on. I called to him: "Would you believe everything Harold says?" He turned back and cocked his slim face questioningly. "He calls himself a Sempie, after all." He grimaced, bored by the comment. "Did the Sempies ever own a mine?"

He shrugged and screwed up his face: "In a way. They owned land above one anyway. Why?"

"Because they would have claimed they did, I guess."

He shook his head. "You don't know anything do you?"

"How little did Martha not mind Aidan?"

He grimaced again, turned away and walked on, his straw shopping bag banging against his knee.

*

I have a dream in which I am just on the verge of being discovered of having murdered someone, on the point of being found out. It has nothing to do with being twenty-five and deciding someone must die. It started before then. In my mind I assumed it was to do with the fact that I was unfaithful to Donald.

He wouldn't have believed it, of course. It went so much against the grain of how he saw me, how he wanted me to be seen, his naïve girl who didn't know how to be independent and then, when she was, was wrong. Perhaps that's why I did it. That and difference. A respite. An affair has no future, no reality, so you can make yourself up, be as the fancy arises. With Peter I had no fears, no misgivings, but then I had no past, just a pleasure seeking present. Perhaps all of life should be just such a fantasy, but then, perhaps it already is.

We met in the deaf club. To be honest he wasn't the first. I don't think I had a reputation for promiscuity, but I can't say for certain. I know I had a desire to lay the ghost of Somers Town church dances and put Michael's charity to rest. I was deaf, extremely hard of hearing, relatively skilled in lip-reading, capable at signing, with Grade II, certainly IIb, hearing, not a freak, inferior or stupid. The occasional relationships with boys from the deaf club eradicated the whole business.

232

Following the disastrous night in Hampstead Donald was more abrupt and angry than ever before. We only saw each other a couple of times leading up to Christmas and rowed on both occasions. I started going to the deaf club more. I didn't see him at all over Christmas then, a few days after New Year, he called in on his way from work unannounced. I was just about to leave. He wanted me to cancel. I shook my head. It was already arranged. How could I not go? He flew into a rage. He told me I didn't need the club – I don't know that he ever called it the deaf club – I was having them on, scarcely deaf at all. He accused me of being attitudinally deaf.

He was so pleased with the charge that he calmed down. I thought he had actually made it up, one of his own, a clever swipe. I didn't answer. He must have thought my silence a victory. He went on more reasonably, describing the club as a form of segregation, apartheid, surely I saw that. I didn't need it, I was post-lingual deaf.

I asked him who he was trying to convince, me or himself.

With that he flew into another rage. He said I only went there for pity, and it disgusted him.

He was wrong. I was deaf, am deaf.

I wasn't going to the deaf club for pity, I was going for sex.

There is something thrilling about making love in sign. Peter could mark my whole body with pleasure, his shape fastening across me, the tip of his tongue on my clitoris, then my nipples, his knees either side of my torso, one way then another, rump and groin, his hands extending down, then up, forming a signature of himself, a presence, and then penetration, a double sign, pleasure and identity. He also smoked, smoked a great deal, so we could taste addiction in each other's mouths.

I didn't love him, though, and never felt any need to.

I didn't think I loved Donald, until I returned that night and found him still there. Bizarrely, I had walked out on him, but left my own place. I hadn't expected him to stay.

He made the caustic comment that the club went on late. I shrugged. He wondered if it always went on so late. I replied that it wasn't usual, not the norm, but it was the New Year. He scoffed and said we must all be such party animals. As he spat that out he went for a drink and the penny dropped; he had been drinking a great deal, probably all night. I wondered why and asked him, why he felt the need to drink.

Because I had abandoned him.

The triteness of that disappointed, rather angered me.

I told him that I had simply kept an appointment.

He flared, and raged that it was an appointment over him.

I shrugged and carelessly accused him of jealousy.

His rage intensified, but to my amazement he agreed. Yes, he was jealous, insanely jealous, jealous that I wanted to go off with my own kind.

Even that didn't disgust me. I reminded him that he had insisted they weren't my kind.

He turned on me, his eyes ugly with drink, flabby, unfocused, his mind greedy on crumbs. He retorted that I wanted them to be my kind, though, wanted the whole stinking world to make out that we were different, disabled.

I smiled and said that if I had been born in another country at another time I would have been gassed.

He evidently knew his history, because he immediately countered that I wouldn't, I personally would have been all right.

I shrugged.

I would have wanted to be gassed, though, he added snidely, wanted to be a martyr, a saint.

How could I have said, I just wanted sex. The thought was amusing. I was being accused of all the wrong things. My faithlessness was of a completely different order. Maybe I should have said it, blurted it out, confessed that I had been with a deaf man for the last six hours and we had drunk London Gin, smoked Rothmans and had sex twice. As the admission formed itself in my mind though, the thought struck me that he didn't even believe it possible. His jealousy wasn't about sex. He didn't associate any such possibility with the club. The very notion was incredible. He just didn't want me to belong to something, anything, certainly not of his making. It was the usual contradiction with him.

I chose not to pursue it. I made light of it. I said the deaf club was pleasant, that was all, a break, a chance to just . . . I ran out of words, because I didn't quite know how to finish the sentence without being contentious. In the end I said it was a chance just to sign and be happy.

He came up to me, face to face. He smelt of whisky, his breath hot and acrid. He spoke slowly, a deliberate speech. The problem of opposition, he said, was belonging: to be against something forces you to belong to something, even though that something might not be natural at all.

I told him I wasn't against anything, I was for something. I really did believe in the deaf club, insisting on the word deaf. Deaf clubs had been the guardians of the deaf for generations.

He shouted out his objections. I wasn't deaf in the same way.

I simply nodded.

I had no need to scream.

In that moment I was politicised. I understood what belonging meant. I knew then that I had to go home and do what I had to do. They had to pay, those who had made Abby suffer. My love called out for retribution, correction, restitution.

I burst out laughing. Donald flared. I immediately reached out and touched him, tracing my fingers along the outline of his face, the face that drink was making slack and flabby. I smiled coaxingly and told him everything would be all right. He actually fought against my touch, or made a show of it, as if it were magical and he couldn't quite free himself, despite his twists and objections.

I gazed at him sympathetically, fulfilled by my mission, my desire to kill.

He met my gaze with weary, pleading eyes. He asked

about the baby. It was obvious from his expression that he just couldn't make sense of the baby.

What, what about the baby, I prompted?

Will the baby be able to hear?

I shook my head.

He wailed incredulously.

I smiled, thinking to myself, how would I feel if it was Peter's baby I was carrying, if the chance the baby couldn't hear was greater.

I didn't have an answer.

I said that I meant I didn't know, that was all, didn't know. There was perhaps more deafness in my family than I thought.

He said he wanted me to have a termination, he would arrange it, insisting it wasn't because the baby might be deaf, not that at all.

So what, I asked, gesturing the question, what?

He wasn't ready, that was all. He wasn't ready and didn't know if he wanted to stay with me.

In that moment, having not loved enough, I loved too much, spurred on in imagination by his absence. I felt it in my stomach, absence, the emptiness absence creates. I touched him as gently as I could and suggested he leave.

He did go, without speaking, but gesturing the need, the desire to put something into words, something that wasn't near the mark. I shook my head. There was no need. The discomfort and the relief were writ large for anyone to read.

The very next day I set off home.

I don't think, now, that my dream, a dream I still have on a regular basis, was the fear of being found out for having an affair. It was about being found out as a fraud. It was about discovering that the grown-up woman known as Judith Salt was really that same Judith Salt who traipsed a coal infested shoreline thinking this is the extent of the world, the extent of knowing, deaf to all else. Judith Salt, nothing and never. I have suspicions. I surmise that is true.

236

Chapter Sixteen

Judith Salt made a weapon. She needed an act of creativity to make sense of Abby's life.

Strange that I should disassociate myself like that, by naming me, casting myself in the role of character. Judith Salt and all that went into the understanding of that name made a weapon. As if her mind had reverted to the most archaic period of human development, she took herself off into a cave and fashioned an implement that she endowed with magical properties, a weapon charged with the mystical task of vendetta.

I need to correct myself. I made a weapon. I have no intention of trying to suggest that I wasn't in my right mind, my actions those of an automaton, driven mad by vagaries and skirmishes. I am not about to claim that Judith Salt would have been a wholly different woman if circumstance had only allowed. Circumstance did not allow. I was what I was made and acted on that mission. I made a weapon, a weapon capable of killing my enemies, who were legion but had to be made specific. I made a weapon; I was creative.

I went to the old mine buildings at dawn. They remained as I remembered, dilapidated locked sheds and the tower, its iron gate long breached, still twisted on its hinges. Appropriately the sky was blood-red, deep red, black-red, the air bitterly cold, the iron soil solid, though devoid of visible frost. I waited by the tower entrance, viewing the morning sky, thinking of Abby, the day we lost her close by, and Grace Powers crying for her mother, neither of us yet knowing Abby had discovered burial, the hidden history of our world. Eventually there were spangles of yellow light across the horizon, their sudden brilliance veining the crimson, then overwhelming it. It was time to seek shelter.

I ducked through the door, a brush shank in my right hand and small tool-bag in my left. The tower still had the same stink of rotten vegetation and clay as it had years before, as if its atmosphere were caught in time. I climbed to the upper chamber. A streak of brittle winter light poured through one of the square openings, a shaft insufficient to eradicate the gloom. It was colder than I remembered, the outside world more intrusive.

I lay the shank along the ground, measured it with my eye, walked around it three times, then knelt on the clay floor and measured it with my two hands, spreading them from the centre to the two apex, mythologizing it, personifying it. After that I picked it up and placed the base into my lap, which had a metal clasp for the brush head to fix into. I tipped the contents of my tool-bag onto the floor beside me. There were a pair of pliers, a ball of string, dress-maker scissors, a roll of electrical tape and a carving knife. Everything had come from home, but only the knife would be missed, the rest having been stowed away in an old shed in the yard. Still, the knife would be returned soon enough, put back in its drawer to become another everyday object, having been washed of its ritual significance.

I took the pliers and eased open the round clasp to make room for the thicker, square shaped knife handle, which I jammed in as far as I could get it, carefully avoiding grasping the blade with my fingers. It went in almost two thirds of its length. I tapped it firmly against the rear of the clasp with the pliers, using them as a hammer, and then pressed the clasp with the pliers to seal it as best I could. Then I took the string and plaited it around the clasp and the handle, criss-crossing it from front to back until there were two tight, neat chevrons to either side, then I cut the string with the blade of the pliers and knotted it together.

I stood up and thrust the blade into the clay. The fixture remained solid. I pulled it out as if I were dragging it back through viscera, measured its height against myself, which despite my stature, was up to my ear, and then laid it against the wall in readiness. I put my tools back into the bag and put that with the weapon and left, risking their discovery.

I didn't think it was so great a risk. It was a weekday so there wasn't likely to be any kids exploring there, and I didn't envisage anyone else blundering in. It would have been very unlucky.

I wandered to the pond and walked along its bank. I considered walking along the back of the drainage tube, maybe even climbing inside, but dismissed the idea as fanciful. I didn't need to look for Abby, she was everywhere, shapes of her, patterns, her figure rotating against the early morning sun, substance and shadow, action and result, indelible – evidence.

Pulling myself together I quit the place and went into town, where I acknowledged Mr Drake, much to his obvious annoyance, which wasn't helped by my saying that I would be seeing him again soon, and bought myself a shoulder bag with a great silver buckle in the shape of a lozenge, from a market-stall-holder for a fraction of the price I would have paid in Camden Lock.

*

I asked my delightful hairdresser whether she would ever marry, settle down, have children. She stopped what she was doing – the spirited sprint around my hair, the scissors moving so quickly as to be invisible – and gazed at herself in the mirror. For a moment she was transported somewhere. I rather regretted the question because she lost something of her eccentricity standing rapt like that.

I guessed she must have been imagining herself in the role, not of wife but bride, in a bolt of ivory, her two-tone hair as vivid and singular as always, set-off beautifully against the subtle shades of the gown. She must have been seeing herself stepping towards the altar, imagining the man waiting for her. Was he of the same crop as her current boyfriends, or would those adventures have ended, to be replaced by an altogether more solid animal?

As I gazed at her, lost to her own thoughts, I craved admission, but for that to have occurred we would have to be more than purchaser and provider but friends, and that really can't be.

Judith Salt is a good customer, but an old woman, slightly batty – certainly in no need of such grooming – her life belongs to a different time, a different era, the substance of it to a different geography, though parts of me object to such assertions. I would love a moment of friendship with that valiant girl, that jigsaw piece in the crazy, cut-up individuality of modern London. Or is it that I just feel motherly towards her, shyly concerned, mildly shocked and surreptitiously jealous? I would hope not. Besides, I am old enough to feel grandmotherly about her.

At that moment I considered confessing. I would tell her about the substance of my life, the terrible crime, the long punishment, my motives, my vision, but would that have bought friendship or merely notoriety? Would I not simply have become an example to be cited of never judging a book by its cover, an exposition to be returned to from time to time with her other paying clients? The risk was too great. Besides, I had no right to intrude onto her world.

She addressed me with a look of genuine sadness, perhaps tenderness. No, she did not see herself married – certainly not that, meaning the institution, presumably, which she reinforced with a sharp smile – did not see herself with any man particularly, but the prospect of no children was horrifying.

I sagely nodded my agreement. But why not a particular man, even if not the trappings of ivory?

Because, she said, as if it was an admission rather than

flippancy, she saw herself as a little mad. After all, she talked to mirrors all day about hair, holidays and him indoors. Was she not a little too frivolous to be the marrying kind?

I told her there was nothing remotely frivolous about her and that she had affected the most courageous of all acts, a lifestyle. I suggested that if the world was not of your making then all you could do was confront it the way she did, and then, following a brief pause, I went on to add that it would never cross her mind that she might exist through the virtues of others.

She shrugged dubiously. This was not hairdresser talk. If it was in her training it was certainly on the afternoon given over to difficult situations. Of course, I didn't do her justice and as so often she was quite equal to it. She fearlessly threw it back to me. What about me, what did I have to say about men and children, surely I should have been giving her advice?

I nodded and smiled, but said nothing. She shrugged and apologised, and said, of course, if I would rather not, then made to carry on with her minuscule trim.

No, I said immediately, halting her work, though without any idea of how I would follow up that prohibition. Eventually I made a short statement, as if I were in a court of law, not the domain of my delicious hairdresser, at all.

We don't ever forget the past: we change our relationship to it; sometimes it is friendly, more usually fraught.

She waited for more, eager, unashamed and comfortable, and, which is very fanciful of me, though I'll forgive myself because I am at that age, took on a look of Abby, quizzical and visionary, capable of seeing through walls.

Would Abby remember herself? She ran along the lane, turned, waved, ran sideways until the corner and was gone: except she was never entirely gone. An outline remained carved invisibly in the invisible air, despite her running through it, time after time, spreading and reforming herself, a woman and child tied together in infernal togetherness.

I whispered, Ms Sempie, I love you – not wanting anyone to hear and so get her into trouble – but even if I shouted it she wouldn't hear, so what kind of protection was that? Who could ever have predicted such a dead-end?

I smiled and shook my head.

It was an invitation to talk to mirrors.

Nothing was unfriendly.

*

When Abby returned she was the same and different. We were teenagers then, not exactly women but not children either. We were still sisters, but I think somewhat estranged.

Grace was pretending she wasn't deaf, which gave Seamus some hope, though deep down he suspected it was a lie. She was working in a thermometer factory and Phillip was with her. They were a pretty couple and got on well enough, despite Grace's failure to persuade him to stop using sign. He just laughed and teased her, calling her a snob, though we all knew by that stage that it was more fundamental than that.

I was working in a bakery, six days a week with early starts, so I couldn't see Abby, not as I would have wanted, though I did have two half-days a week. I would try to be with her then, but it wasn't always easy.

Sometimes I couldn't find her, though I wasn't aware she had found any new haunts, only that she had resumed the old ones. She didn't prostrate herself before the angel anymore, though, simply sat there, indeed, more often stood, gazing at her, as if making inquiries the angel wasn't equal to answer. Her preference remained the shoreline, though she did go to the tower quite regularly, which I took to be a grownup preference for shelter. I guessed at times she was in The Shed, lured by the promise of silent films and boiled sweets, forgetting entirely that she never had taken Mr Drake's sweets.

Of course, I didn't know about Stephen then.

My mother told me she had returned home under something of a cloud. I assumed that was inevitable. Harold and Agnes could hardly have been pleased by her return. Somehow they'd managed it that she hadn't even been home for holidays. She might as well have been dead, except there was no mourning, no sadness. They lived as if she had never been. The last thing they wanted was to have her back. My mother said it was more than that, though: something had happened at the residential home.

Abby never gave any hint of it, but nor did she deny it. Then I found them together. They were on the beach, sitting close to the water line, slumped down, looking across the dark surface, hand in hand, Poppy across both of their laps – I had kept her safe for Abby for all those years. Abby had taken possession of her as if it had only been a matter of minutes since they were separated. Time could never dull her.

I was surprised and a little annoyed. My first instinct was to tell him to let Abby go, but quickly realised she wouldn't have thanked me for that. In fact, they both ignored me. In the end I had to sit down directly in front of them, an obstacle between them and the horizon, to gain any response, which in Abby's case was to actively look away and in his to smile.

After a moment's hesitation I smiled back, then the gestures became fixed and ridiculous, the two of us simply smiling.

It was Stephen who had the sense to break off that communication. He looked down at Poppy, placed her more fully in Abby's lap, then jumped to his feet and ran back to the shingle and began throwing stones into the oncoming waves. I think, once upon a time, Abby would have deplored that, but she simply watched them land, Stephen behind her, with a look of quaint forbearance on her face.

Later, Stephen let me understand that he had walked a long way to be with Abby. I smiled at his gesture of exhaustion. He had no idea where he was going to stay or what he was going to do. They just wanted to be together. It was a touching, if hopeless story. It struck me that it wasn't a Sempie story at all, but a Shaughnessy story, so everyone was bound to disapprove.

He told the tale in primitive signs, because he couldn't speak at all, had no recourse to the beautiful and intricate word play Abby was capable of, but he was a wonderful interpreter. He read Abby's poetry with all of its complex metaphor and intricate syntax as if it were the simplest of human utterance. He thought her brave, defiant and eloquent. It took me a while to realise that those things meant love, that an abstract word is made up of so many component parts, some complementary, some contradictory, but each one needed: so love has no dictionary meaning, no discrete meaning, only relative and dependent meaning. They loved each other and they were full of images.

I tried to help. He slept in the tower and washed in the pond. I brought him bread and rolls, but it was difficult to find anything else. The situation was as ludicrous as it was romantic. He might have slowly starved if Harold hadn't spotted them together, hand in hand, lovers wandering along the lane to St Bridget's.

Harold didn't give it a second thought but thrashed Stephen on the spot, despite Abby's attempts to save him, and her success in tearing Harold's left cheek with her nails, only just failing to gouge out his eye. Harold threatened Stephen with worse, much worse, if he ever saw him again, and then dragged Abby back to the pig farm, which wasn't as easy as it once had been. Surprisingly, he didn't hit her but locked her in a shed, putting a crowbar across the door, where he kept her for the next ten days.

When she was released Stephen was no where to be found. Foolishly I thought he must have taken Harold at his word, despite the fact that he wouldn't have heard any of what Harold had said, and decided to leave her alone. (I knew that despite her incarceration he would never have believed her capable of abandoning him.) Abby knew differently though, knew he must have hidden himself away, as she had so often done herself, nursing his wounds, nursing himself back to health. I discovered her in the tower with Poppy aimlessly drifting round the room as if it had some secret passage hidden behind the wall that even she couldn't penetrate, her expression fixed into a stare of hypnotic determination.

It dawned on me then, that she rarely said her name anymore, so rarely insisted on identity.

Chapter Seventeen

I reckoned I had one chance with Harold and one alone, after which I would be dead-meat. I knew that many things had to come into play at once, many pieces of luck, which in itself was an archaic thought.

Of course, he might not come at all, deliberately shunning the opportunity, or inadvertently unable to keep the appointment. I don't for a second think he doubted my sincerity. He was too arrogant not to think I meant it – a poor, deluded invalid, still capable of giving him what he wanted. I hadn't thought of him as arrogant before then, a bully and a thug, but not necessarily arrogant, but since seeing the way he had eyed me I had changed that opinion. Certainly he reacted to everything on impulse, but that didn't exclude arrogance, not as I had thought, anyway.

I had to trust to surprise and belief. He had to believe in my intention, the certainty that the weapon I had fashioned was destined to slice through his entrails. Otherwise he might just snatch it out of my hands, break it across his thigh and deal with me as he felt fit. The prospect was terrifying. I felt my guts wrench, and on a number of occasions thought my bowels were going to empty. I told myself, over and over, I hadn't done anything yet; I didn't need to do it. I could turn around and return to London, leaving the weapon behind, a strange, mystical object to be discovered at some point in the future. Then I remembered the bond of sisters, the obligation, and my guts froze up and became heavy and I didn't fear shame anymore.

I needed moonlight, the brilliance of a three-quarter moon,

a waxing moon. I had to be able to see him in the doorway, because I certainly couldn't listen for him, hear his step, his whispering. The moonlight had to come through the square openings. The forecast was favourable, clear skies, frost, moonlight and stars, but forecasts are so often incorrect.

Above all, I had to do it, had to perform, had to set in motion the sequence of actions I desired, or else his expectations would remain in existence, and how would I defy those? If, at the last moment, I panicked, I was doomed. I had to know that, had to believe it. It was the spur that would keep me focused, keep me true.

Of course I went to the tower far too early. Agnes didn't go to Aidan and Hazel's before six. Harold wouldn't appear before quarter past at the earliest. I couldn't stop my mind running wild with the idea of his reaching the tower before me, couldn't stem an image of him holding my javelin, its point towards me, his face creased up with pleasure. It was nonsense, naturally. I had said to come when Agnes left. He couldn't come at any other time. Why would he? Nevertheless, I was there at dusk.

The day was circular, beginning and concluding with the same crimson intensity at the fringes, blood-red daubs outlining the jagged earth, a slate-grey density above, with tendrils of whiteness sketched through. I guessed it had sequences of sounds, call and answer, but I made no attempt to listen, indeed I refused the possibility. The world was a surface, but sound was inward, a succession of names, Abby's name, hammering inside me with its own dreadful music.

I was relieved I'd brought a blanket as I'd promised, otherwise I would have been too cold to move, too cold to act. I'd had no intention. The very thought of it was repulsive, but at the last minute, I'd thought better of it. For show, I told myself, though without defining just what show that was going to be. I lay it on the clay floor, sat on it with my knees up, and brought it up around me, keeping my hands wrapped in it, the weapon clenched between them, raised in front of my face, the shaft cushioned by the fabric. I was a soldier, a sentinel, an ancient guard watching the gate, ready, no retreat possible. I just had to wait.

He was later than I expected. I'd begun to assume he wasn't coming, my whole being relaxing at the thought. Different ideas went through my mind, the uppermost being that he'd decided I wasn't worth it, maybe had never been worth it and he'd being playing a game, like me.

Then, just after a quarter to seven, he appeared in the doorway. The moonlight lit up his face, a pale, luminous grey, his expression amused, playful, uncertain, I really couldn't say. It was important that his expression was always beyond my comprehension. That was the only way it made sense.

Although everything happened very quickly, within seconds, it was all very distinct and clear to me. Luckily he didn't stand in the doorway simply putting his head through, but kept coming. As soon as he was halfway across the threshold I leapt to my feet and jabbed the blade at his neck. He reeled back against the door frame, but I went with him, pressing him against the wall, the blade resting comfortably along his left scapular, the point just at the skin. A smear of blood appeared beneath the blade where I had obviously nicked him. He twisted his head back trying to keep away from the point, his eyes flashing between the weapon and me.

I told him to lie on the floor, face down. He didn't move. I screamed the order. Slowly he inched forward, all the time the blade pressed heavily across his shoulder. I kept on shouting my orders, instructing him to his knees, then down onto his belly, his hands behind him. He moved as slowly as he could. I shook the shaft, drawing a new spurt of blood. He winced in pain and anger, and began shouting back, swearing at me, threatening. I sliced him more deeply. With a yelp of pain he lay flat. I kept on shouting all of the time. I wanted his hands. This was the moment I was dreading.

248

Keeping my left hand firmly on the shaft I reached out for my tool-bag which was alongside the blanket. I took the string and lay the end across his back then made him lay his two hands over it. I told him that I was going to tie him and if he tried anything I would kill him straight off, his only chance being to humour me. I repeated it so that there was no doubt, impressing on him the fact that if he didn't humour me I would certainly kill him, I was so scared.

Still with the spear at his throat I began to wind the string in and out of his clasped wrists, a tight figure of eight binding them together. When I was pretty sure he wouldn't be able to seize me, I eased my left hand over, still trying to keep the blade in position and held the string with it, and cut it with the dress-making scissors with my right hand. After that it was relatively easy knotting the end.

I stood up, put both hands onto the shaft, and stretched my back. He began to moan and wail, certain I was about to thrust the weapon deep into his throat. I made no attempt to pick out words. I snapped at him to shut up. After all, I was only relaxing, trying to rid my body of the strain of taking a prisoner. The fear, the expectation, in his expression was wonderful to see.

I lay the weapon to the side, within easy reach, then took the string and with both hands wound it tightly around his wrists, the first lot not likely to be enough, just a holding measure. Then I wrapped his ankles together. When I was happy with the knots I took the electrical tape and wrapped layer upon layer around his wrists and ankles. Then finally I bound his fingers together on each hand, so he couldn't pick at anything. When I was happy he was securely trussed I told him to roll over and sit up. I gazed at him for a moment, enjoying the look of hatred apparent in his face. He said something, presumably threatening me again, but I simply smiled and signalled my incomprehension. I took the string and leant over him wanting to tie him around the knees. As I did he kicked out but didn't manage to unbalance me. In a fit of temper I picked up the weapon and slashed him across the cheek. He screamed in agony. I screamed back that he shut up, just shut up.

He fell silent and stared at me, his entire expression seized by doubt, his face constricting, the realisation of what was possible hitting home. His left cheek was smudged with blood, an uneven line sprouting from a straight gash, its colour hidden in the gloom. I raised the javelin again. Terrible, tantalising thoughts burst in my mind. If I chose I could ram the blade right into his heart, or I could slice him portion by portion, reducing him, snipping away at his weight, cutting him down to a manageable size. I could disfigure him in any way I chose, make his body vile, unapproved, tortured, messed up, mutilated.

I had to say to myself: not here, not now. I could decide when. I could describe it, name it, keep it safe and keep it secret. Not here, not now. Only I knew when. I was in charge: I defined time and place.

I made him shuffle beneath the window. Underneath the frame, probably where there had been a shelf or ledge of some kind, there was a line of long, rusted nails. I had already curled some of these into hooks with the pliers whilst I was waiting. I wrapped more string around the point of contact of his wrists and secured it to the hooks. I just had to trust that they would hold. If he did manage to break free I assumed he would have a difficult job negotiating the steps, almost certainly likely to fall and kill himself. He wouldn't take any such risk. I could see it in his eyes, a bully but a coward.

I was satisfied. I had successfully taken my first prisoner.

I went up to him again and leaned over him. He made no attempt to kick out this time, obviously having learnt to respect my rage. I told him to put his lips together, press and pout them so they could be kissed. Then I slapped electrical tape over them so that I didn't have to hear another word from him. It didn't stop him trying, but there was no point at all.

I rifled his pockets until I found his keys. Then, before leaving him, I took the blanket and wrapped it about him. No sense in letting him die of the cold.

I was waiting behind the door for Agnes' homecoming. By then I felt every inch an ancient warrior, having run through the dark, across mine slag, and along the lane from St Bridget's, holding my weapon at waist height, a hunter and a soldier. I let myself in through the kitchen door and waited. There were lights on in the house, which troubled me at first, until I reasoned that Harold would simply have left them out of laziness.

I had a moment's trouble with Agnes as I led her from the modernised living-room into the kitchen. As I guided her through the doorway, my blade behind her back, she had the temerity to try and make a dash for it. I hadn't let my success with Harold go to my head and never underestimated Agnes for a second. I suspected she would try something so as soon as she moved I was onto her, and caught a thick bundle of her hair in my hand. Naturally I hadn't been fool enough to hold the weapon anywhere but at the knife-head so that Agnes was always within reach. Of course I had to teach her a little lesson. I swung her round, bent back her head, exposing her slack neck and brought the knife against it. I told her plainly that if she tried anything like that again I wouldn't hesitate to run the blade right across her throat. I gave her a small nick for good measure. It was unfair not to let her know how serious I was.

I bound and gagged her, tied her to a kitchen chair, then tied the chair to the table. I had already closed the curtains in the kitchen. I switched off the light and slipped out, locking the door behind me.

Mr Drake was a much easier proposition altogether. His kitchen door was unlocked. I let myself in as quietly as I could, tip-toed into the living-room, put my arm around his chair and held the blade at his throat. He made no attempt to speak, or defend himself in any way. As well as the malice that lay just beneath the surface of his expression I sensed something else, resignation, expectation, maybe even perverse hope. I wasn't prepared to ask.

I couldn't hear their defences; I was deaf. If they had pleaded, discovered an eloquence completely alien to them, I am afraid it could only have fallen on stony ground.

I wasn't listening.

I deposited my weapon in one of Harold's pig-sheds, and then I went home to bed. After such exertions I needed an early night.

I would like to say I dreamed of birds in flight, mermaids swimming, Siren songs, but I don't remember dreaming at all, and refuse to lie about that.

*

The next morning I went to a phone box and rang Donald. He was vague and bleary. Had I woken him, I asked? Yes and no, he said, it was early, but he should be up, getting ready. I told him he would have to shout to be heard. I couldn't hear if he didn't shout, not on a phone. I think he said something about not wanting to shout. I wondered if he was alone. He threw the question back at me. Was I alone? I told him he didn't have to be angry, I was only asking, wondering if he didn't want to be overheard, and then I assured him that I was alone, very alone. He didn't pick up on the semi-dramatic addendum, maybe because the pips went for more money or he hadn't heard. I told him that I missed him. I said it quietly, so quietly I failed to hear it myself, so maybe he didn't catch it either, or if he did, decided to ignore it. He wondered if I'd had time to think, then immediately snapped that he felt ridiculous shouting down a telephone line. You're right, I said, there should be something more for us. He tried to speak reasonably, but couldn't quite manage it, having to shout. He said he couldn't do it and had to go, had to get ready. I didn't interrogate that idea that he couldn't do it. I said it was all

252

right, I had some pigs to feed anyway. The pips went again. The last thing he said was that he thought I was joking. I held the phone to my ear for sometime, listening to nothing but the idea in my head that I was joking. Then I put the receiver down. I really did have some pigs to feed. There was no reason they should be overlooked. Besides, I had a weapon to collect.

Chapter Eighteen

Harold had wet himself. He cursed me when I tore the tape from his mouth. Unperturbed I strolled quite calmly to the other side of the chamber and leaned against the wall. I told him I'd fed his pigs, so he didn't need to worry about that. He swore again and threatened to kill me. My calm spirit sank. A child's refrain of *sticks and stones may break my bones* petered away in my head. I wasn't prepared to treat this as a game. Someone was going to die. Besides it wasn't remotely true. Of course a name could harm you. It claims you, fixes you to its own doggerel history; makes you something you can't help.

I lifted the weapon and held it like a javelin, eyeing it along the shaft, aimed at his chest. "How do you like being called names?" I asked. "Sempie, for instance. How do you like that?"

He stared at the point of the blade, as if it were the object that had to be watched, outfaced, and not me, not my shifts of expression, signalling now or maybe later.

I lowered the weapon, made my way slowly to him then waved the blade in front of his face. I leaned close to him. I could smell his breath which was fetid. There was dry black blood smeared across his cheek. I smiled and uttered: "You don't even know your own name, and now I possess your body as well. There really isn't much going for you today. No name, no body. Nobody. Tut, tut. And you such a big man. Christ, I've such a desire to slice your face into a pattern, but I'm fighting it, honestly, but I'm not sure how much of a fighter I am. Do you get that?"

"They'll be looking for me."

"Speak up, all right, speak up."

"I said they'll be looking for me."

"Who? Who'll be looking for you? The last time I saw her Agnes was all tied up, so she won't have missed you."

"What have you done, you bitch?"

"Names again. Now, what do I make of that? What should I do with my acquisition?" I stood up, holding the shaft of the spear loosely in my hand, the blade dangling over his chest. "You see I'm in charge, I own the weapon, I own you." I turned and walked away from him. I was serious. The urge to make him pay straight away was so great I had to put him out of arms length. I resumed my position against the wall, watching him, his patient interrogator, the weapon upright beside me. "I'm prepared to listen to you, if you'll speak up. My hearing aid is in and switched on and the batteries are new, but you'll still have to speak up. That's the only chance you have, to make yourself clear. So, why did you hurt Stephen?"

He gazed back at me, at first blankly, then with a quickening of his eyes, his dulled intelligence obviously working, and then he slowly shook his head.

"You don't know, do you? You know you've hurt so many people you can't work it out, can you? But I don't for a second believe you hurt people just because you can, there has to be more. Christ!"

*

It shocks me yet that I was banal enough to believe that Stephen could have deserted Abby. I should have known better. I had seen the way they loved each other, that relative and dependent union of the two of them, an image made up of so many moments of time – residential school, the shore, the tower – a rebus. I should have known he would never have deserted that. He would have been deserting himself. I wonder if that was why Abby had stopped declaring her name, because she shared an identity.

I saw them together after he had returned, strong and

healthy again just as Abby surmised, in the room in the tower, lying on the blanket that I had brought for them, their accomplice. They were rolling together, stretching and colliding, like kittens or puppies, creating spontaneous, arbitrary shapes, so that it was difficult to know where one ended and the other began. It was the most primitive of all gestures, that animal caress, playful, profound, uncontrived. It couldn't last. They were illicit lovers, illegal.

At the time I was guilty of thinking it fortunate that I was the one to interrupt them. I shuddered to think what Harold would have done if he had been the one to discover them there.

As Stephen stood up and approached me, signing something like welcome, I saw Abby's face contort with the gnawing pain of absence, absence rather than separation, because she understood, recognised in her sister's fault, that they weren't free to be together. What chance did they have? They weren't even able to listen out for an intruder.

Like a fool, I thought I had saved them, saved her: I was as culpable as the rest.

Abby stood up and came beside him, pushing her head beneath his arm, her eyes peering at me as if I had hurt her. I reached out, signalling a need to touch her, but she looked at my hand as if it were an alien object. She said nothing, and that nothing was wretched.

They must have come together, though, despite the likelihood of discovery.

When they realised she was pregnant they locked her up.

*

"Why did you lock her up when you found out she was pregnant?"

He stared at me for a moment, wanting to defy me, yet at the same time wary of me and uncertain. In the end a moderated defiance won out and he retorted: "Why do you think! We were ashamed."

256

"Ashamed?" He glared at me, indicating that the word didn't need explaining. "You could have married them off. You didn't have to leave him wandering round the pig-sheds, grieving for her. That was vicious, spiteful." His expression remained defiant, but again shot with uncertainty. I stepped towards him. "It was strange you didn't beat him up! Did you enjoy his suffering that much?" I kept on walking.

"I don't remember," he called out, successfully stalling me, the weapon. He shrugged and repeated: "I don't remember."

"Just a shrug," I uttered. "What happened is just a shrug."

"I wasn't really involved. It was Agnes. She thought it better, that's all."

"You always live to someone else's plan, don't you, but you don't really know whose and quite frankly don't really care. You'd smile at God, be ignorant of science, scoff at politics and screw your face up at fate. You're just here in a permanent present."

"She was right," he called, moaning it. "She wasn't fit to look after herself, wasn't fit to have a baby."

"But she did. At least you never stopped it happening." He didn't respond but stared straight at me, his expression again balanced between defiance and uncertainty. I peered at him, probing him. "But you tried, didn't you," I said. "I can see it in your face, the fact that you tried to get rid of the baby. You did, didn't you?"

He considered for a moment and then snapped: "She wanted it for the best."

"She?"

"Agnes, for the best, and it would have been better, wouldn't it? But it was too late, and . . . well, it didn't happen."

I smiled: "And she would have bitten your hands off. You would have knocked her out though, wouldn't you? Presumably whoever you got wouldn't hear of that, a step too

257

far even for your hired help, a drunken vet I suppose, not likely a midwife. I see, another shrug. You dispense with the past so easily."

"It's over."

"No Harold, it's here, I'm here, not permanently, maybe an existence you can't conceive, but you'd better believe it."

He screwed his face in frustration, despair and sheer ignorance. I don't suppose he had ever felt so powerless, so impotent, so entirely out of control. I went closer to him. His eyes fastened on me, vigilant and panicked. He tried to back away, but it wasn't possible. He was in confined space, imposed in it. I went closer. I lifted the spear. He looked terrified. It was obvious he wanted to speak up, but even he realised the insubstantiality of that, the inaccuracy. What would he have managed, his repertoire was so seriously lacking? He gave himself to instinct. His face showed it all.

"How could it be for the best?" I demanded.

"Agnes said," he wailed.

"Said what?" I shouted, feeling suddenly exhausted, the weapon indescribably heavy. "What, what did Agnes say?"

"That she wouldn't understand, wouldn't behave right. That she might hurt it."

"She wouldn't have hurt Stephen's baby."

"She did."

I rammed the blade an inch away from his eyeball. "No, she did not."

He looked along the upper edge of the knife and slowly uttered: "But it wasn't Stephen's baby." Then he glared at me, his eyes wide with fear, loathing and temper, and screamed: "Who the hell is Stephen?"

*

Memory unites and divides us. It is the truth and the lie we stand our ground for: and it is the thing from which we hide ourselves away. We are editors of time, who don't really understand time at all, can't unravel its shape or pattern.

I search for Abby, and for me, and Grace Powers in the days before she was ashamed of her language, in the places we used to be, but what exactly am I searching for? The simple answer is, I suppose, enthusiasm and disappointment, the steps that fell either side of a very slim divide. Did it all turn out as we said, or was it never remotely likely to?

At first we had very few words at our disposal, then we gained some more and lost others. We were like so many village kids at their supposed play, in the main bewildered, sometimes bemused, often afraid, attracted by a very limited vocabulary indeed. It took us a long time to realise so much was acquired by rote and a rulebook, though we were always aware that Abby's poetry was of a different order, of a different place, better than anything we were taught. It was at least honest. I could do with some of her creativity now, lines of verse that would make everything, if not worthwhile, at least possessed of space and motion.

So I interrogate the landscape, standing on slag banks, eyeing the surrounding escarpments, troughs, spoil and the enclosing thread of horizon, but its contours quickly merge, blur into oneness, rock and soil, mountain and sea, its possessing silence pierced by something I don't recognise because I have been immune to sound for so very long, but might be a curlew, oystercatcher or wren, certainly a dying breed, to add to all the other dying breeds, the earth voicing its discarded ghosts.

Iron Age settlers crafted long straight fields here, which the Romans took as their own, who then left forsaken altars, fractured brickwork, mosaics, splinters of people, fragments of belief. Then three, maybe four hundred years later the Norse renamed it, made it Viking land, hunting deer, hare and fox, and farming, after which there were hundreds of years of mixed arable and grazing, producing a self-sufficient Medieval people immune to kings and popes, until the growing Elizabethan markets demanded sheep, cattle, pigs, domesticated meat in abundance. Two hundred years of

259

selling; and then there was ore and coal, new industries to place alongside farming, though the iron-ore and coal mining boom quickly degenerated into a hundred years or more of decline, to a point of no history, zero time, which we always conceive for ourselves, convinced that we represent the end of the line.

It's all sham, though. Of course they bruised and scarred the landscape, but what of themselves, their personal intrigues, their skirmishes and desires? There have been so many lies told here, so many abuses and so many deaths, and it has all passed away as if it were nonsense and of no consequence, and the history that survives is too short to recall leaving only a degraded here and now. Without witness and record that too will pass away, of course, and I find myself saying, thank God. Like Nora, I crave freedom, the undifferentiated crowd.

I prefer to live with scepticism. I don't know why scepticism became the norm, but for me it seems there was no other way.

Then my sister signs to me, and I can't help but sign in return. Like everyone we have our attributes.

At some point you have to deal with yourself as a stranger, and strike away the permanent present and lay bare all the paths, conduits and sewers that led to it.

I could never abandon my sister.

*

I fished around the kitchen drawers until I found a satisfactory knife – I couldn't really have made my way across the countryside like a warrior in broad daylight, even one as grey and misty as that one was, so I had left the weapon among gorse bushes at the mine buildings – then I went into Mr Drake. He had also wet himself. He didn't seem to care, unlike Harold, who I think cared a great deal, though he was too self-conscious to say. I didn't know what I expected when I ripped the tape from his mouth. Harold was predictable – filthy language, limited, vicious – but Mr Drake wasn't. He did what I least expected, he defended himself.

His style was vulgar and ugly, woven with reproaches and forgiveness, but was certainly a defence. "Look, it's not your fault," he began, "but you've got it all wrong. I didn't do anything. That was made up. You know that. I don't know who's been telling you things, but it's all wrong. I really don't blame you."

"Stop," I demanded, though not brutally, just a simple command. There were too many words, too great an attempt to swamp me. I would dictate the quantity of words. He looked instantly perturbed, a thin film of sweat forming in the angular creases of his face, miraculously, like moisture on petals. His skin had turned a lustreless, grey-yellow colour overnight. He tried to avoid eye contact but couldn't stop himself from darting furtive glances at me. I smiled, without generosity, listlessly, and asked: "Do you suffer with your liver?"

He looked confused, but obviously felt compelled to answer, replying: "I take salts."

"Salts. I wonder if I'm interested? Probably not. Not what I need to know."

"I didn't do anything."

"You said, and that is interesting. I'm interested in that, because it's an admission of a sort, isn't it?"

"I didn't do anything, I'm telling you. No, it's not any sort of admission."

"But something happened. You see the logic. I didn't do anything means, but somebody did. I didn't do anything, but I oh so know what you mean."

"Not me," he replied moodily, and then again more quietly, trying to avert his face as if aggrieved by the suggestion: "Really not me."

"I've just had an interesting chat with Harold."

"He's a liar," he retorted instantly.

"A liar?"

261

"He always had it in for me. Of course he's a liar, and a bully."

"But you don't know what he said. Maybe he didn't lie at all."

Once again he lowered his head, looking sheepish and hurt, his eyes flicking to me all of the time, then uttered: "You know he's a bully."

"He told me you tried to pay him off."

"That's a lie," he snapped.

"I haven't said for what?"

"Well, it's a lie whatever."

I moved closer so that I was standing over him. I could smell his urine, which I hadn't with Harold, an acrid, cloying must. I had intended to lean down close to his ear but thought better of it. I remained upright, his bread-knife crossed over my chest, and said: "I don't want to play anymore games, I've had enough. You're the sort of man who draws people into games, confusing what's real and what isn't. Maybe you've watched too many films, but I've had enough. So, do you understand, I'm impatient now, and I feel stupid and cheated, letting you wrangle with me, so I don't know what I might do. Now, he said you tried to pay him off."

He lifted his face, its sharp lines contracted, the expression weary. "He said he would tell Mother."

"What?"

He twisted his head upwards, towards me and snapped: "That I messed around with kids. But I never did. Never. It was all lies, filthy lies."

"Lies, you, sitting in The Shed, in the dark, sitting with the kids, touching them."

"Don't be disgusting. I love kids." Suddenly I sprung the knife to his face, crossways over the bridge of his sharp nose, so that it was almost against the skin, incensed, I suppose, by the fact he should use the word love. He looked straight ahead, past it, though not disputing it, and again defended

262

himself. "I was scared, scared of him, scared of what he could do. It cost me The Shed all the money I gave him. They'd kill you around here for something like that."

"He said it was your baby."

He smiled, the gesture strong and uncontained, liable to become laughter. "That's ridiculous," he said, "you know that, ridiculous."

"I don't believe anything," I replied, going closer to his ear to say it, regardless of the stink of ammonia, his stink, and at the same time lowered the blade to his throat.

*

I wondered whether the child would take after Abby, share her airy truculence, her avowal not to please, her singularity. I tried to share that wonder with Stephen, but he was too crushed by Abby's confinement to be able to think about things he couldn't visualise. I tried to tell him that everything would be all right; they couldn't be kept apart forever. After all, I didn't expect Harold and Agnes would want to keep Abby now that she was an adult. I couldn't work out why they'd locked her up at all and hadn't just sent her off to fend for herself.

It was painful that Stephen refused to speculate about the child, but then he had never seen Abby as a little girl, viewing the horizon for its meanings, the landscape for its cryptic clues, plumbing the depths of both, the hidden life of which they were only signs. Nothing had ever silenced her and she had laid claim to everything, giving it her name, making it correspondent with her identity, its witness.

Like any auntie I was already in love with the child, and planned to pamper and spoil it. I could see it in my mind's eye, exploring the shore, the granular sands, the strange corrugated surface, not a place of confinement, but of openings, doorways into any sphere it dreamed of. We would make sure of that, three sisters – because Grace would not remove herself, though she might insist on describing everything in her own particular way. I never considered whether Abby would have a boy or a girl, because it would inevitably be a girl, though if the inevitable didn't happen, it wouldn't matter at all.

I never considered whether the child would be able to hear or not. What did that matter? It would be possessed of Abby's poetry whatever. Stephen never mentioned it. Like Abby, her child would never be deaf to the joy and suffering of this joyous and suffering world.

I tried to convince Stephen that it would never be a Sempie. They could never insist on that, not three generations of inaccurately defined life. Abby and Harold never had the choice – in that one thing they were related – but they couldn't maintain the deceit indefinitely. The child would have its true name: but Stephen didn't believe it for a second, and of course Stephen was right.

They took the child the same way the matriarch had taken her, claiming it, owning it, deciding how to dispose of it, and she did the only thing her mind could tell her – she fled.

I found her in front of the angel cradling Poppy, little deaf Poppy. She was completely quiet, neither sobbing nor uttering her name. She had opted for silence as if sound answered a demand to please, and she just wasn't prepared to do that. She simply gazed, wide-eyed, scarcely blinking, rocking Poppy back and forth, with her usual rough, indefatigable love, after all she had learned the sign so long ago.

*

"You haven't wet yourself," I said, slowly strolling around Agnes, tied to her chair at the table.

"Do you think I'd give you that satisfaction?"

"No, probably not."

"You're going to pay, you know. You're not getting away with this, I'll make sure of that."

I smiled, though deep down I felt as if I were back at school, scared of what was next. I stopped in front of her, showed her the knife and said: "I have the knife, you're going to pay."

"Are you sure?"

"I'm in charge."

She smiled grimly: "Are you sure?"

"Don't rile me."

"Are you not simply crazy too?"

I slammed the knife onto the table in an outburst of rage. She smiled again as if the gesture proved her point. I wanted to slash her, but didn't go an inch closer. "And what if I am?" I blurted out. "How does that help you?"

"I'd be right."

I threw back my head and glared at her, the desire to pounce drumming through me: "I care about so much and nothing at all, all at the same time, but I don't know which is which, so don't push me."

"You should seek help, medical help, they might show you some regard."

"There's more to you than I ever gave you credence for. I always thought you were nothing really, Harold's slops, but you're really quite a bitch. Surprising. You come from a decent family, as far as I can tell."

"Leave my family out of this, they're none of your business. Now untie me." I shook my head. "You're just making it worse for yourself by the second. So, I'm telling you, stop being hysterical and take these bands off now."

"No, Agnes, you're not telling me anything, in fact, if I choose I'll just turn you off."

She screwed up her face, dismissive, impatient, maybe bored. She even had the front to yawn, and then demanded: "Are we through now?"

I looked at her coldly, feeling myself choke up with her indifference, but I was determined not to concede, not to break down, to give her that triumph. Without emphasis I said: "I haven't begun."

"Oh Christ," she complained, looking towards the

curtained window, "get it over with, will you, whatever it is."

"Are you not scared of death, Agnes, not even a little bit?" She turned back and eyed me impassively. "I'd be scared of it if I was you." Still she continued to gaze at me, conceding nothing, not a quickening of the senses, perhaps only a marginal alertness. "It intrigues me, the fact you take death, dying, so lightly, and I'm not sure whether I envy you or despise you. Which should it be?"

"I don't know," she replied quietly.

"You see, someone's going to die and it very well might be you."

"You're off your head."

"Does that change things Agnes? Are you scared of it now?" She scowled in response, still putting a defiant face on it. "Maybe you really don't care about death, and you were the one to kill it. Was it you Agnes, smothered your own grandchild?"

"Oh, I see. That's what all this is about. Untie me Judith and we'll get you some help. This has gone far enough."

"Did you smother it?"

"She did it," she snapped. "She did it and you know fine well she did."

"She would never have done that."

"But she did."

"No!"

"She was lucky to be put away and not hanged."

"You put her away."

"And do you think it was easy, watching them take her and her struggling to be with her father."

"With Harold?"

"It was horrible, her reaching out, twining in that voice of hers. It was lucky they brought that man McBride. She went along for him in the end."

"Signing, she was signing."

"She was ill."

266

"And Harold found her, with the baby, I mean?"

She put back her head and inhaled deeply, her nostrils flaring wide. "Give me a cigarette, I could really do with a cigarette."

"Harold found her, in the tower? He did, didn't he?"

"No, he didn't," she said, her voice lowering, but still strong. "When she took off with the baby he wouldn't lift a finger. He'd had enough. To hell with her, he said, and he wouldn't budge. We had to do it ourselves."

"Who?"

"Me and Martha, who do you think? It was always left to us to look after her."

"And Martha found her?"

"Too late, yes, Martha found her, found her with the rags from a pot doll pressed across the baby's face."

"She didn't love Poppy enough for that."

"Give me a cigarette."

I plastered tape across her mouth again.

*

Sometimes we long so much to hear someone again that it threatens to tear us apart, rip our fragile organs straight through our chest cage, but even if I could affect the trick what hope would there be for Abby? The chance was never hers to take, to stand up, neck slightly craned, chest out, her small convex breasts pushed up and out, to make the bewildering, blatant, beautiful assertion: I have voice, speech, word, language: I am a witness, and I will rend you all to pieces with what I have to say. That was never to be her stage, her role, her identity. She only had a single vowel.

My spirit is breaking with forbidden, unsanctioned love. No one on this ridiculous planet, on any of its islands, big or small, should die without being afforded the opportunity to live.

They took it away from her though, denied her that right. What hope was there when they took her baby, took it before it was even named, so that it didn't even have a vowel? She could never have lived with that. She wasn't even allowed to be there when they buried it – a boy, surprisingly – one of the nails bending as they hammered it in, which they unsuccessfully tried a number of times to straighten out, until Harold told them it was enough and they should press on.

They said it was a bitterly cold night, everywhere white with frost and a full moon low in the sky – to which I concur, having checked the records. Agnes said Abby would have remembered the pond from when she was a child and the ice broke one Christmas time when she took her skating. She said it as if Abby were really quite unlucky in that way. No one suggested that Abby had come looking for the baby; after all, she had smothered it and must have known there was no going back.

According to all of them, though, she never had been in her right mind. They fully made that point to the coroner, as well as insisting that she obviously must have wanted to die, why else would she have made a sixty mile journey on foot when she escaped from the hospital. At the same inquest the hospital apologised. They simply hadn't thought her capable. So, it was concluded that Abby made a sixty mile journey for water, the particular water where Agnes said, by rights, she should have died as a child, presumably contradicting herself and meaning that Abby was as lucky as she was unlucky, though Agnes was always ambivalent or really quite limited with language.

I don't know why Abby never came for her sister, came to my bedside and whispered her name. I would never have let her go.

Dreams she had though, of depth and weight, of narrow space, a world that would define her, so maybe she looked and saw herself answering, the two of them calling each other, saying her name as she exchanged places, swapping element for element, yet still occupying both.

It has to be the case because I hear her name in everything and I am very hard of hearing. My name is E.

If you remove a life, take a piece out of the mosaic, the jigsaw, the absence doesn't simply close up, heal like a wound, a wound on life, the life absented. The essence isn't so frail. So, I'll spit Abby's life, praise her, announce her achievement, her perfection, the tissue winding around her, staunching her. We play it, sing it, our unhearing role. I will be the arbiter. I refuse to allow her piece such easy repeal.

Someone will pay for this with their life.

*

My gorgeous, enthusiastic hairdresser brought snaps of her sister's wedding and offered them to me to look through. I asked whether it was recent, but she shrugged in the mirror and said it wasn't recent at all, more than a year ago as a matter of fact. I smiled appreciatively. The snaps were a symbol of our pseudo-friendship, which isn't really allowed, contravening as it does numerous professional boundaries.

The snaps were of the usual wedding groups, two families brought together, whether successfully or not the snaps didn't reveal. She generously pointed out who everyone was, allowing me access to quite intimate details of her background, her parents, two brothers and a sister, privileged knowledge. She even conceded that when she looked at them she did see herself married and couldn't really conceive of not having a similar sort of day herself. I responded by telling her that she would make such a beautiful bride. She shrugged, but didn't deny it. We are on that scale of friendship that doesn't need polite modesty.

There were other snaps slipped in that had nothing to do with the wedding. She apologised for those and admitted she was such an untidy person, her photographs ended up in all kinds of mess. I wondered how she could tell the sequence they should be in. She confessed she couldn't. I told her I had rarely seen so many happy photographs. She shrugged again and suggested, without saying it, that photographs only ever have one truth.

Without being able to stop myself I began to cry. I always cry at other people's snaps, whether they are formal or informal, obviously happy, or neutral of all emotion.

Of course I don't possess a single photograph of Abby. None of our families had cameras, nor had any inclination to take us to one of the shops that made up formal portraits. I have no evidence of a past life at all, no source material, only a trust that it happened. I do have later pictures of Grace, Grace and Phillip, and then Grace with her two children, both hearing, yet capable signers, but none when Grace was the best signer of us all.

My incredible, dissident hairdresser did the unthinkable and bent down, wrapped her arm around me and tried to console me. I didn't know whether to reciprocate or not. Would it be going just too far? There was something so splendid in her embrace, though, I had to return it. I laughed as I held her and said it was silly but I was not sad, quite the opposite, very happy. She actually wiped away my tears with the backs of her fingers and said I had a funny way of showing it. I conceded that people's photographs always make me cry, and that sometimes they make me sad, particularly when they are black and white and formal, but on the whole I am happy to see them: in fact, I am never bored as some people are, but I had a friend who died and I never had a single snap.

With such knowledge she began to cry herself. I admitted it had been hard over the years not having a single snap, but then there is always something to break you and something to sustain you. I told her she was a great help. She skewed her face. Perhaps I was being indiscreet.

She stood up, saying she didn't do anything really. But she was an enthusiast, I insisted. I went straight on and told her it was enthusiasm that saved me. She smiled in the mirror and asked me for what, enthusiasm for what? For poetry, I

270

said, and smiled in return. My friend, I explained, the one who died, taught me about poetry. She was a poet herself. A good poet, my hairdresser wanted to know? I thought so, I said, without insistence. And with a great open arm embrace of time, my efficient, insightful hairdresser said she must have been then.

I returned to the snaps. I didn't mind crying.

I'm an enthusiast and so was my friend.

Chapter Nineteen

Martha was feeding her chickens and bantams. The ground was frozen hard so the seed lay on top of the mud. She ignored me and carried on, her poultry pecking madly around her feet. I leaned against my weapon as if it were a staff. I had covered the head, the blade, clumsily with a bag, which must have made me seem mildly eccentric. I watched the feeding birds until Martha's seed bag ran out then called to her: "Agnes tells me that it was you who found Abby and the baby."

She looked towards me, making no gesture of surprise or irritation, no gesture of pretence. "Sadly," she said without emphasis.

"Were you not pleased?"

"Pleased?"

"Yes pleased, pleased you'd got rid of them both. You never did want our kind to breed."

"You're not her kind, Judith Salt, so don't claim it."

"Oh but I am, Martha. I really am." She shrugged and began to fold her empty seed bag. The birds were ranging more widely, searching out the food. Martha was preparing to go. I called: "You haven't said you weren't pleased."

She turned to me again, her head held back, refusing to show impatience. "I wasn't pleased, but I wasn't hurt. I'm not going to pretend that. What life had she had, and for the child maybe worse, certainly worse."

"So you killed it."

"No I didn't. She did."

She turned away and made towards the kitchen door. I

followed, making my way through the still pecking poultry. Before she reached the door I called to her: "She wouldn't do it, so you can't tell me that."

She carried on. I thought she wasn't going to stop. Perhaps I would have to pursue her all the way, but then she turned impatiently, looked me in the eye and said: "I don't want you to come in, so go away."

I ripped the ridiculous bag from the end of my spear and rammed it up against the side of her neck. "I always knew it would be you," I said. "Deep down I knew you would be the one I'd have to come for. You told her too much."

She looked more shocked and vulnerable than I had anticipated. It aged her. She backed away, nervously feeling for the doorway behind her, but came up against the corner where the lean-to kitchen joined the house. She had no where else to go. I pressed the flat of the blade firmly against her neck. She gazed upward, beyond me, as if help must be somewhere at hand, though in reality knowing it couldn't be, because no one came there informally. Never having made anyone welcome, she had brought this on herself.

She made a number of attempts to speak, but failed each time, her lips and tongue moving but no words materialising. I smiled and gestured for her to speak up. Still she failed, so I gestured again more forcibly, my free hand waving in front of her eyes demanding greater volume. Eventually she stuttered: "What do you want me to say?"

"What do I want you to say? Oh I don't know. Try telling me I've been a good girl."

"You're a good girl, Judith Salt."

"Excellent, my name as well, identified. That really is good. Now tell me all the secrets you told her."

She began to tremble. Not in my wildest imaginings had I expected the matriarch to display such fear. In its own way it was unnerving. I wanted her death to be devoid of pity. In order to eradicate any misplaced sympathy I pictured her crimes. She was steeped in them. In the same moment she shook her head, as if defending herself, and from deep in her chest asked: "What, what secrets?"

I moved closer to her, leading myself along the shaft of the weapon, crawling my way towards her: "Harold's father?"

She shook her head, though I didn't get the impression she was refusing me particularly, rather refusing the knowledge, refusing it to herself. I demanded again, reminding her that she must have told Abby when Abby was a baby. "I can't say," she stammered, then looked squarely at me, her expression horrified, appealing, and again shook her head, again refusing herself.

"You told her and hated her for it, now tell me."

She looked skywards, her face contorting with the name, her torso heaving. I wasn't unconvinced that she was about to expire, stealing her secret away, but then she looked me in the face, almost smiled, sighed and said: "Aidan Shaughnessy." She immediately repeated the name as if needing to confirm it to herself.

"Then they are brother and sister," I said, spelling it out slowly, with frank amazement, crazily really, as if she might not have realised the significance herself. "Harold and Agnes are brother and sister."

"Half," she insisted, as if the correction were everything.

"Brother and sister."

"Don't you think I know? Don't you think I did everything I could to stop the marriage?" She looked at me with furious intensity. "Do you not think I know why she was like she was, the child, an imbecile, a deaf-mute imbecile, born of such a marriage? Do you not think I've had to suffer that?"

"Why didn't the two of you marry, you and Aidan, I mean?" She shook her head firmly, her expression obdurate, defiant. I peered at her, dumbfounded, yet impressed. "You've always given the clue, haven't you? Never as hateful of Aidan as the others? I should have picked that up, but never did. But I don't get it. You were going to evict them."

She glared at me, her usual temper flashing in her expression. "Why not?"

I looked at her, the shifting expression, scarcely discernible but certainly there, the fine muscles in her features firing as memory flooded her, memories that she had probably prohibited for years. Naturally I was gifted at reading such signs, such faces, I had had a lifetime of it. There was bitterness, resentment and pain, the latter unmistakable.

"He didn't want you, did he?" I suggested tentatively. "Aidan Shaughnessy didn't want you."

She made no reply, but gazed at me coldly.

I went on, trying to piece her hatred together. "I suppose you thought he couldn't refuse you, after all you owned the lease to their property, to their survival. You didn't count on Nora though, did you, didn't count on her determination to make sure they came through. Is that why you hated her so much, because she got in your way, took away your power?"

She glared at me, her habitual gestures rejuvenated, her terrible contempt for everything restored.

I lifted my head slightly, fixing her with my eyes. I felt enraged. What I'd learnt didn't alter a thing, changed nothing, excused nothing. She had vindictively, systematically and persistently crushed and hurt my beautiful sister. She was as guilty as hell. I pressed the blade against her. All I had to do was swipe it across her throat, pierce her clearly defined wind-pipe and everything would be complete, my mission fulfilled. There would be recompense for what she had done to Abby. Someone had to die. It had to be her. I snapped at her, shouting it aloud, that it didn't make any difference. She had killed the baby.

"No," she snapped back. "I was going to bring it back after she stole it. It couldn't have been left with her."

"You were going to take it from her?"

"I don't know. I don't know what we would have done. Found somewhere for it, I suppose, God knows where, I

275

don't know. It would have been worse than her, I know that. It wouldn't have had any life, not a proper life, not what would be considered a proper life."

"Did you say that, that it would be worse than her? Did you say that to her, to Abby?"

"I don't know. I suppose so. And it was true. Of course it would have been worse than her. But she smothered it, not me."

"And you watched."

She made no reply. I shouted it aloud, the fact that she had watched, shouted the accusation, the crime. I stood tall, stepped back and held my shaft at the end, the spear projected downward. The time had come. There was nothing more to say. I was finished with language, with explanations, meanings. I had one act to perform then it would all be concluded. It was my privilege to execute the matriarch. All the secrets she had shared with Abby would be done with. That portion of time would be completed, dismissed, dispensed with.

I pushed my arms into the air. The spear was poised earthward. I stared into her face. I wanted to see how she would encounter death. There were to be no last rites, no chance of absolution, no last words. Her life was going to end as it was.

I summonsed all of my strength for the thrust. I screamed my intent, a long, agonised vowel. I heard it gather around me, filling the air, saturating everything, the seen and the unseen, the myriad secretive spaces. It was Abby's note, her name, a single profound and beautiful syllable, her name finally achieving recompense, control, justice. I rammed the spear through the air, my hollered note of identity following it.

*

At my age what I have discovered is discernment: I choose my leisure; my television and music, my hairstyle and

276

makeup. I don't have to take what's there simply because it is. I can say no. I can say that this, that or the other is no longer of any interest. I am less discerning about speech. That is an old habit and seems impossible to break. I find myself agreeing and disagreeing with people out of laziness, laziness of words. My gestures suffer from the same laxity. Recreationally, however, I have developed my own culture, broken ties, released myself from my historical bind. It's a start. If I live to a hundred I may yet achieve freedom, though I doubt it, in the extreme.

*

Inevitably the tragedy remains in the things I could do and not those I couldn't.

When the moment of retribution was to be realised I failed. The spear went hurtling across the yard, falling harmlessly amongst the poultry. I can in all truth state that it wasn't the look in her face – the terror of pain, of dying, of an unprepared soul – that stopped me. Certainly I pitied her, in many ways pitied them all, felt sorry for their belief in nothing but existence as it is, like so many eager moths at a flame, trapped in their perpetual present, accustomed to brilliance but ignorant of its meaning, but pity wouldn't have annulled my revenge. Pity drove it on.

I had Abby's oppressor in my grasp, her startled expression begging for mercy, and I had no intention of conceding. Oppressors have no rights that the oppressed should respect. If I had executed Martha though, maybe even returned and punished Harold, Agnes and Mr Drake for their parts in the crime, would it have made Abby's past legitimate? Would it have been the corrective I sought? In that moment I understood something that Abby had always understood, that correction is not about vendetta: it is about the future, not the past. Inevitably it was Abby who said it to me, Abby who provided the revelation. I heard it as I screamed my intention, that loud, tortured, angry syllable, and it was her name

I heard, that beautiful identity with which she announced her rightful place in everything, her name that called to me. Abby, my sister, speaking to me, her name, calling from a world as yet unannounced, calling me away from a primitive past.

I threw away the weapon and told Martha that Abby reprieved her, though offered no forgiveness, and then I told her where she would find the others and left. I went to a phone-box and rang Donald. I told him I was coming home. I told him I agreed with what he wanted. He wasn't ready. That was what he had told me. He was pleased that I had seen sense. It was the last conversation we had together, though I guess he knew I would be true to my word.

*

So, the last time I stood here I was twenty-five and pregnant and determined to kill someone, though in the end all I killed was myself, a part of myself, probably the greater part, and when all is said and done the discriminatory world colludes with my murder. It has time, scope, understanding and sympathy for it. There was no objection to a deaf woman terminating a potentially deaf pregnancy.

Personally, though, I have done time for that death, solitary confinement, penance and, despite never rectifying it, I have reached a peace that requires no forgiveness, though I would never consider the crime legitimate. I could never think that.

What if the entire world were illegitimate though: what if its random, tribal customs, its everyday practices, were rescinded and found culpable? Where would the perpetrator stand then? Condemned, naturally. Our punishment? Well, that is impossible to say. Contemporary, of course, whatever the contemporary world might be. I would stand alongside Martha, Harold, Agnes and Mr Drake and face the accusations, found wanting, found guilty, found able.

I realise I can't summons them back, though, can't tell

them their acts, their crimes and their perverted personal passions, were of another time and that time has disposed of them; that it is always in the nature of time to rob us of our relevance: though when I was younger, when I stood on this same shore subscribing to a different age, that is exactly what I believed I could do.

Time is the miracle, the coincidence, the omen, the tragedy and ultimately, the triumph.

Finally, Martha is dead, a very old woman, dead at last. I wouldn't intrude on her funeral, – better attended than I might have wished for, but people have their own reasons – or on the lives of Harold and Agnes, both old and failing themselves, not this time: nevertheless, I insist on my right to lurk in the shadows and watch, not to make sure or to garner any satisfaction, but simply because I am a part of it, an inescapable player.

When they are all dead, and that day must arrive soon, the worst that could be desired of me is reconciliation, a reconciliation I can never offer, never give, never accept because as long as there is no reconciliation the past will always exist, always be there spiralling into time gone, time lost, time removed, time future.

And I spin with Abby in its writhing, anxious discord, bodies, sisters, with depth and weight, mermaids, after all, listening beneath the waves to a low groan that repeats endlessly: My name is E. My name is E.